AMERICANITIS

RENARD PRESS LTD

124 City Road
London EC1V 2NX
United Kingdom
info@renardpress.com
020 8050 2928

www.renardpress.com

Americanitis first published by Renard Press Ltd in 2024

Text © Miles Beard, 2024
Permission has been granted to quote from other copyrighted works in this book. For copyright holders and licensors please see 'Credits and Permissions' on p. 263, which forms an extension of this copyright notice.

Cover design by Will Dady

Printed and bound in the UK on carbon-balanced papers by CMP Books

Paperback ISBN: 978-1-80447-104-3
Renard Press Edition (limited printing) ISBN: 978-1-80447-105-0

UNCORRECTED ADVANCE-READING COPY

Miles Beard asserts his moral right to be identified as the author of this work in accordance with the Copyright, Designs and Patents Act 1988.

This is a work of fiction. Any resemblance to actual persons, living or dead, is purely coincidental, or is used fictitiously.

CLIMATE POSITIVE   Renard Press is proud to be a climate positive publisher, removing more carbon from the air than we emit and planting a small forest. For more information see renardpress.com/eco.

Americanitis

MILES BEARD

RENARD PRESS

AMERICANITIS

for
S J M-B
(1989–2016)

MINGUS AT THE SHOWPLACE

I was miserable, of course, for I was seventeen,
and so I swung into action and wrote a poem,

and it was miserable, for that was how I thought
poetry worked: you digested experience and shat

literature. It was 1960 at The Showplace, long since
defunct, on West 4th St., and I sat at the bar,

casting beer money from a thin reel of ones,
the kid in the city, big ears like a puppy.

And I knew Mingus was a genius. I knew two
other things, but as it happened they were wrong.

So I made him look at the poem.
"There's a lot of that going around," he said,

and Sweet Baby Jesus he was right. He glowered
at me but he didn't look as if he thought

bad poems were dangerous, the way some poets do.
If they were baseball executives they'd plot

to destroy sandlots everywhere so that the game
could be saved from children. Of course later

that night he fired his pianist in mid-number
and flurried him from the stand.

"We've suffered a diminuendo in personnel,"
he explained, and the band played on.

—William Matthews, 1995

I

I RESENTED THE term widower in the same way a postwoman might. Not only did I object to its antiquated invoking of gender but also its inability to connote me accurately and succinctly. I was only 27. Sarah had been dead for just over a year. It was almost farcical to describe myself as such, and yet, again and again, was I asked to do so: on bureaucratic forms; in the news media; at the GP; or to well-meaning but ultimately damaging shop assistants inquiring as to whether my partner and I have the same preference of mattress – hard or soft? Well, currently she's in hard box beneath the soft earth and I'm not sleeping at all, so... And much like Kodak or Bic or Coca-Cola it felt like a word sprung from an unexceptional boardroom with that singular goal in mind: profit.

Everything had been paid for in full – Sarah's life insurance policy through her work had seen to that and then some – but still I felt my vulnerability seized upon at regular intervals. I finally got around to cancelling the phone line after a few too many cold calls asking if I or a loved one had been in a serious accident recently and even then the man at the telecoms company pleaded with me to reconsider. Life's too short, I'd supposed, so I thanked him for his help and left our contract intact, only dimly acknowledging later that, whatever my intention, I was invoking neither a genuine nor ironic spirit of the phrase by using it to justify continuing to pay for something I didn't want and actually found quite painful. It was just a phrase that played upon my mind quite a bit in that time, I suppose.

It was something of a joke between us that she would die before me, despite my mysterious ailments, my immediate onset of anxiety at the slightest indication of some nutritional deficiency, some neurological twitch. And yet she never could grasp what would and would not frighten me. I could scrape a knee in the park and throughout her beseeching that I not worry she would stare at me like I was a madman, as I did the same back at her. A scraped knee did not bother me. A jammed finger could never bother me. A blow to the head? Of course. Anything involving my sex organs? Perish the thought.

When Sarah died I had so many feelings. To untangle some such, I even visited a therapist. She (I knew that I would see a woman; I don't know how I knew and I don't know what it means that I knew, but I knew despite never consciously looking) suggested that I write down what had happened to me, everything that had happened to me, even events that weren't true or those that I had wished to be true, but to use our real names, to be myself, and to therefore take ownership of every aspect of our story.

I smirked. You mean autofiction? I teach a course on it.

She returned a puzzled look so I explained that the most exciting authors of the moment were interrogating the subjective experience of being alive and the audience's insatiable desires for authenticity and celebrity, even while praising their ingenuous imaginations and fidelity to artful language. (I should say this happened a couple of years ago, before the form began to dominate basically all the serious literary production in this country. So please don't think I was, like, trying to explain what an epistolary novel was to an attuned reader in the eighteenth century. Or, you know, something else that's really obvious.)

But she replied that she was familiar with the term. What she was actually curious of was why my first impulse had been to name the form, to genericise the task she was setting before me.

I felt a twinge and adopted a hurt look. Sarah was the same, I said. She thinks – she thought – I was always over-intellectualising things.

We can discuss that at some point, the therapist said, and we should. But to be clear I wasn't suggesting that you were intellectualising so much as attempting to exert a level of control that isn't necessary; to absolve the personal functions of a journal in the service of the literary, distancing yourself from the task before you had even started it. Whereas I am trying to give you the space to put your whole self into your story: your fantasies; your desires; your moral corruptions, even, if you have any. You're a lecturer?

Yes, I responded, too quickly. (It wasn't true. I'm only a teaching associate, languishing on rolling fixed-term contracts.)

She pushed the button on her pen and wrote this down, retracting it afterward. And your doctoral thesis?

I jumped into the thirty-second 'elevator pitch' we had been taught to prepare and memorise for our interviews, throughout which her pen remained painfully retracted.

…and so it mostly focuses on Nadar, Tennessee Williams, and Charles Mingus, whose archives in Washington, D.C. I was very fortunate to visit on a six-week stay, I finished.

All men?

Yes, I said, guiltily, putting my wrists out before her as if manacled, an expression of mock anguish on my face. Oh, and there was that pen again. What fun we were having!

I left feeling heavier than ever. I was a magician with a secret pocket stored inside of his chest that no number of coloured handkerchiefs could ever fill. I was an anti-archaeologist, covering the portentous artefacts of knowledge before him in the sand, looking away, distracted by something glittering in the far distance on the horizon ahead. A lumbering birdwatcher whose tears obscure the lenses of his binoculars. A warrior monk with a heavy conscience…

But at home, I opened this abandoned jotter and tore out its pages on Propp, the old Russki fool. The first lines I wrote, the only lines I could write that night:

Sarah. Sarah. Sarah. Sarah. Sarah. Sarah. Sarah. Sarah. Sarah. Sarah. Sarah. Sarah.

Write it!

Sarah.

Sorry. I just realised I forgot to include my own name in this. It's Miles, as in *miles gloriosus.*

II

NONE OF OUR friends would believe us but when Sarah became pregnant again, this time carrying it past the first trimester, I too gained weight in my stomach and struggled with mood swings and nausea. She thought it was sweet at first but one morning, when I was violently retching in the toilet, I heard her call me something darkly under her breath. (A ponce, maybe? That can't be right...) It didn't stop how I felt – nothing could – but I wouldn't talk about it any more with her after that and tried to disguise the very real symptoms I was experiencing with ostentatious displays of my prior eating habits: chips piled into polystyrene containers slick with orange grease from the coloured cheese, a battered sausage. Stuffing it into my mouth I would intimate that it was all behind me – silly, really, wasn't it? – while I thought of an excuse to go out. Into the hedges, beyond the view of our sitting room window where she watched television, I would spew everything. Eventually, when she lost the baby, my symptoms subsided.

Though we wanted a child more than ever now, we didn't have sex for months after. I was still finishing my thesis at the time and Sarah had returned quickly to work. It was a pain neither of us had experienced, almost everyone we knew up until that point having lived full lives, and we were helpless to each other. It wasn't real, I would say to myself in that time, over and over again. It was never real.

Only a small taste of what was to come, after some time I did start to get over it. Not her. I remember one night we were staying in with a bottle of wine when I put on a funk record I had got earlier in the day at the vinyl record fair we had walked through on our way home from the park where we still liked to go and throw the frisbee. I didn't know anything about the album itself but I had liked all of the bandleader's output that I was familiar with, and his group's infectious zaniness always put me into a good mood. But, as we sat there, when the first track opened with the spoken words, 'Mother Earth is pregnant for the third time,' I knew I had made a mistake. As guitars started to wail – truly wail – over an arpeggiated melody of profound grief and longing, I watched Sarah begin to weep, shuddering as she did so. I didn't know what to do. Almost five minutes in, without any tonal shift at all from the band – the drummer especially insistent in the lugubrious, absurdly funereal pace he set – she stood up and left the room, calling me a bastard on her way out. I wasn't offended. I knew I would have to rise above it all or drown in my own shit. But, still, my heart went out to her, even if in the end it couldn't quite reach.

So I just sat there and let the song play out. There was nothing I could do. My glass again empty, my head slightly spinning, it was another five interminable minutes before the bloody thing was over, pounding in my temples, field of vision decreasing almost imperceptibly. As the music transitioned without counterpoint into the next track, an uplifting gospel-style rock song asking a meaningless question over and over, I let this play out as well, if only so that Sarah might intuit the complete lack of intention in my actions: I wasn't trying to bring us down; I wasn't forcing her to confront anything. But she didn't return. And when we woke up the next morning, neither of us mentioned the incident.

There's something you should know about Sarah. You've probably wondered why we got married when we were so young, for instance. Young for people our age, anyway. Well, as you might already know, her parents are a bit religious and she used to have to go to the village church with them every week growing up: service and bible study. When they became suspicious that we were living together (we were) it seemed easier to just get married rather than keep lying to them whenever they came into the city to visit us. But Sarah had a lot of lingering questions, more than I had been aware of. Around this time we had been out on one of our 'constitutionals' talking about something or other when I made a pun about a soul musician we both liked, putting the word into air-quotes with my hands.

Wait a minute, she said, stopping. You don't even believe in souls?

Of course not, I responded, laughing a little too absently, my mind faraway in that moment as I wondered if I had put enough sun cream onto my face and neck. It was then that I realised she'd had tears in her eyes when she asked me. I'm really sorry, I said quickly. Do you?

I... I don't know now. I thought I did. But I guess I had never really thought about it, to be honest.

Suddenly connecting this to the debacle of our unborn children, I started to backpedal. (It's more of a philosophical question than anything else, isn't it...) But she stopped me and took my hand in hers – my hand devouring hers, really – and said, As long as we have each other, that's all that really matters, right?

I kissed her on the nose as the traffic roared around us where we waited on an island in the middle of the road, her exasperated arms stretching out towards me, the top of her forehead meeting the bottom of mine. Right, I said.

If you look closely, you can still see some tear splotches on these pages, here and there.

III

AT OUR NEXT meeting, the therapist started our session by asking me to tell her more about my thesis. This surprised me. No one had wanted to talk about any of the research I had done ever since the *viva voce*, and even then it felt like I was being indulged: I was given the polite number of corrections you would expect, a cheap bottle of fizz bought by the department, and then sent on my merry way with very little regard for what I would do next, left so I was at the end of the student's road. Though I had already successfully interviewed for a post at another university, I hadn't told anyone about it. You would think they might have thought to ask about my plans, but whatever. Bastards.

After I had outlined my argument in a little bit more detail than when we'd first met (basically, that the autobiographies of artists tend to present the quotidian sides of the practitioner as metaphors for their craft rather than deal explicitly with that craft) she asked me to locate the centre of my interest in the topic. I couldn't. Faltering as I spoke, I touched on my own youthful ambitions in music, the chance to go to America, the career prospects for interdisciplinarity in academia, and, finally, the role of the persona in literary interpretation.

Mingus tackles this directly, I said. His book begins with him in a therapist's office, actually, where he's told that there are in fact three of him, all real, all to be taken seriously.

Who are the three? she asked.

Um, one is just standing there, unflappable and watchful. One is like a frightened rabbit that's attacking others out of fear, I think. And then there's the big gentle giant, innocent and naïve but who can turn violent when he realises he's being take advantage of.

And who are yours? How many Mileses are there?

I was quiet for a moment.

Alazon, I replied.

She judged the word carefully in her mind, eyes betraying her as they darted around, cuing some memory or secret knowledge from long ago. Alazon, she said aloud. Who is Alazon?

He's who I am on message boards. Online, I mean. It's the name I use.

Anonymously.

Yes.

Alazon is, well, he's a stock character in the theatre. From ancient times. A kind of... figure of ridicule, yes? Is that right?

That's right, I said.

But why?

My heart started to pound.

Well...

She didn't cut me off.

No one can...

The terrible silence pervaded.

No one can ridicule you if you're deliberately setting yourself up for ridicule.

I see, she said. Where does Sarah figure in this?

I didn't say that she does.

No, you didn't. That's true. But I'm asking.

Well, literally speaking, not very much. Alazon isn't married.

Alazon isn't married, she repeated, spacing the words apart like a line from some exquisite, bittersweet haiku.

I don't... Or, I didn't... talk about Sarah. Ever.

Online.

Right.

So what does Alazon talk about?

He, uh, flirts, I guess. More than he 'talks about something', if you know what I mean.

I think I'm starting to understand now. Did Sarah know about Alazon?

No. Not as far as I'm aware, anyway.

Let's leave this there for the moment, she said. Let's just leave it in the air and see if it's something we'll return to at a later point.

I nodded, grateful.

When you came last week, you said you have been experiencing some health anxiety since the death of your wife. That's perfectly natural – and well done for seeking help – but I'm curious to know when it these feelings first started.

Like, from my whole life, you mean?

Sure, if you wish. Had you dealt with this kind of anxiety before Sarah died?

Yes.

Tell me about it. Can you pinpoint it to a time or place?

I told her how it had started when Sarah and I were apart for six weeks during my research fellowship in the States, three years into the PhD. How I couldn't even recognise it as anxiety. Just a shortness of breath brought about by something lacking in my diet: iron, B12, folic acid, all that shite you're never really sure of at the chemist's. Or maybe something that had been introduced to me. A parasite. Over and over, in the shared house in Georgetown where I stayed, I would sit bolt upright and try to yawn, or otherwise just breathe deeply: anything that would allow me to reach that fullness in my lungs, that fullness that my own body was cruelly denying me, and thereby the sense of comfort that only knowing – truly knowing – that, yes, there was still enough oxygen left in this world for me, could bring.

When did you learn it was anxiety? she asked.

When I realised it went away whenever we spoke. Or if I was preoccupied with something else.

Like your research.

That, yes. Also, I had made a friend there and I noticed it disappeared whenever we were together.

Our time was up. She said talking about this might have shifted something for me and that it would be important to watch my own thoughts for the next little while, keep an eye on myself. But in the lift going down I felt more dismayed than ever. I had no idea what we were talking about. I wasn't sure why I had brought up my forum activities at all and the only thing that seemed to be shifting for me was the growing awareness that with each day that passed Sarah was further from me. I looked at myself in the video screen next to the door that projected the surveillance footage of the camera above me in real time. I stood without moving, watching myself. I was alone.

At home, I went into my study and turned on the computer. As I drew the curtains, the browser auto-filled with my username and password. Gratified, thrown again into that miserable space where I could be anyone I wanted but somehow always still chose a version so close to myself, I visited the familiar pages.

board/hotdepressedchicks
@alazon: i am the floor pile. walk over me.

Degrading myself further, the words weren't even mine.

IV

IN AN OVERPRICED Capitol Hill bar, we had agreed to meet at five o'clock to laugh about the foibles of our respective subjects and their apparently equally obsessive bookkeeping/hoarding. It was my first day in the Madison Building of the Library of Congress and I was utterly overwhelmed. Having completed all the necessary pre-registration forms online weeks beforehand, after retrieving my Reader Identification Card, I made my way to the Performing Arts Reading Room only to find that there some kind of altercation going on inside. I could see through the great glass panes of the door a couple of policemen speaking to a wearied man who remained seated but was gesticulating wildly with one arm while his other rested proprietorially over a vinyl record. Nevertheless, I started to enter on the basis that I had been directed to this location at registration and, in any case, was curious to see what all the fuss was about. But I had only opened the door about halfway when a librarian inside quickly stopped me and motioned me back into the hall with her, where, giving no indication of what was happening inside, she told me that she was familiar with my request and that several boxes for me had been taken down the hall to the Manuscript Reading Room around the corner from where we were standing and that she hoped this wouldn't be too inconvenient. But before I could respond, she turned back into the room. I stood for a moment, still watching. It seemed like whatever excitement there had been had tapered off and a stalemate was emerging that seemed to wear thin for every person involved. And as the door swung behind her I was given a glimpse into this disturbance, though it didn't make much sense to me.

Sir, I will tell you, again, for the final time: you cannot take the Goldberg Variations home with you.

But the humming! he shouted. With the software on my computer, I can remove his godawful humming!

In the next room I was ushered quickly to a table where a trolley was waiting for me. Actually confronting the number of boxes I had requested was staggering and it was far fewer that the number that would be available to me throughout my time. As I gazed upon them in all their beige and unhelpful cardboard glory, my head began to swim, and what had started as a nice excuse to go abroad suddenly appeared a herculean, if not Sisyphean, endeavour that I would surely never find the strength to rise to. I felt very foolish for thinking that I would get much done in six weeks and I wondered if anyone from the university would notice if the trip they were part-funding didn't result in the lynchpin to my thesis it had been planned for. With only my battered copy of Mingus's book sporadically underlined and scribbled on during the plane rides over, a pencil I had bought in a gift shop, and that neat yellow lined paper you only saw on American legal dramas before me, I wondered what the hell I was going to do.

Then, on a table not far from me, I saw her. I hesitated. She was clearly engrossed in her task. But she had mounds of material at her table too. And I was very attracted to her. I won't lie about that. It had only been three, maybe four days – I was also jet-lagged – since I had left home, but already I was craving some socialisation. My new flatmate never seemed to leave his room or was never there to begin with – I couldn't be sure of which because his door remained closed regardless and he never made a sound; only occasionally dirty dishes would present themselves in the sink – and I didn't know anyone in the city. So I'll admit right now that I knew exactly what I was doing when I walked over to her, leaned down next to her, and asked her, quietly, How do you start?

She looked at me, laughed, and then stifled herself. What do you mean?

How do you start? I repeated, indicating the trolley next to my chair. I have no idea what I'm doing.

You're a researcher?

PhD student, I said.

First year writing the thesis?

The third.

Oh, that year is the worst. But it doesn't matter where you start. You just have to start somewhere. Who've you got over there?

Charles Mingus – the jazz player. His memoir draft is literally over a thousand pages long. It's outrageous. You?

Philip Roth. This is just what he lets you see and it's still almost three hundred boxes.

What an arsehole. Who keeps all this keich?

I know.

Listen, I'm going to take your advice and get started but do you want meet at the end of the day and compare notes? Who knows, Mingus and Roth could be more alike than they seem.

She agreed and wrote down the name of a place she said was nearby and told me that she typically didn't leave the library until the close of each day.

I hadn't taken my laptop with me (stupid) and only had the burner phone I bought near the airport to use while I was in the U.S. But when I looked up around closing time she was engaged in a conversation with a librarian that seemed to be distinguishing the boxes she was finished with and the ones she would need the next day. I didn't want to interrupt, or seem like I was hanging around waiting for her, so I sorted myself out in the Performing Arts Reading Room – no, I'm not finished with anything yet, unfortunately – and made my way outside with zero indication of where I should go. I remember it was crisp and bright and I was becoming a little giddy. (Desiring simply could not compare with feeling desired!) I walked around aimlessly, hoping that I'd just run into the place, but in the end the assistance of a rowdy crew of men my age all wearing tailored but slightly ruffled suits was required.

In particular, she told me, she was interested in Roth's treatment of women in his texts, and especially the letters he had written to them, but, officially, she was focusing on the ambiguous fictionality of his narratives. Our drinks were in hand and we'd found a table outside on the brick-lined pavement. Laughing ruefully, she told me that one of his correspondents, a well-known English author who wrote only subtle, nearly sexless novels about lonely women, he would savage later with an artist friend, as they faxed each other sketches of her in various compromising positions. Only her side of their dialogue was in the archives, so it goes, but she had heard all about it from Roth's official biographer with whom she was sporadically in touch. Now that she was able to read the woman's cordial and effusive letters to him first-hand, she felt devastated on her behalf.

He actually called me once, she said. I had already received provisional copyright permission from his agent – an assistant of his agent, anyway – for my Newark article and even when that notice came through it felt like I had received a direct transmission from Jehovah Himself. But I guess Roth was made aware of my project and he had decided to dig deeper into what I was doing. So he calls me up. Random number from Connecticut. I didn't think anything of it, obviously. (I don't know if it's the same in Scotland, but we get these tedious scam calls all the time here in the U.S. that come from numbers similar to yours so you think it's someone you'll know.) Anyway, I say hello? And this surprisingly soft, almost tender, voice goes, It's Philip Roth. And I'm like, Okay... How are you Mr Roth? And he just starts laying into me. Says he's never heard of me; the proposal I wrote doesn't make any sense; I shouldn't believe what I read in the accounts of his jaded ex-lovers; how he's already discussed 'the woman thing' at length, etc. – some real *senex iratus*-type stuff. You know, just circular, obsessive nonsense about himself. Eventually, he pauses for breath, so I'm like wait a minute: do you want to hear my side of this or did you just call me up to yell at me? Clearly, it was then that he realised that he was talking to a young woman because his tone changes completely and he says, Well, I just don't think you're getting the full picture here. I can tell you're at the start of your career. Why don't you come up and visit me, blah blah blah, I'll cook you dinner and I'll show you why you're wrong to pursue this. I didn't go, of course. It has nothing to do with him! Everything I need is right over there. So I politely declined and tried to explain: I'm a serious scholar; I'm not writing anything gossipy; and he'll never hear anything more of this anyway because, like he said, no one has heard of me and probably never will. Except him, I guess! He didn't seem convinced, but the permission has remained intact ever since – thank God – so here I still am. No idea how he got my number.

I can't imagine what a phone call from Mingus would have been like, I replied. I don't believe half of what he says happened to him. I'm approaching it allegorically out of necessity more than anything else.

You probably don't remember, she said after a pause, but Bret Easton Ellis had this website up back when he was promoting *Lunar Park*. You know, that horror/faux-memoir thing he did. On one side was the biographical details of the 'real' Bret and on the other side it had the novel's 'Bret'.

She was flattering me to suggest that this was something I had once known but since forgotten. I'd read a few books by Ellis, it was true, but I wouldn't have thought to do a search of him on the internet that long ago, I don't think. But I enjoyed *Lunar Park* a lot and remembered it well.

Ha, I said, neither confirming nor denying any awareness on my part. I can't tell if that seems dated now or if it's actually quite an avant-garde way to go about it. You can interpret it as either a defensive move or an offensive one. But I wonder how much input into it he would have really had. I doubt it was a personal site. It was probably set up by his publisher.

What I can't remember, she said, is which one was on which side of the screen.

Do you think it makes any difference? I asked. If I had to guess I would bet that the 'real' Bret was on the left.

Well, he probably was. But the implications of that are still worth considering, don't you think? Because we read left to right, placing it there would presuppose the notion that our fake selves are springing forth from our 'real' ones; not the other way around. Isn't it possible, or, to be even more direct, plausible, to say that it's actually the images that we hold of ourselves that have the greater impact on who 'we' are? Or who we are to become? I am who I am because of who I think I am or who I think I want to be. I remember when I first read *Lunar Park*, I wanted to believe so badly that a version of those events had really happened. The text inculcates this desire, even as the author flagrantly fictionalises himself. And though I knew it simply couldn't be true – even back then everyone could see Bret portraying himself in a suburban, heterosexual homestead for the piss-take that it was – I was disappointed by how openly he announced it as an homage to Stephen King in his interviews. There was no attempt at the verisimilitude he so deftly portrays in the novel.

I guess for Bret any entanglement there was just a more abstract yet paradoxically more literal layer of what Barthes called the reality effect, another way to signify to us that the story he wanted to tell had 'happened', I said. All the through lines he establishes in the narrative to himself, and to his previous works, texturises for the reader what's really a story of grief for his father and longing for the reassurances of childhood. We're made to feel closer to him and therefore experience the pain he's trying to express all the more acutely, as in between old friends whose personal tragedies may not be able to compare, quantitatively, to the staggering atrocities that happen on the news every day, yet because of the trenchant connection that exists between them, what is essentially only a personal woe of, usually, not that much suffering, this tender outpouring of empathy and affection can be drawn, whereas an entire genocide somehow becomes this detached event of unfathomability and meaninglessness, of scorn almost. How dare this disaster intrude on my life? Etc. But outside of the confines of the book-object, blurring those lines has no use. As you say, his website formally separated the two.

But what I realised, she started before pausing briefly, is that it is true. Truer than any autobiography he could have written. What better way is there to convey your ambivalent sexuality in the wake of a stuffy upbringing in an upper middle-class WASP's nest than to portray yourself struggling within the same traditional family structures you were taught to idealise? How can we talk about the role of the father in our society without talking about spectres? The once-powerful tyrant whose vigour will inevitably fail him, his presence still felt long after his corporeal absence. To know Bret, you must first understand 'Bret'. I checked, and no cover I could find has ever declared the work to be 'a novel'. That would be too reductive. *Lunar Park* is the window into someone's soul. King, horror fiction, pastiche, they're all just the pathways into it. And what you're saying, she continued, correctly points to a real limit of the human condition, but it still seeks to depict these aspects as formal characteristics rather than at the heart of the reading experience itself. It's not just 'and now Bret is signifying the ways in which I should be moved'. It is also 'I am moved'. It's both and it's neither.

I think Faulkner might have written something similar about journalism, I said, not knowing quite what else to say.

I knew my instincts were too structuralist to keep up with her on this. To me, everything was just a device. Even at my most inventive – and I've never written much fiction – I was still Geoffrey Braithwaite trying every literary trick in the book to hide myself from the dissolution of my marriage. Everything was a game to me, like I assumed it was for everybody else as well. But there was something about what she said that spoke to me; chilled me, even. It seemed to imply a certain unknowability in the other that only the exceptional artistic act could reveal, and what it then revealed would say as much about the artist as it did about us as an audience. This was information I didn't know what to do with. What did I really know about anyone? About myself?

I'm sorry, she said. I'm boring you with my earnestly held opinions on authorship.

No, please, not at all, I said. If anything, I'm simply too boring to come up with something interesting to say in response. You've given me a lot to think about with my own project.

A moment passed while a dog next to us barked into space, exciting itself.

So have you published any of this, then? I asked.

On Bret Easton Ellis?

She laughed incredulously.

No way, that dude sucks.

Back at the house, I logged on to my email and sent a message to Sarah, telling her about my first day in the library. The first half of it, anyway.

V

THE YEAR BEFORE Sarah died we were invited to a Halloween party thrown by a work colleague of hers whom she didn't know very well but had wanted to befriend since she had joined at the office where they were the two youngest by far. As we're both big fans of the whole Village scene in '60s and '70s New York, which seemed to us the most ideal time and location for artistic creation and consumption in modern history, we decided to go as Sam Shepard and Patti Smith. I swept my hair back, put some ratty jeans on and a tartan shirt with pearl snap buttons over a vintage tee I had bought for £20, soft and faded from a thousand washes. Basically, I looked like myself. Sarah spent hours with a curling iron and product getting her hair perfectly ragged like an old mop and then dressed herself blindly, having decided to thrust her arm into her closet and wear whatever came out so long as it was black, which was most of her wardrobe, and to throw her leather jacket on top of it all. From this, out of its pocket, flopped a raw steak, folding over on itself, rubbery and thick and revolting, an homage to a key moment from Smith's memoir when she met Shepard for the first time.

I have to admit we were both excited. Never typically thrilled at the prospect of spending long periods of time with people I don't already know very well, I warmed to the occasion as we dressed, drinking some beers and laughing a lot as we did so. Sarah clearly wanted to make a good impression on her new co-worker. It was also our first time out of the house in a while.

Everyone was actually really personable, I thought. Helped in part by the abundantly distributed alcohol and drugs, of this there was little doubt. But I was wary of getting wasted. A lot of the drama in people's lives, I felt, they brought onto themselves with their own unimaginative impulses, and, as in a horrible *danse macabre*, they paraded fragile, almost ironic senses of their own mortality (the skulls are always smiling) before everyone else as if it was some cute quirk that would make them special. Thematically, I guess, that just didn't appeal to me. I was also constantly aware of the limited number of braincells that I would be capable of firing in my lifetime, and fervently wished to preserve as many as I would be able to during that lifetime, within reason of course. Sarah partook freely which was fine.

After an hour or two, having lost her for a moment, I walked into the small back garden for some fresh air, which, to my dismay, was mostly filled with cigarette smoke. I was about to turn back inside when I heard someone call over to me, Hey are you supposed to be Charles Bukowski?

Christ no, I replied, turning around to see a woman wearing a suit. I'm Sam Shepard.

But she was right. While the hair and perfectly unkempt outfit might have been working in my favour, going unshaven plainly wasn't.

Wait, is that your name? she asked. Or is that who you're dressed like.

It's who I'm supposed to be dressed like, I clarified.

Who is Sam the Shepherd? she asked.

He's playwright, kind of in the same period as Bukowski, actually. He's an actor too, though. Have you seen *Days of Heaven?*

No, she said.

The Right Stuff?

Uh-uh.

The Notebook?

Yes! she cried. I thought it was trashy as hell and way too sentimental though, so if that was some kind of film buff test, I promise I didn't fail it. I know who Terrence Malick is and I think Tom Wolfe is a fraud. But I'll freely admit I didn't know they had adapted that into a movie. Not that I would see it regardless.

Fair enough, I said. Astronauts are boring. But I have also seen *The Notebook* and not *The Right Stuff,* so no worries. I only mentioned it because Sam Shepard won an Oscar for it. And *Days of Heaven* is excellent, you should definitely watch that. Anyway, he plays Ryan Gosling's dad in *The Notebook.*

She laughed and said, This is getting ridiculous. I don't even remember there being a dad in that. I'm just going to look your shepherd boy up.

She pulled her phone out and I leaned over her as she started typing.

Wow, he's fit, she said.

Don't I look like him? I asked, facing her, presenting myself.

She appraised me for a moment and then said, Maybe if you had shaved and contoured your cheekbones a bit.

Ouch, I replied.

I'm kidding, she said. You've got that Wild West thing going on with your shirt, I guess. And you *are* a bit rugged, like a coyote.

Thanks, I said, thrilled with any approximation. Who are you dressed as? John Major?

She playfully pushed me away and shouted, Hey! Just because I didn't know who you were...

Okay, okay, I replied. Not Tom Wolfe either then, I suppose. One more guess... Annie Hall.

Yes! she cried. I'm very sorry to say you're only, like, the third or fourth person to get that.

Couldn't the tie be a bit longer? I asked.

Well, I did have some trouble with it, as you might imagine, she said.

Here, I'll help, I responded, walking around behind her, loosening it all the way out and then starting to remake it around her neck. The tension between us felt enormous as I did this. Throughout our conversation we had been maintaining eye contact far more steadily than any casual dialogue required and it seemed to be building a palpable sense of propitious expectation. It would need to be broken, one way or another. But for now I planned to avoid it.

So why do you hate Wolfe? I asked. There, that's better. Very Diane Keaton.

First of all, I didn't say I hated him, she said. I just think his 'fictional novels' schtick is weaselly and indicative of a mind that has general difficulty coping with ambivalence or ambiguity. Like, would Joyce's 'kindly lights' of Dublin really be rendered more acutely through a caricature of some historic Irish resistance figure nobody even remembered five years later, especially if the cost of it was pretty sentences that could actually mean something? I mean really mean something? There were so many people writing the books Wolfe claims he wanted to read in that crap essay of his, too – women especially, hello! – they probably just recognised that there isn't actually a tension between realism and something that's enjoyable to read, you know? Something that can help you to see something more about yourself. Or at least there doesn't have to be. Modernism did exist, by the way? We're not going to just forget about that because it would be convenient for his argument. But I'm not at all convinced he's actually very interested in literature, so maybe this is way beside the point. Anyway, don't get me started.

I laughed. You kind of already have, but that's okay. I've never read anything by him myself, so this is all new to me. I just think he dresses like an arsehole and I'm generally sceptical of people that lean that heavily into their own identity.

Except Woody Allen, she said gravely, grabbing my arm with the fixed stare of mock concern.

I think I'd agree with that, actually, I said. I certainly prefer his aesthetic over Wolfe's.[1]

Her hand remained at my arm as her face softened back to its blasé, slightly haughty neutral expression that really was quite attractive to me, as it seems I have a bit of a thing for posh English girls.

Unfortunately, you don't look at all like Alvy Singer, she said, inspecting me first and then herself. Together we're probably closer to Simon and Garfunkel. If they had dressed in each other's clothes, or something.

---

1 Going back through this little episode, I feel the need to make absolutely clear that this conversation took place before Dylan Farrow's open letter against Allen, which was when the whole thing got put back into the public consciousness. Regardless, I wouldn't intentionally dress like him. Okay?

She looked up at me and that sense of a newly formed yet seemingly unbreakable connection suddenly returned. She put her arms around herself like she was cold. We had been out here for some time and were the only two left in the back garden. My heart started to pound and it was as though I could perceive my pupils dilating in the growing darkness.

That reminds me, I said, stammering slightly. I should probably go and find my wife. Our costumes are barely recognisable when we're together, let alone separated.

Yeah. Sure, okay.

I could tell this was new, unexpected information to her and I felt bad that I had given her the wrong impression. Or, rather, that I had purposefully given her the correct impression, even though on paper it had been a perfectly innocent interaction and one throughout which I had maintained a veneer of plausible deniability, if I needed it.

You don't wear a ring, she said.

Well, I always figure I might decide to become a dentist one day and then I couldn't wear one anyway, I joked.

She didn't laugh. Which one is your wife?

She's got long dark hair, I said, realising as I said it that it wasn't very descriptive. And she's wearing a leather jacket.

You mean Patti Smith? I think she looks incredible. Well done, she said punching me lightly on the arm where previously she had held it.

Cheers, I said. The crow thing works for her, I guess.

We walked inside and were both surprised to see how much of the party had cleared. A couple of stragglers stranded on the couch in the main room told us that most people had moved on to a club down the road but a few had gone upstairs to hang out.

Sarah wouldn't go to a club without me, I muttered, starting to feel a little nervous. I couldn't remember the state she had been in when I had lost track of her. Nothing had seemed out of the ordinary to me at the time but things could turn quickly for her if she accepted a shot of spirits or hadn't eaten enough.

I climbed the stairs but I didn't call for her as we were always wary of coming across parentally to the other. There were only a couple of bedrooms in any case and when I heard laughter from one of them and that old Lee Hazlewood album describing a lonesome town where most people are good and bad most of the time that my parents used to listen to, I approached it instinctively even though I couldn't hear her voice from inside of it. But she wasn't there. A small group were sitting on the floor spinning a dark green wine bottle amongst themselves – a joke, I presumed. (We weren't all just pretending to be adults, were we?)

Has anyone seen Patti Smith? I asked.

I think she went in there, one of them said, pointing across the hall to a closed door.

Hey, wait a second, who are you? Harry Dean Stanton? I heard as I turned and walked out of the room.

Some light was shining through to the landing, beneath the frame of the door. I opened it slowly. From the glow of a bedside lamp, I could just make out a man dressed in a *Phantom of the Opera* costume standing against a wall, his face partially obscured, his trousers at his ankles with a dark, amorphous figure squatted round his crotch in front of him. He didn't notice me there and moaned lowly while wet noises emanated from beneath him. Finally registering what I was seeing, I revolted backward and started to turn away

– maybe in search of Annie, I honestly don't know – when I heard the Phantom say, That's it you dirty bitch, such a good little slut.

I waited to hear her reaction to such demeaning language, the kind of thing I'd never said, out loud, to anyone. And when all she returned was murmur in acquiescence, I erupted.

Sarah! I yelled, my voice sharp in aggrievement and so pained, so clearly pained, so declaratory of its own misery it was: like a child; like a hurt, lost, pathetic little child. Even now it embarrasses me to hear it ring out inside of my own head; as I type this on my clacky Smith Corona, I can't help but cringe and recoil.

What the hell do you think you're doing? I demanded, my words bursting forth from me now like I was reciting them from some high school drama script we were still rehearsing and wouldn't understand for years.

They both leapt away from the wall, straightening themselves out instinctively. He began to say something conciliatory to me, patting me on the back aggressively all the while, but I told him to just get out of there. As he left, I realised that my interruption had taken place in full view of the group in the other room, who presently sat quietened and slackjawed. For fuck's sake, I shouted, slamming the door, adrenaline now coursing rapturously through my thirsty veins. In such a wrathful state, I was at risk of becoming unmoored. My eyes, adjusting to the room's dingy golden glow – a dull, dismal fool's gold – cast about the place as if I expected a queue of men to appear before me from beneath the bed or out of the wardrobe like a demented children's story.

Is this a joke? I yelled. Who the fuck was that?

She looked down, playing with her fingers, shoulders slumped, hair a mess, body ashamed, and without warning crumpled desperately towards the floor.

Sarah, I asked you something.

Crying now, she blubbered that she didn't know who he was. She hadn't even seen what he looked like without the mask. He was just some guy who in that moment had wanted her, and she had wanted him for it.

Before I could compose any reply to this repulsive detail, I was taken aback when a noise of chortled, frustrated anguish burst forth from somewhere deep inside of her, reminding me of a confused and distressed urban fox. She was obviously drunk, and probably high too, but, still, it didn't seem a satisfactory explanation for this outrageous encounter, to either my wounded ego or to basic logic. Here? Now?

Why? I asked quietly, her propulsion of despair finally stilling me. Why would you do this to me?

It wasn't going to go any further, she said, wiping her nose on her jacket, the jacket I can see now she would have been keen for me to realise that she was still wearing, its lurid meat flapping away at the motion of her arm.

You were just going to go down on the guy? I asked, trying – trying – to be gentle. While he calls you a slut? How, exactly, is that any better than you fucking him? It's disgusting.

I could feel the venom start to coagulate inside of my throat again, choking me.

Answer me, Sarah.

Because it's not real! Because it wasn't procreative for once! she shouted.

I backed away from her, almost involuntarily. I could feel my eyes bulge in astonishment. As I walked down the stairs and out of the house, I could just make out the record in the other room running now a desultory, circular void of empty needle scratching. Sarah's heaving sobs would provide the house's new soundtrack, it seemed; everyone having retreated elsewhere, to someplace far away from such disturbing theatre.

We walked home in silence, she a few paces behind. Every now and then I would glance back to make sure she hadn't collapsed or something, but never would she look up at me. It was as if she was all alone. The streets were so quiet, the waters of the snaking river next to us so calm. I could have fallen to my knees and cried into the night like a wounded animal and no one would have taken any notice. I could have thrown myself into its watery depths and sank like a stone.

But I didn't. I led us home. I opened the door. I made myself a drink. And, yes, I put on the record again, the song that had upset her some weeks beforehand. For ten minutes it just rang out, relentless and doleful. I was going to deal with this in my own way, I thought. If she wasn't going to deal with it at all, well, I couldn't help her. I wouldn't be able to help her.

But when I woke in the morning, I was ashamed. I got up from the couch, crawled into bed next to where she still lay, and I held her; my hand on her stomach, my breath in her hair.

I must admit I initially wrote this as justification, for exculpation of the actions that I would later be asked to take. Only reading it over again now can I see that it is anything but. Mother Earth was pregnant for the third time. Because I had knocked her up.

VI

THE 'NOT JUST a dalliance but a full-blown affair', as it was later to be called, was, I suppose, inaugurated on the second day of my stint at the Library of Congress. It was a grey morning, and the bus passed the White House, through the National Mall, holding a kind of significance for me that made the institutions of my own country seem somehow quainter and more distant than ever before. That they were plainly visible, that you could even walk through, the settings of the scenarios that had rocked the world, some seemingly so innocuous to our sophisticated minds today that it is only with the benefit of our knowledge of the events to come that their ramifications can even begin to be understood – lying about a blow job, for instance; a national investigation hinging on what one broken man's sophistic definition of the word 'is' is – would continue to dazzle me throughout my time there.

And when I saw her through a glimpse at the door of the Manuscript Reading Room – she had arrived there before me, as expected – I was unsure whether I should approach her again while she worked. Although I wished to settle into that table I had sat at previously – I can feel myself yearn to call it 'my table' in my head, even now; to call her 'my girlfriend' – I was instructed at registration to continue my research amongst the other performing arts materials, as was originally intended. There, I set about arranging the files I would be going through. By now, I had at least started this monumental task but still I was in search of the direction that my time spent here would take. Though I had come to terms with the fact that I could not meaningfully engage with the eighty-four boxes available to me over the six-week period – and that it wouldn't necessarily be helpful to try to – I knew that I nevertheless needed to get to work on something. The problem, such that there was one, in the grand scheme, was that while I understood the manner in which *Beneath the Underdog* was situated within the shape of my thesis, I was at a loss as to how my study of his manuscript could actually prove any of the things that I would need it to. I had argued so vigorously for the necessity of the trip in the funding applications, and to my supervisors, I had lost sight of the fact that it was only ever just that, merely an argument in support of something that I had wanted. Though in the evenings, on the weekends, when the close of business would leave any and every administrative affair at the university at a standstill, I was able to admit to myself, and to Sarah, that it was hardly the essential element of my thesis that I was making it out to be, I still assumed something critical would be learnt as a matter of course, and that whatever it was would surely take the prominent place in my research that I needed it to. But as a result of these dual forces – on the one hand, the need to prove my case and justify the expenditure; on the other, the presumption that things would work out for themselves once I was there – it seemed I had misplaced my awareness of how much of the idea had spawned from the happenstance of the library's location in a faraway place that appealed to me, and the free availability of money that could take me there.

The truth was, I didn't actually know how to talk about Mingus. For some reason – besides simply our completely diverging demographics, I think – I had been finding it more difficult to produce the metaphors I needed which had seemed to arrive so easily to me with Nadar or Williams. The massive manuscript, alongside its factual record, I had rationalised, would illuminate all the myths for me. The edits would be clear, the novelistic embellishments in stark counterpoint to the sober reportage. With my flimsy and irritating airline-provided eye-mask on, I had imagined that I would see them, literally, side by side. But the boxes that confronted me now only taunted my mixed-up mind further, so cruelly did they seem to blend fact with fiction, as the 'Writings by Charles Mingus' and 'Writings about Charles Mingus' sections overlapped in their absurd stories, or contradicted each other with competing but no less outlandish claims to his actions and behaviours. While at the time it had been taken for granted in critical circles that some of the more shocking descriptions of moments during Mingus's childhood had been, at the very least, exaggerated, many of these same moments would be seen to become validated by his sisters, years after the book's publication, after his death – though they would also claim to have never witnessed his temper, a quality as legendary as it was well documented. I just didn't know what to make of it all.

Creativity isn't necessarily straightforward in its dealings with the world. To put it another way, no one has ever convinced me that the geniuses who have the lasting human touch we call art are either monsters or role models, or even that they should be. Shamans don't have to be horrible or nice. They just have to work effectively in their surroundings, account for some of the planet's mysteries in ways the people they live among can understand.

What counts about artists is that they perceive reality differently. In any clinical sense they're not schizophrenics (although historically some of them have been that too) because they produce something coherent in its own terms that is valued by their communities – their art, their strikingly individual contributions to human culture. Artists don't simply reflect their lives and times like mirrors, but if they're worth anything they light some way we haven't seen from quite that angle before. That takes a genius; otherwise everybody would be doing it.[2]

But was Mingus a genius? I wasn't sure, and I was even less sure that it really mattered one way or another. But while one of my supervisors warned me against any kind of hagiography for any of my subjects, the other encouraged me to lean into it, to wear my allegiances on my sleeve, and to avail myself of my biases so that any replications of them in my thesis could be read by the examiners within their authentic context. But the more I thought about this, the more detached I began to feel from my writing and from my own sense of self. 'Myself When I Am Real' – that was the title of one of his most accomplished pieces. But what is Being Real? And who or what is My Self? Mingus was implicitly asking us some compelling questions, but, for all I admired it, I doubted if the music, for all its artistry, could hold many answers for anyone other than the Self himself. While aspects of his personality can certainly be read into the multiple movements of the beguiling piano piece – it

---

2 See copyright page.

jumps from the delicate, to the wild, to the contemplative, to the unsettling, to the beautiful, to the impatient, to, finally, unexpectedly, the dissonant − none of it made any clearer for me how I should disentangle the man, the music, or the text. By now in my studies, I knew that to respond to a performative work one needed to write performatively, but nevertheless something nagged at me, insisting that if I didn't know Miles, I could never know Mingus, and that any search for a methodology while the grasp of the subject − the Real subject − was so tenuous would inevitably prove futile.

And what was Nel King's role in the book as co-author? Before the narrative has even begun, Mingus writes, 'I would like to express my deep thanks to Nel King, who worked long and hard editing this book, and who is probably the only white person who could have done it.' Yet few of his biographers even mention King, and it's apparent that the manuscript had passed through many hands before it ever reached her. Perhaps there was something to this. The life lived first for oneself before then being lived for − and through − those close to us as we start to take on the roles of biographer and editor for everyone else's stories. Yet here I was caught betwixt both and neither, muddling my way through the documents as an interpreter, a translator, and, ultimately, I felt, a charlatan. I thought I would find some comprehensive evidence of her involvement, whatever it might have been: new writing, perhaps, or some significant cutting, the introduction of its multiple points of view, an altered voice − that I could mine for my discussions of how his anecdotes seem to reify the methods of his jazz compositions. But the years and dates never made sense, and her typescript draft was so similar to the final copy, I felt suddenly thrown back to where I had first started. I sat there dumbfounded, furtively fingering a lock of his son Eric's hair that I had stumbled upon in a thin, yellowing envelope. The hair was soft and illicit. It was a stranger's.

What in the heck is that? she asked, suddenly appearing above me.

It is, unfortunately, exactly what it looks like, I replied. His son's. From the Personal series – subheading Miscellaneous, which I suppose is accurate. You can also find Mingus's divorce papers and some credit card statements too, if you're curious.

Roth wishes I had access to those, she joked. See, she said, imitating his voice, I didn't take any of those women out to dinner. None of them!

I laughed. What are you up to, then? I asked.

Still wading through his correspondence. The other side of it, anyway. Seems unfair that he didn't put any of his own letters in the collection, but I don't suppose he was making carbon copies. Of course, email has superseded that problem with its organic threading of replies. We'll forever be read in complete context, alas. Hey, do you want to take a break?

Sure, I said. What do you have in mind?

Well, the weather still isn't great – you'll be used to it, actually; it's a lot like where you're from! – but we could go check out one of the exhibitions in the library's other building across the street?

Okay, I said, smiling, ignoring the comment about the weather which I was already sensitive to as it seemed so frequently remarked upon by Americans, often in what appeared to be demonstration of some strange superiority/ inferiority complex which in either case confused me as our countries supposedly had such a special relationship. Sounds good! Should we go now?

But the weather was, in fact, very much like what I was accustomed to, if slightly more humid: it was quite windy, spitting with rain, and what would appear unseasonably chilly. The difference was that it would last for days here, rather than a few hours at home when it would go away and return and go away, all over again, and again. But as she had only done a semester abroad at Oxford, I wasn't quite ready to accede to her expertise on the subject, not least because of a story she had told me the day before in which she'd gone *down* to Edinburgh for a weekend.

As we stood on the corner waiting to cross, both groping to fill the silence between us, I mentioned that I'd recently had something about Mingus published in one of Britain's most prestigious literary magazines. She seemed impressed and told me she had emailed the editors there three times in the past year with book review proposals, but they had never once responded to her.

It was true: in the letters section, in response to a short article by the magazine's editor at large that had touched on the diversity of personas represented by the jazz greats, I speculated that far from ever being an actual pimp, Mingus returned to the activity over and over in his self-mythologising in order to relate his growing inability to make the aesthetic goals of his artistry distinct from those of the music industry's relentless profit motive. But, as I told her this, I realised I had made it sound like it was a commissioned article, like I was some kind of authority who had been sought out for his invaluable perspective on the subject. Then, she pulled out her phone and started to search for it.

It's only a small thing, I said, a sense of dread creeping onto me. It was just a letter. Really, it's nothing. It's really not worth reading. Please.

(What I also didn't say was that days after it was published I realised I had made a mistake in my sourcing, mixing up two different accounts I had been drawing my material from. While it didn't change the substance of my contribution, still I had agonised over this for months, never owning up to it with the editors, checking each subsequent issue fastidiously – my heart thumping – for someone to call me out on it in indignant reply. In hindsight, this is of course preposterous, but such was my guilt.)

Her face didn't register anything when she'd found it. Then, after a moment, she said, It's good. It's funny. It's Adorno, right?

Huh. He was probably an influence, yeah, I conceded unsurely, suddenly registering that I hadn't even considered the Marxist angle when I was feverishly drafting it the night I'd emailed it in. Writing to their standards of tone and content had been the first priority; the theoretical context of the points it was making a distant second. But Adorno didn't even like jazz, I sputtered, recovering slightly. To him it was just another ideology that only exhibited the ornaments of change, rather than any true development beyond the confines of its rhythmic or melodic structures. Those critiques would hardly apply to Mingus, in my opinion, but, of course, Adorno wasn't exactly known for being compromising. (Phew.)

Trees dotted the wide streets where we walked. Reaching above us, cast iron lamplights stood impatiently in the static, penumbral haze, waiting for darkness... A few tourists admired the building to which we were headed, or perhaps merely the haughty flag flapping above it. I thought of my own allegiances, torn so they were at home. Sarah, a fierce Scottish nationalist brooked no dissent on the matter and I loved her for it, even as I obliquely flirted with a further-left politics that rejected borders entirely. That we, the people, had been called determine such a huge, binary question on Europe only two years after the one on independence was faintly ridiculous to me, but before I left, I elected her as my proxy in full knowledge of how my vote would be cast while I was away.

But I wasn't led to the steps where I had assumed we were going and instead we broke away momentarily as I started up them before registering the path that she was still on was leading to a small but intricate fountain display next to the pavement and situated directly below our ultimate destination. I turned around and walked over to meet her there.

A muscly Neptune was staring past me – hard and handsome with bronze beard flowing – from a seated posture of ambivalence and sensuality. On either side, two sea nymphs on horseback were racing fast as they could away from him, all the while blinded, being sprayed in the face by two of his servile turtles. Nearer to him, resting their arms on his rocky perch, two tritons lackadaisically blew their conchs, also tormenting the nymphs with their own relentless streams. Centred beneath, Neptune's long, twisting sea serpent spat towards us a puny little jet, and, carved into the stone behind this whole scene was a sentry of thirsty fish holding their mouths luridly open in anticipation.

We took it in, standing next to each other rather close. We were the only ones in the vicinity who'd stopped to look. I shifted on my feet, looked away and then back again at the sculptures.

This is why I'm not such a huge fan of oral sex, I blurted after a silence, immediately regretful of the words even as they ventured from my mouth. Too much politics.

Mercifully she laughed and even met my overtures in kind. I know what you mean, she said. But I think our generation can overthink some of these things, especially wherever pleasure is concerned. You probably just haven't met a genuinely enthusiastic participant yet.

(This is when I should have said something. I see now the space for a simple if perhaps slightly tenuous segue to my wife and our own proclivities, or whatever; a coded reference of some kind, a backing away, an admission. We had only known each other for a day and a bit. The pretence of platonic connection we'd established had yet to be breached in any meaningful sense and we could have carried on the rest of our time together at the library in the same stifled, licentious manner that I was able to maintain with several colleagues at the university on our late nights in the shared space: flickeringly charged moments across an electric kettle, eyes meeting in secret over a bank of computers. But never more. There would be some remark about how I don't wear a ring, I'd make the same joke about how it's because I might one day decide to get into dentistry, and then we'd move on, separate but together, bound in an erotically miasmal strain all the more rewarding for its endless possibilities that would never have to be tested, never forced to come up against the disappointing realities of, well, reality. This outing would be our last like it, perhaps, or maybe, just maybe, everything could have carried on much the same as it did, but with a greater sense of transparency and trust, bridging some of those gaps between fantasy and actuality without profoundly disturbing either, and, ultimately, without some of its most painful consequences.

Neptune's impassive gaze fell onto me as my nervous system – now reacting only to language, to suggestion, and to the sexually charged atmosphere of this moment – drained blood perceptibly downward to my hardening penis.

Yet I dissembled.)

Maybe you're right, I said, letting the words dangle and so drawing myself deeper into my strange, unfocused game.

VII

THERE WAS SOMETHING dazzling about the Jefferson
Building's lobby where we were that distinguished it totally
from the bland courthouse-like Madison Building where our
materials were stored. In the foreign press, it seemed as if
Americans were routinely told that their country was poor,
or that the governance itself was of such a low standard that
even the most simple problems couldn't be solved without so
many sops to special interest groups and 'compromises' with
lobbyists that everyone in office pretty much gave up on doing
anything and just let those with the most money have their
way with the basic functionings of society. I was thinking in
particular of an article I had read in a newspaper back home
about the predatory payday loans industry in the U.S. that
was ravaging the most impoverished communities. This was
once a problem in Britain, too, but after several high-profile
incidents, regulation was swift and had slain many of the most
egregious lenders, leaving those that remained much more
cautious and amenable. But in the U.S., the dragon of greed
was a hydra, and every knight a coward. I could have wept
for some of the poverty I saw on my trip when so much of
it was so clearly beyond the trickier culpabilities of addiction
and mental illness like I was used to coming across in the
indigent at home. In the streets of America, you could see it
plain on their faces: they simply didn't have enough to live. To

survive, yes. Not live. I'm not saying things are perfect here – the response to the crash was dreadful, though Scotland was hardly alone in being bullied into accepting austerity (funny how I catch myself now parroting Sarah's talking points) – but I did get the impression more of us are able to live fuller lives than our transatlantic counterparts. America was a classless society, maybe. But hardly a casteless one.

What to think, then, of such a richly decorated interior, packed with motif-laden marble structures, elaborate murals, intricate friezes, and towering statues of staunch literary figures? I stood in wonder at it all and tried to imagine where everything had gone wrong. I felt if the period still existed, I would fall into it utterly beguiled and weave myself into the fabric of its unique intellectual life, like an Eliot in reverse.[3]

I whipped my head around as if I was an officious foreman looking up at a stalled building site in frustration. Big Government's really got its tentacles in here, huh? I said, adopting an approximation of an American accent.

She laughed.

Shut it down! I yelled, waving my hands, startling several tourists and attracting the bemused glare of a lone security guard.

---

3 Look, I am obviously aware that there's something a bit problematic, for a variety of a reasons, about seeming to glorify the artistic output of the American Renaissance which, like today, was a time of vast inequalities, and, in any case, isn't really my field or period. But what I'm only cautiously approving here is the state's apparent regard for aesthetics and scholarship in public life at that time, rather than endorse any whole movement or institution unequivocally. Regardless, I think most people can agree that the idea of the U.S., today, establishing anything remotely as ambitious (and non-belligerent) is pretty much unthinkable. Right?

Wow, you're really embracing the Land of the Freedom to Have Nothing, she replied, taking my hand into hers.

We walked past a Gutenberg Bible open to the Book of Esther – an odd and, as a result, seemingly deliberate choice, and no less cryptic for it, I thought – on our way to the exhibition, which, as it turns out, was called 'America Reads', a response to a survey put on a few years beforehand that had asked the public to name which books they believed to be the most 'important' in shaping contemporary life in the country, displayed in tandem with their chosen favourites from a curated list that had been compiled by an panel of experts for a previous exhibit.

Oh, we can have fun with this, she said.

In the first room there was a kind of introduction-*cum*-disclaimer by the library. On the one hand, it seemed reasonable and justified. On the other, it was also rather pathetic and seemed to acknowledge a discomfort with democracy conspicuously incompatible with the exhibit's stated aims:

The books chosen were not what critics would consider to be 'the best', we were told.

Of course.

Nor were the selections representative of the diversity of the country.

Okay…

And Ayn Rand occupied the top two spots.

Ah. Right. Got it.

I think I'm starting to understand what this exhibit is really about, I said. The infiltration of right-wing hegemony in what until recently was considered the purview of over-educated liberals.

I can't help but wonder about those thousands of responses they claim to have gotten, she said. I guarantee you that was not an in-person paper survey of visitors to the previous exhibit. Definitely online, probably with multiple votes allowed. In fact, I'd love to see the IP clusters. 95% within a five-mile radius of here, I'd be willing to bet.

To be fair, I said, they were only looking for books that 'shaped' America. You can't really argue with that, even if there was foul play. Or, should I say, especially if there was foul play.

True, she said. Plus, I really think even reading has become so politicised that just buying a certain book is, like, an endorsement of your politics, whatever those might be. The equivalent of wearing your team's jersey, or something. I absolutely refuse to believe that any of these Senators who are totally somehow not at all embarrassed to say that *Atlas Shrugged* is their favourite book have read it more than once or considered anything more about it than the ideology that they believe that it espouses. It's all a shorthand way of saying, Vote for me, I'm an asshole just like you. Even with our current president, who claims to read fiction, they still release these clearly focus-grouped bullshit 'summer reading lists'. You can just imagine the conversations they've had about what each choice *says* to their voting bloc. But can you imagine if somebody in public life came out and said that, actually, they really admired the provocative style of Knausgård's *Min Kamp* series?

She'd get my vote, I said.

Smooth, she replied. Too bad you can't vote here.

I stood there looking at her. We were quiet. The only sound in the room was our own breathing, and the occasional shrieking child somewhere in the far distance. I had a choice. No, that's not true. I'd had a choice about half an hour ago. Now, I had a duty. Not quite an obligation, and not at all a command, but neither at this point did I feel truly capable of exercising my free will towards any question other than when, how, and where.

You're so awkward, she said, laughing. And she kissed me. It was a rush unlike anything I had experienced since I was a child. Because even in the time before Sarah and I met, I had been going out on the pull with my mates from school fairly regularly, so whatever newness the weekend would bring was never in itself the thrill, not any more so than the fact that it was happening at all, and – better still – would be witnessed by my peer group. Not like now.

But I couldn't kiss her with anything other than Sarah's kiss. It had been too long, and we were too practiced for me to give to her anything other than what I only knew now to give. Perhaps she was doing the same, returning with the remnants of some cherished but doomed love affair, or the lasting passions for a hated but fuckable ex. I don't know, because to be honest I never once asked her. But we were negotiating this here, with our lips, with our flitting tongues. Figuring out together when our teeth were open for a dart, when the lips started to close in osculation. Where to put our hands. When to stop.

It didn't stop. Maybe we were compensating for something, maybe our bodies were just that urgent, but she broke away only to pull me around the giant room divider made to look like the page from a book that we were standing in front of, dragging me drastically forward in time from the birth of the nation to the beginning of its end: *Capitalism and Freedom* by Milton Friedman. She pushed me against its duplicitous description, kissing my neck, unbuckling my jeans. I helped her with the zip as she reached below and began to yank vigorously.

She looked down, giggled a bit, leaned towards my ear, and whispered, How European.

I stood there with laboured breath and that prickle of pleasure extending like an itch from the locus of its physical sensation all the way to my brain, and to my heart.

I can't believe this is happening, I said.

She grinned, glanced behind her, dropped my trousers to the floor, and lowered herself beneath me. I just stood there and let it happen to me. It was incredible, in every sense of the word. And, at the time, what I regarded as possibly one of the best things to ever happen to me.

As the orgasm began to build, and I edged closer to the Point of No Return – a Very Serious physiological phrase that continuously startled me whenever I came across it online – I caught her eye, held her hair in my hand, and groaned, Where do you want me to come?

She released my cock from her mouth for only a moment to say, Where do you want to?

Before I could answer – before I could think of an answer – the security guard turned the corner of the big, stupid page where we were loitering.

Jesus Christ, he said, jumping back away from us.

I'm really, really sorry, I said while she gathered herself together and I stuck myself back inside of my clothes.

In this moment, I was terrified. I saw myself like a cartoon character dripping great beads of sweat with tremorous lines of nervousness zagging at my sides, my long furry ears drooping in disgrace. But her? She started laughing. Laughed and laughed, so that I started laughing, and then, eventually, he did too.

Y'all are crazy, he said. But seriously, this is a family place. Go do that shit somewhere else or I'll be the one who gets in trouble.

We thanked him red-faced and left the library quickly, never reaching the exhibit's final display, *The Things They Carried*.

VIII

THE DAY HAD cleared while we were inside and we went to sit on the stone wall above the Court of Neptune, facing back towards scene of our crime in all its beaux-arts majesty.

There, she said. Now you're an American sex offender.

I don't know, I replied. I'm pretty sure I'm the victim of one.

Oh really, she said, and we leant in towards each other to kiss, gently now, and with feeling.

The sun was above us, my testicles were tender, and I felt so light it was like some side-street marionettist was drawing me up to full posture in the moment of great dramatic triumph before the show's inevitable comic denouement.

Hey, she said. I know this is kind of weird… but can I take a photo of your Reader Identification Card?

Um, I guess, I said, pulling it out from my pocket. Can I ask why?

I know it's dumb. But I was talking to my roommates about you last night and they were all freaked out because, you know, everyone meets on apps and stuff these days and – I don't know – there's, like, no verification of who anybody is in this kind of situation. I said to them, Well I know he has access to the special collections. That must mean something, right? But they insisted that if you murdered me they'd have no way of tracking you down because you could've told me a fake name. So, uh, is this okay? I trust you, I swear. It'll just save to my cloud. I promise I won't give it to them or anything. They've obviously been watching too much TV.

I smiled and handed it over. She inspected and held her phone out towards it.

I'm jealous, she said. You have such a writer's name. Beard is a little... unusual, obviously. But you're a boy, so you can pull it off. If you were a girl you'd get the Nabokov treatment – *Lolita*, I think? – 'What a name for a woman!' that kind of thing. So, basically, just don't have any daughters and you'll be fine. Not that we should really care what Humbert Humbert thinks.

It's two commonplace nouns, I pointed out. It's hardly even a name. But, yeah, this is me. Funny that it's become anomalous and sinister to meet someone spontaneously. I'm doubtful of the 'checks' your friends think any of these big tech companies are doing though. Someone could upload a fake ID pretty easily, I'm sure, if they really wanted to get away with something. But, still, I get where they're coming from. And you can't deny that true crime is having a moment.

It honestly would have never crossed my mind, she said.

We walked back to the Madison Building a bit bashful with each other but not uncomfortably so and agreed that it had been enough fun for one afternoon and that we'd see each other the next day. Settled back in with my material, I finally started to develop some kind of argument that I felt could be situated within the thesis. The quotes as I pulled them seemed to fit within a cohesive and coherent whole, and, when contextualised in a certain way, were almost obvious in how they would support the story I wanted to tell. Normally, such a revelation could leave me aching for hours as I questioned the absurd human desire to find narrative in everything, and the way in which any one quote could say pretty much anything you wanted it to, if you framed it in just such a way. But today I accepted it all as it came from me, writing my confident pronouncements and aphorisms as if I had no doubt that they told something not only important but urgent as well.

When I got back to the house, I yelled for my flatmate, who, again, wasn't there or simply didn't feel like responding. And after I had written about my encounter online (board/ truesexstories) and checked some of the replies as they came through almost immediately after posting (yo this is awesome. soooooo jealous, one said) I laid on top of the bed and finished what she had started, a single question playing out in my mind all the while as I pumped away at myself, full of longing, conviction, and a kind of misery, too.

Where do you want to?

(When I come it's like a river. First I can feel it building up inside of me like a biological omniscience, or the grandiose vision of some forlorn prophet that will, when an even halfway adequate context is found, burst forth in rapture without any preparatory warning or desultory preamble. Then, as the performance reaches its morose crescendo, my toes flex, my heart breaks. My thoughts are a jumble, my legs wildly akimbo. And for those precious few moments my secret wishes would never seem so pure, my spiritual longings never so fulfilled. But when it all finally starts to chortle out, I would gaze down the way at my own efficacious little manoeuvres, so stalwart and sure of themselves, so practiced, like the sacred ritual of an ancient but forgotten people, like a freakishly unaccompanied waltz, a feeling arises inside of me like shame or remorse. A poor solo nevertheless uniquely voiced, the act sings its declaration of messy attitudes: a manifesto of confused protest, inchoate and sublime; a mournful call to arms for all the Peeping Toms who sneak among us, humiliated but no more chastened for it.

What a rush! I rise and stumble from the bed towards the toilet, my private prayer dripping from my clumsy hand, my scattered DNA falling to the floor, my bastard half-formed children squiggling in vain.)

One aspect of the surveillance state was an unlikely source of comfort to me when I was away from home. Though it seemed to scare a lot of people, I quite liked thinking about the web of connections I was drawing with every search term I entered, with every address I bookmarked. What was the only possible connection between the trainee H.E. teacher with long red hair who I heard got off with one of my classmates and the new book on post-Hiroshima poetics by the ludicrously sexy postdoc who came up from London to tell us about early career research opportunities in England? Me, of course. At the centre of my own digital universe, I could maintain this web no matter where on the planet I was, geographically. And because I never thought any human would ever actually try to make any meaningful sense out of the data I was producing, the targeted ads it would regularly prompt – reliably off-target for the most part but occasionally close enough to give pause – never really bothered me much.

But a few hours later I checked my post again. There was notification alerting me to a private message from one of the moderators.

Pretty sure you've said before that you're married. You really need to put an infidelity tag in your title so our subs know what they're getting into.

Why? I wrote back. It's not relevant to this story.

A couple of minutes passed. I stood and paced around the room.

Because, was the reply, it could be traumatic for someone who's been cheated on if they were to look through your post history and see that your wife is sitting at home in Scotland while you're blowing your load at a historic landmark in D.C. It should be their choice whether to read something like that.

Scotland! D.C.! Had I actually said all that? There was no way, absolutely no way. And, 'sitting at home'? What was that supposed to mean? It was one thing to drag me like this, but to make out like Sarah was some kind of '50s housewife...

I stood again, and, lightheaded, suddenly became far too aware of my own vision. It was like my entire periphery had simply vanished, or that everything outside of my immediate focus had gone dark and become draped in shadow. And yet the more my eyes revolved and tried to revive the sense of this full optical view that I would need to be able to tell myself that I was all right − that everything was all right − the more I seemed to see nothing but dim trails of light surrounding each new angular object that my eyes alighted upon. Beyond the curvature of my nose, only tiny bubbles like pinprick freckles, and a faint snow inhabiting everything in view as if forced again to watch painful home videos on the antique television at my grandparents' house.

I held the phone to my mouth and started a voice message.

Sarah, I said. Sarah, please call me. I can't see anything and I'm scared. I don't know what's happening to me. I'm going blind.

Dizzy now, I collapsed onto the bed, trembling. I stared at the shimmering clock on the phone and calculated our time difference. She was asleep and I knew I wouldn't hear from her until the morning.

Eventually – maybe thirty minutes or so later – I regained my composure and sent a second message to her saying I was fine and that she shouldn't worry.

With a slight headache, I went back through my post history to see myself as others would see me if they were to click through to my account. For the most part, I was right: I hadn't ever said that we lived in Scotland, I didn't say I was in D.C., and the only reference to Sarah was fleeting, a single comment buried amongst countless others about a new tax break for married couples if one was earning significantly less than the other. But, to my surprise, little of our situation was very difficult to infer once you started to take in the whole picture. A regionally-expletive rant here about the upcoming referendum, a question there about the best places to eat in Georgetown, and it was all patently obvious. In fact, once you factored in the topics I'd started on the jazz page about my working theory on how we should interpret Mingus's double (or triple) life in regards to his compositions, it wouldn't take much cross-referencing at all to find me, the Real Me. If one were to guess that my musings were in a professional capacity and then happened upon the short bio I had been told to write for the Library of Congress's fellowships page, boom, there I was, photo and all. As it turns out, I had been Alazon the whole time.

Needless to say, I covered my tracks. I didn't delete my account entirely and start anew because I was secretly (yes, it was a secret even to myself back then, somehow) proud of the high score I'd accrued for my contributions. But I took out some of the more identifying posts and even appended [cheating] to the title of my story, as requested.

What did it matter? The word was meaningless, just something we used to say in high school to sound grownup and American. *Did she cheat on ye, aye? What a slag.*

And the truth was I never wanted to traumatise anyone.

IX

BEING A HYPOCHONDRIAC means becoming a voyeur to one's own exhibitionism. Never is this truer than in the therapeutic setting as you listen to yourself perform not just your experiences of the symptoms themselves but, to a greater extent, your awareness of your need (ultimately unfounded, this you know even at a conscious level, most of the time) to believe that the experiences of those symptoms are both true and justified, even as you occasionally falter, acknowledging at inadvertent moments that you could sometimes steady the mind by slowing your breath, or with simple thoughts and commands like, You are okay, Don't worry, and, She loved you. She really, really loved you.

Fearing I would be late, I rushed from the subway and in doing so forgot to stop to get cash out of the machine to pay for our session. While the therapist had suggested early on that I set up a standing order to draw the balance automatically on a monthly basis, I couldn't bear the thought of getting a bank involved in my mental health, even minimally. Though this frequently proved inconvenient, it simply wasn't a breadcrumb of data I was willing to offer, and, besides, I knew by then that the webs we created weren't nearly so simple as I had previously thought: though the possibility of snaring others into your own was indeed limited, the likelihood of entangling yourself was vast.

When I finally arrived she was waiting by the door with an expression I found difficult to read. At the time it seemed like annoyance but isn't it interesting (listen to me: I'm starting to sound like her) that I'd instinctively hunt for criticism when concern would be so much more natural? In either case, as soon as I sat down she started to speak.

It surprised me the last time you were here, she said, to learn that your earliest memories of anxiety were from adulthood. Most of my patients (or was 'clients' the word she chose?) who have had significant difficulties in this area, as you have, can recall some moments from their childhood that they associate with their present condition. Can you go into a bit more detail about the first experience you had, when you knew what you were feeling was anxiety?

I didn't want to answer this question, obviously. But I was starting to doubt the efficacy of any talk therapy in my situation if I couldn't be honest about the thing that, really, I had come here to talk about. Because, basically, I knew what had happened, even if I was still having trouble verbalising it then. But it seemed to me at the time that through this knowledge alone I should have just been able to get over it by myself, a thought that called into question my desire to speak to someone in the first place.

At its simplest, I was overwhelmed with guilt. Towards Sarah, of course, but there was something quite generalised about it as well, like I was guilty somehow for my own existence: to my parents who had raised me reasonably okay but continued to aggravate me; to my teachers for always disappointing them with my lackadaisical, often disruptive, work ethic that never met the standards for some reason expected of me; to all the books on my shelf that were left neglected, unread, and therefore purposeless, reduced to mere talismans of my own aspirational but unrealistic nature; and to life itself, for taking such a meek approach to what was, terrifyingly, an infinite set of choices backdropped by what I considered the only philosophical text that had ever really spoken to me, a spinning 3D gif I saw once that proclaimed, movingly, spartanly, lol nothing matters. The truth was I felt I didn't ever know what I was doing: in a cosmic sense, sure, but on a day-to-day level, too, like I was paying penance for obscure charges no one had bothered to explain to me; like I lived my life inside of an austere country house I could never quite believe was now home, playing the good guest on an endless loop, forever worried that I'd stain the couch or break a distant relative's expensive heirloom.

Nonetheless I demurred, abandoning the relevant context of these sensations in the service of describing only the sensations themselves.

A sudden shortening of breath, I said finally, followed by a rapidity of thoughts – you know, all the things I'm worried about suddenly coming true – and then fear, I guess. Fear that everything is going to engulf me. As if I've been pushed to the precipice of a complete disassociation and might just fall over into it at any moment.

Complete disassociation? she repeated. That's an evocative phrase. Can you tell me what would that be like? Or how you imagine it would be?

Just, like, I'm not in control of myself, I tried to articulate.

And what might happen if you weren't in control of yourself?

Uh, well, anything, I guess. That's – that's what's so scary, I stammered.

We sat there looking at each other for a moment. I wondered if we were about to enter one of those prolonged periods of silence you see sometimes in films where the analyst and the analysand both wait for the other to start speaking; a waste of money, in my opinion.

Instead, she changed tack.

Was going to Washington D.C. the first trip you ever took to America? she asked, scribbling a new heading onto what I had started to regard as *my notepad*.

The question surprised me. What did this have to do with Sarah? I crossed my legs. No, I went there on holiday once with my parents, to Florida. That's the only other time.

Whereabouts in Florida? she asked. Can you remember?

Not really, I said. Somewhere on the Atlantic coast. It wasn't a super nice place or anything, but my parents had booked this little house for us right near the beach. I was too old to be interested in the theme parks and that. They mostly sat on the patio and read.

And what did you do?

Without quite meaning to, I found myself telling the story to her, as much as I still knew to be true; how the night had unfolded, a confluence of events I hadn't given serious thought to in a very long time but was, without warning, coming back to me there like the threaded pattern of a stonework Celtic knot, intricate and unyielding, with a sense of order derived only by virtue of its deliberate disorder, as entangling and entrapping as beads on a chain only without the comfort of fixed points to denote any beginning or end.

I had been standing on a sand dune, looking out into the sea – don't ask me what I was thinking about – when, suddenly, I heard someone behind me shout that I wasn't supposed to be up there, that it was a protected area or something. I turned to see a boy about my age, stationary on a bike with a few friends, a couple of other boys and a girl, all looking up at me. I clambered down, and as I did, he started to explain the importance of dunes to the ecosystem, speaking in that faux-busybody way kids do when they're repeating something they've been taught at school or were scolded for once themselves, mocking adult mannerisms while equally relishing the opportunity to employ them for once.

Sorry, I muttered, trudging back towards my parents who had probably opened their beers by now, meaning I'd be allowed to help myself to a fizzy juice.

Hey wait, the girl called. It's okay. We've all done it. What's your name?

Miles, I said.

They repeated this to each other, looking quizzically.

Oh, he means Miles! shouted one of the other boys, eliding the word into a single syllable, adding a southern twang to the 'i' sound. Are you from a foreign country?

Scotland, I replied.

Cool! the girl exclaimed. My family is Scottish.

Mine is too, each of the boys said quickly, forming a semi-unison chorus.

Do you want to hang out with us? the girl asked. We're going to a party later.

No, we're not, the boy who'd lectured me about sand dunes said. It's not a party, Clarissa. My brother told us not to tell anyone, anyway.

It's one more person! the girl shouted. He's all the way here from Scotland! You should come, she said, turning to me.

Naw, you're all right, I deflected. Cheers, though.

There was a pause.

I have no idea what he just said, one of the other boys said, laughing.

Okay, the lead boy started, forming a pyramid with his fingers that he held close to his face. You can come. But you have to keep talking like that.

Fine, I replied, trying to look unbothered. But I need to check in with my parents first. Where shall I meet you?

He said 'shall'!

Again, the boys looked at each other and laughed.

I like the way he talks, the girl said. Meet us down by the ocean in half an hour?

Back at the house it was, indeed, cocktail hour, a misnomer they deployed in a casually ironic manner that failed to convey their drink of choice or the typical duration of imbibing. But they were on holiday, after all.

I took a shower and put on the most American-seeming clothes I could find, eventually settling on a polo shirt and a pair of chino shorts.

When I told my parents I was going to a party, they looked at each other, smiled furtively, and pretended as though they wanted me to stay, dining out on a bit I had heard many times before.

Oh, you mustn't! my father cried. What-ever will we do?

You don't really want to spend time with children your own age, do you, dear? asked my mother.

While they continued their false entreaties, chortling at their own increasingly absurd comments, I crept into the kitchen out of view and helped myself to two of their beers, stuffing them quickly into my short pockets. Subterfuge probably wasn't necessary at this stage but growing up with them was something the three of us were still negotiating and I couldn't be sure of their reaction to such a flagrant display of my desire for maturity and equal status.

Look, Clarissa: *Mahls* changed for you, one of the boys said, as I walked towards where they waited by the water.

The girl blushed. Before either of us could respond, the boys raced ahead on their bikes, leaving clear tyre streaks in the damp sand. She walked hers next to me.

Don't listen to them, she said, eventually. They're just jealous.

Why?

Because you're more interesting than they are.

The sun was setting into the palm trees next to us, illuminating the sky in brilliant orange hues the likes of which I'd never seen and casting our shadows like monstrous rivals stretching across the shore. A harsh glare refracted off the darkening water, hurting my eyes.

It's not as blue and green as I had expected, I said, gesturing.

Oh, it is on the gulf side. You've never been?

No.

I was afraid to speak. Every comment I might have made would seem fatuous the more I toyed with it in my mind, and I was hyper-conscious of my accent in ways that I'd never experienced. I wasn't used to being misunderstood like this, and the resulting adoption of an awkward personality was only compounding my struggle: the further I retreated into accepting being thought of as a quiet person, the more difficult I knew it would be to pull myself out of it, to ever let go of myself around them.

I brought beers? I mumbled as a question for some reason.

You did? she asked unsurely.

I have two. Do you want one?

She gave this some consideration, looking slightly terrified.

Okay, she said, finally. But I've never drank before.

There's nothing to it, I said, flooded with relief at her affirmative response. You just swallow.

I handed one to her and we opened them simultaneously, just like they were Cokes.

Cheers, I said, tilting my can towards her. Chin-chin.

What? she laughed. Chin… chin? What in the heck does that mean?

I took a sip of the gagging liquid, bravely forcing it to slide down my throat.

I don't know, I admitted. It's just something my parents say.

I watched as she raised that first taste of alcohol to her lips. I was by no means a seasoned pro, but I'd had enough experiences in parks at home hiding in the overgrowth with other middle-class delinquent youths to feel somewhat accomplished in my ability to get a bit sloshed. Even then I think I knew I was witnessing an important milestone for her.

She began to cough.

Do you like it? I asked.

Uh-huh.

The beer tasted as dirty and foamy as the water looked. I remember feeling very grown-up in this moment, like I'd begun to inhabit the stations of older people on telly, graduating from my precocious, ancillary, and incidental status to one at the centre of drama and romance, a primary role. The long-time child actor on a soap with his first real storyline.

She told me that she had told her parents that she was staying over with another girl she had met at the pool of the beach club the other day, that the girl was a local, and that her parents were home and they were gonna order pizza and watch a movie, *Titanic* probably, but the local girl had never existed, she'd made her up. She seemed impressed when I told her my parents had simply allowed me to come, no questions asked.

It took almost an hour to get to wherever it was we were going. A couple of times the boys would double back to us, imploring that we hurry, repeating that we needed to make it there before nightfall, or they wouldn't be able to find the place. After several attempts, they persuaded the girl to let me sit on the saddle of her bike while she pedalled ahead of me. I held her waist, confident now in my placid tipsiness. And it's impossible to know how much of the effect on us was the alcohol itself and how much of it was our teenage projections of the ways in which the substance might change a person's behaviour, but we had become comfortable with each other in the haze of that one illicit can, and – I don't know – though I couldn't recall much of our conversation later, I thought about her a lot after this. For a little while, anyway. Everything that happened that night was so stupid and it still isn't clear to me what I should've done. Send me back as an adult, and, sure, I'll figure this out. Ask me to relive it as a child and all I can see is the same awful result, over and over again.

A few guys, probably two or three years older than us, were waiting in the sandy carport of a beachfront house that was partially obscured by blue builders' tarpaulin. We were introduced to them as the elder brother of the boy who had shouted at me and his friends. I remember they were each holding a clear plastic bag containing a bottle of spirit, and I remember thinking, This is new, This is unexpected, and, I have no idea what's going to happen next.

How obvious it would seem later.

They led us into the house through a corner of the tarpaulin that wasn't secured to the house's foundation like the rest of it was. It appeared a palm tree or something must have fallen onto that section of the house and the repair efforts were ongoing. The partially-built room where we entered was very dusty, and there were some snack wrappers strewn about the wretched cement floor and an old, paint-splattered boombox was plugged-in through an open door, as though workmen had only just left.

We retreated to the rest of the house which seemed totally normal, with furniture, running water, and electricity, though the lights we agreed to keep off in case the neighbours noticed. No one paid me much attention, and, despite my earlier misgivings about fitting in, I started to feel a bit useless when I wasn't asked to say anything, like I wasn't even worth a novelty value any more. The older guys were quite focused on the only female member of our fragile troop, but I couldn't blame them, fixated as I was on her myself. Then again, I didn't have much awareness of the disparities in our ages or experience. Girls taking up with lads from the older years seemed normal to me at the time, and, really, it was. Back then, anyway. Probably still is, I suppose. Growing up without siblings meant I never had much of a frame of reference for these kinds of things. I guess I just assumed she was keen to go along with everything. But, honestly, I wasn't thinking about any of that. I won't sit here and pretend like I was. The only emotion I would have felt was disappointment that I wasn't the centre of her attention any longer. Perhaps some envy as well.

They found some shot glasses and lined them up on a coffee table for us in the penumbral moonlight. When a crack was made about how none of us knew anything about alcohol, she exclaimed proudly that, actually, she and I'd had a can of beer each on the ride up. They were duly impressed and filled her shot to the brim.

It was disgusting and horrible, and the heat that arose inside of me was like a consumptive fever spreading out from my undersized heart. But, as its effects started to kick in, I could hear myself become voluble. Witty, even. The words seemed to flow from me unimpeded, and I watched as others reacted to my pronouncements with wide-eyed amusement, like they'd never heard anyone make such outrageous and entertaining remarks before.

I'm cold, she said, brushing up against me. I put my arm around her.

After another round or two of this, someone suggested that we play hide-and-seek. She grabbed my hand, slurring, Let's hide together. But somehow it was decided that I should be 'it' first. I stayed sitting on the floor against the rattan frame of the couch. I didn't need to close my eyes, because I couldn't see anything anyway. For the first thirty seconds, I counted aloud, and listened to the creaks of the floorboards around me, on the stairs, and the opening and closing of doors up above. For the next thirty, I just sat there staring at the bottles, dizzy and slightly sedated. I think I must've passed out for a moment, because I remember that I suddenly became aware that some greater amount of time had passed than I had intended, and it felt as though I was waking from a dream. Or that I was falling into one.

Ready or not, here I come! I shouted, to no response.

I stood and walked through the house silently, as if it was important for me not to be detected as well. My body was moving as if of its own volition, and I marvelled at the inherent sense of space I seemed to be exhibiting, as though even my stumbling contained its own liquid balance. *You're drunk*, I thought to myself. *This is what being really drunk is like.*

First, I cleared the ground floor. With half of it blocked off and me having occupied one of the only available rooms while I counted, there weren't many good places to hide, but I figured it would make sense to start there before working my way up. Then, on the stairs, my foot slipped and I fell forwards, only just catching myself on the smoothed driftwood bannister as my head hurtled towards the sharp edge of a landing.

I swore a bit theatrically, and when I still couldn't hear anything – no stifled laughter, no calls to see if I was all right – a terrible thought occurred to me then: what if they left me; what if this has all been a set-up, even her.

But there was only one way to find out, so I had to keep going. At the top, I was faced with a long hallway branching off into several rooms. There was no reason in this moment for me to have changed so drastically from my previously ebullient state, but standing there like a malevolent figure in the dark made me realise that, now, things were just about out of hand, and that it was time for me to go. I think a part of me knew that I was afraid of the emptiness I would find behind each closed door, and that if I left before opening them, I'd never have to confront it. But as I glanced behind me to the stairs I had just climbed and started to turn, full of resolve to beat them at their own game (such was my adolescent logic), I heard a muffled cry. A whimper, almost.

Hello? I said.

Nothing.

I opened the door nearest to me, finding only a small washroom. A streetlamp beyond the window didn't reveal anyone inside, just as I'd suspected. I looked at myself in the mirror above the stone basin sink and thought, Either they're playing tricks on you, or you're playing them on yourself.

Again, I turned back to the staircase, but, as I did so, again heard the same sound.

This isn't funny, I said in a raised voice.

Nothing.

The next door along I stood outside of before opening, terrified here more than ever. I placed my ear to the door and heard some sounds of shuffled movement coming from within.

I knocked on the door.

Game's over, dude! one of the older guys yelled from inside. Everyone's gone!

I didn't reply but stood there for another moment, still listening.

Please... don't, whispered a sleepy voice I could only just make out.

The voice was hers.

I pushed the door open a bit and, as I did, he turned from his position on top of her to look at me with a curious glass-eyed expression, like he couldn't see me at all and was reacting to a presence he only sensed, like I was a ghost. They were both still clothed, I could see that, and I remember registering this as an important detail, though I wasn't sure to what end.

I said, get out! he yelled. We're just having a little fun. Leave us alone.

I started to close the door when I heard, once more, softly, that word, plaintive, deadened. *Please...*

I didn't know what to do, but before I would have had to make a decision to do anything, something came over me that can only be described as an out-of-body experience.

I felt myself fall onto floor in front of them, and then to begin to writhe, moaning as I did so. I started to pour sweat, and to tremble in small, hypothermic motions, even as I gyrated in larger ones, as if in the midst of an illness-induced fit, or demonic possession. All the while, my inebriated inner voice seemed to narrate my own actions to myself as if I was viewing the recording of some other sad soul through a screen, providing a clinical commentary with a detached mindset that compensates for an awareness that you are without any agency in a matter whatsoever.

Oh my god, what's happening to him? I heard her ask.

I... I don't know, he said, staring down in disbelief.

I saw the lights turn on and I looked up into them as the brightness obscured my vision, desperately trying to catch my breath as I tore at the dampened collar of my shirt.

He's dying! I heard her shout, and then she began to cry. Do something!

Frantically, he phoned the emergency services and told them someone was injured in the house, a possible alcohol poisoning. After he did, declining to leave his name, he told her that they needed to leave, that there was nothing they could do for me now. She was kneeling beside me, looking down into my eyes, but he pulled her by the arm, dragging her away from me. I'm sure I don't need to tell you the word that she was, now, screaming to him. *Please!*

When they had left the house, and when I heard sirens approach in the distance, I found my breath, turned the lights back off, and made my way downstairs. I put the shot glasses back into the cupboard and I placed the bottles beneath the sink behind the cleaning supplies. Through the unfinished room and the unfastened tarpaulin, I left the house and found the palm-lined alley stretching towards the beach.

I stumbled back along the black coast by myself, wet and shivery in a dusty wind. I never saw any of them again.[4]

One thing you should know, Miles, the therapist said when I had finished, is that I'm not such a believer in explanatory motifs: the one big moment from our pasts that can reveal our psyches or that will determine our trajectories. I think things stick into our minds for a variety of reasons, and that sometimes they stick in our minds just because they happen to stick in our minds. That shouldn't make any difference to our sessions, but I'm telling you this in case it confounds some of your expectations of what my role as a therapist should be. What I find more resonant – and many of my colleagues work from a similar perspective – is their cumulative impact. So, in this instance, your story is poignant – and, frankly, would be disturbing to anyone – but what strikes me most about the fraught situation you found yourself in is – while you saved the girl, and of course should be applauded for that – who was there to save you? It doesn't sound like your parents ever looked for you or asked what happened to you at the party. Did you often find yourself having to deal with these big, adult situations on your own?

---

4 An account of this evening, minus the attempted rape, was fictionalised in my first ever publication, a short story entitled 'Just Walk Away' which won first prize in my undergraduate university's literary competition amongst all eligible entrants, including faculty and alumni. It was praised by the judging panel for its 'believability' and 'the lushness and grandeur of its well-chosen setting'.

Saved her? I didn't save her.

Didn't you? What would have happened if you weren't there? I'm not saying you necessarily chose to do so at the conscious level, but your body reacted to something it perceived to be wrong, and the actions it took as a result prevented her situation from going any further. Whatever initial reluctance you might have exhibited is perhaps more archetypical than you realise and shouldn't diminish the result.

I mulled this over but dismissed its implications. I still wasn't ready to accept any responsibility, one way or another. The memory was like a stalled film I couldn't fix without reshoots but all the principal actors had already died, and, much as I might wish to, it was far too late to cast myself as the valiant hero.

I guess my parents have always been pretty laidback about that kind of thing, I said.

I understand, and often that is a good attitude to take. But remember: you are a child in a foreign country who doesn't return home for an entire night.

Hmm, I replied, unwilling to acquiesce to this new interpretation of the events.

We sat there looking at each other for a moment. Well, she was looking at me, probably into my eyes, but my gaze, though she might not have been able to tell, was, I realised, actually directed towards her mouth as I waited to see the shapes it would take when she processed what I had to say next.

I need to know something, I said.

From my periphery, I noticed her brows rising in encouragement for me to continue. I steeled myself.

Do you know who I am?

Her mouth didn't tighten as I had expected but instead seemed to slacken a bit and then, pursing slightly, began to form an answer.

I think I understand the question, she replied, and I welcome the direction it might be taking, but I would need further elaboration before I could give you a proper answer. Why don't you tell me who you are instead?

Don't give me that, I said, gruffly, maybe a little too gruffly. Do. You. Know. Who. I. Am?

It sounds as though you're asking if I've approached our relationship with any awareness of potential third-party accounts of what other people have possibly said about who you are at one time or another. But the only things I *know* about you are the things you have told me here and the impressions that I have formed of you as a result.

And you sound like my solicitor, I said. Come on, it's a simple question.

But it's not a simple question, Miles, and that is my point, in fact. I'll try to clarify my response to your satisfaction one last time, but then we'll have to leave it there until next week. As we agreed from the beginning, it's important that we start and we finish when we're scheduled to.

She paused for a moment while she reformulated her words in her mind, holding her hands out before her as if she were grasping for something precious but ultimately intangible. Finally, she started to speak again.

Perhaps what you would like to know is if I keep up with current affairs in Scotland, and if I follow the major news stories as they unfold in the media. The answer to that is yes, usually.

It seemed she was getting at what I had expected her to already know, although I hadn't anticipated we would take such a circuitous route to get there. Why didn't you say anything? I asked.

Perhaps you'll have heard this adage before, she said, but they say that your therapist is the one person in your life who, on hearing that someone close to you has died, won't respond with 'I'm sorry for your loss'. That's because it isn't our place to direct your feelings. Or, for that matter, to indulge in such clichés uncritically.

But of course I'm sorry! I nearly shouted.

She jumped in her chair, clearly startled by my outburst, and then regained her composure.

That probably wasn't the best example, she said, running her hands across the armrests of her chair. And I am sorry if my remarks came across as insensitive. I wasn't referring to Sarah. My point is there's nothing deceptive about letting someone speak for themselves and that I approach the work we do here on your terms – no one else's. We can pick this up next time, if you'd like – and I think it's a good idea – but we'll have to conclude for now.

She stood and I handed her the banknotes I'd been fingering in my pocket before closing the door behind me. Waiting for the lift, I clutched my chest and burst into tears.

And, cumulative or not, that night as I lay in the too-large bed, tormented in a half-wakeful state, all I could see was Clarissa's face, and all I could hear was Sarah's voice, the last words she spoke to me – written, actually, in a text she had sent from her parents' house, the message everyone later heard about: I hate you.

Children. We were, all of us, still children.

X

IT WAS DURING this time in my life that I simply couldn't stop thinking about the future. I couldn't wait to finish my PhD; I couldn't wait to experience America; and, perhaps even more so, I couldn't wait to return to Scotland from there, so that I could tell everyone I knew that I had gone in the first place. Each day that passed I appreciated like a single tile of some vast mosaic, which is to say that I couldn't really appreciate any individual day at all. There were many moments of joy, of course. (You have to believe: Sarah and I truly enjoyed spending our time together, and the regular video chats we would have while I was away were very often quite humorous or sexy.) But it was impossible not to view these at the time as only the transitory glimpses of humanity on a hinterland railway track hurtling me towards some kind of something or other that eventually I would arrive at exhausted, impassioned, and ready: for adulthood; to use my experiences as the basis for a new critical mode of thinking; or even as impressions that I could one day transform into a wild and expansive form of artistic expression. Later, they would become much more meaningful for all that they really were, which was memories.

This next part no one ever found out about. That's right, it's a world exclusive. Not that anyone cares much about me any more, but, still, I wouldn't be surprised if some of it gets picked up by the tabloid press in one of those filler columns that are only an inch wide and seem to restate themselves several times over. Maybe a salacious little splash about it on the front page, that ludicrous image of a pixelated dick pic again. But, anyway, not long into my trip abroad, I was up to my usual tricks online when I saw a new topic had been crossposted to one of the literary subs that I frequented. Hi, it read, I'm Sophie Auster: recording artist, actor, model, and, yes, Paul Auster is my dad – Ask Me Anything.

I clicked through to see that the ongoing discussion was equally split amongst Spanish fans of her career and American fans of her dad's, as well as a confused number of users who took the time to write that they were neither. I decided to wade in:

@alazon: what do you look like?

@sophie_aus: Dude, there's literally a hundred photos of me online. You can just do a search for them

@alazon: no i mean now. what do you look like right now?

I didn't think she'd respond to this, but after a minute or two when I refreshed the page I saw a new post.

@sophie_aus: Like this, creep

She had taken a photo of herself in a bedroom, flipping off the camera with a bored, contemptuous countenance. *Nice!* I thought.

But evidently, and to my slight chagrin, I had fallen into the role of a heel or villainous foil to the rather bland discussion of the new music she was trying to promote, a bad actor male chauvinist exemplary of the worst and most predatory online behaviour. (I received many downvotes.) Yet I was thrilled to have established any kind of connection with her, so rather than issue a grovelling apology to placate the fanatical Spaniards, I decided to settle into it.

@alazon: do you think your dad's books are contrived?

@sophie_aus: Narrative is contrived

@alazon: sure. but do you think his books are more contrived than most?

@sophie_aus: Yes. They are supposed to be

@alazon: i get that he wants to say something about like luck and coincidence and stuff (though what I'm not really sure tbh) but don't you think at the end of the day the only thing he actually does is just expose how banal all those things really are, thereby damning his own books in the process?

A few moments passed and she hadn't responded, though someone chimed in only to say, tHeReBy. I flitted around the news sources at home, feeling my pulse quicken at the release of a poll result placing this seismic issue I felt fairly ambivalent about within the margin of error, when a notification appeared.

@sophie_aus: Wow. It's almost impressive. You seem to pretty much get his life's work without actually realising that the qualities you're suggesting are happenstance or examples of bad writing were done with explicit purpose. He certainly doesn't need me to defend him but, sure, why not? He creates suspense out of "banal" indeterminate encounters and he is able to make inventive use of "contrived" determinate forms by inverting readers' expectations of the relationships between perspective and distance. His most recent novel was *Sunset Park* – everyone go buy it! – and it's a brutal response to the recession, about a twenty-eight-year-old college drop-out named Miles who returns to New York after running away from his family. Any fault you'd find in his commitment to realism would be to find fault in human nature, contemporary society, and our own quotidian lives. Which is fine but has nothing to do with him as a writer. More than literally anything else, we're governed by serendipity and a deeply held need for narrative forms to explain to ourselves the things that happen to us. At least that's what he is saying in his novels. My dad has probably thought more about the craft and purpose of storytelling than you've been alive, bitch

I sat there, stunned. I had no idea he'd written a novel about someone called Miles. It was even stranger to think Auster would have sought to portray someone my own age. The truth was that I enjoyed a couple of his early works, though it's also true to say that the more by him I read the less engaged I became. But Sophie was right to contend that this could just as easily be a failing on my part, or on the mechanics of reality itself. That didn't mean I was going to give up, though.

@alazon: you're probably right but that wouldn't necessarily mean that any of the things he's sitting around thinking about are very interesting, you know? sometimes you can think yourself into circles and mimesis in general is usually shallow. just because you wander in the desert it doesn't mean there's a promised land at the end.

She used the quote function to highlight that last sentence from my post.

@sophie_aus: Haha okay I just looked that up. Are you seriously trying to turn my dad's own words against him in an argument with his daughter about whether he's a good writer? Remind me wtf your problem is again? Log off, man. I'm done with you

All these contributions of mine were, apparently, so unpleasant to the other users that when I refreshed the page I found our conversation to be buried at the bottom of the thread and totally obscured. You actually had to click an extra button in order to reveal my first message, and my profile was haemorrhaging points as a result.

So I took Sophie's advice and logged out, surreptitiously switching to the normie account I'd created for 'impact' purposes which I rarely used. (I had attended a professional development seminar at my university where we were all forced to do this and were then given inane 'tips and tricks' on how to make our research 'go viral'.)

It was time for new tactics. Once more unto the breach, mis amigos!

@mbeard89: Some people are being such a**holes here! Why is anyone talking about Sophie's dad, anyway..?? This is supposed to be about HER. Are you playing in NYC anytime soon I hope my lovely :)

@sophie_aus: Ugh, just ignore them. It's not the first time the fiction of Paul Auster has brought the weirdos out of the woodwork. And yes! I am in Manhattan all summer playing scattered dates, mostly LES venues: Pianos, Berlin, etc. Are you a New Yorker?

@mbeard89: No I'm from Scotland actually, but I'm doing research in the US and am presenting at a conference there next month. (Do you enjoy the compositions of Charles Mingus by chance?) Would be great to catch one of your shows if I can!

She didn't respond for a few minutes, and I started to think about that panel I was on, really for the first time since I got the email saying my abstract had been accepted, when I saw I had received a private message.

> @sophie_aus: Sorry I started thinking that maybe this wasn't the best conversation to play out in front of all my *adoring* fans haha. I used to sing 'Goodbye Pork Pie Hat' during my teen jazz standards phase lol. The Joni Mitchell version obvs. What's the conference? You're a musician?

> @mbeard89: That's a good one! The Joni and Mingus collaborations are fascinating. No I'm not a musician myself. Not any more, anyway. It is a music conference though - at Columbia. 'Sound/Text | Rhythm/Intertext: Music and Literature' lmao. I told them I'd present a metrical analysis of Mingus's autobiography but there's no way I can actually do that so I'll have to come up with something else! Arghhhh. You're welcome to come along and watch me bomb?

I also attached a link to my fellowship profile. Because, as she'd previously intimated, I could know almost anything about her that I wanted to with just a few taps on my keyboard, it only seemed right that she be allowed something close to the same opportunity.

> @sophie_aus: That sounds cool. Definitely something my dad would be interested in. (Not an insult!!) I don't know what I'll be doing that day but shoot me a text that week and we can try to coordinate. Nice pic btw

And she left me her phone number. If you're choosing to read this I assume you have already seen a fair number photos of me by now. (Though it had been my instinct, I was told that covering my face with a jacket would only make me look like more of a criminal.) Even if you haven't, this book probably has one, there at the back. Go on, take a look.[5] In fact – now that I think about it – the one that got circulated the most was of course scraped from that Library of Congress page, so you could very well already be familiar with the one Sophie would have seen before we met. What I'm getting at is that you can decide for yourself if you think I'm attractive enough (or normal-looking enough) to warrant this kind of attention, even though I think the bond we had formed online was more platonic and interesting for that. (Besides, I only sent the link because I feel like it would have been weird not to. Gone are the days you see in those old films where guys pass around phone numbers and call up for dates with women they've never even laid eyes on.) I know what this all sounds like, too. Especially after everything else I've already said happened. Plus, as you may have already found for yourself by now, Sophie is incredibly beautiful. There's no denying it. She's got this kind of feline, Old World thing going on there that I find quite yummy. I'm sure most people do. But even if things in New York hadn't gone to complete shit I don't think I would've tried it on with her, really. So please don't think that I'm just, like, this constant, roving philanderer. I'm not. Or, at least, I wasn't before this period in my life. And Sarah cheated on me first, if you'll recall. Sarah. Sarah.

---

5 It was the first thing you looked at when you picked it up in the shop, wasn't it? Just kidding. Cheaper online, eh. No judgements here! There's no ethical consumption under capitalism, etc. I realise it sounds like I'm joking because that's become such a banality but like most banalities it's also kinda true when you think about it. Anyway, Jeff Bezos thanks you. CHECK IF BEZOS HAS DIED IN SPACE BEFORE THIS GOES TO PRINT

Anyway, we left it there pretty much and I never texted her until the day before I was supposed to leave. That was what she had suggested but also the conversation we'd had was the kick in the arse I needed to start thinking seriously about what my contribution to the panel was going to be so I mostly forgot about our tentative date. The thing about these conferences is that you kind of do them just to do them. I enjoy them myself but I think part of my enjoyment comes from what I perceive as an essentially anonymous opportunity to spout whatever half-baked ideas I wish to a professionally-captive audience. I don't take the piss or anything but I also don't put a lot of pressure on myself over them either like some of my peers I know do. I just don't see the point. There's no scoring – though you do hear occasionally about prizes given to the best paper presented at the postgrad ones where the organisers are probably concerned about the quality – and there's not even an attendance policy for the most part. You typically have to register at the beginning to get your programme and name badge, but there wouldn't be any kind of follow-up if you didn't. It's not a great look to not show up without any explanation but it still happens at least once at every conference, and who cares? Certainly not me. It's just one fewer monologue I have to sit through before I can gain access to the refreshments and, as soon as it's over, add it as a line on my CV.

All of which isn't to say I go in unprepared. Even if you cobble it together the week before, to keep the proceedings interesting for yourself you have to be ready to provoke people a little. Otherwise, it's a wasted opportunity, a bit stilted, and provocation takes preparation. It can be subtle, like being the only person to go in with your paper memorised. The last one I went to was in Lisbon – gorgeous – and I got a wee bit political, throwing in a couple of japes about the referendum which had just been officially announced, visibly flummoxing the international audience by refusing to acknowledge any potential context for Brexit other than its relevance to Scottish nationhood. But it seemed to enliven the round table, like I'd dismantled a *post hoc* safety device everyone was finding rather patronising, and I was grateful that no one asked me if I really thought a life writing conference was the best venue for such unnecessarily pointed remarks. When a courtly English gent approached me in the lobby afterwards to say that he appreciated me addressing the elephant in the room but wondered what I made of Jeremy Corbyn's approach, I feigned a look of confusion, appeared thoughtful for a moment, and said, haltingly, He's the leader of England's Labour Party, right? I'm so sorry, I don't get a chance to read the papers down south very often.

But attempting a rhythmic scan of *Beneath the Underdog* was a complete non-starter. Like most of my ideas it had a promising methodology, but the intended result was fuzzy, and I knew I wouldn't be the best person to enact it regardless: I'd get bored, lose the thread, become frustrated, or, worse, careless in my application of it. Certainly, it made sense to pick a topic relevant to my research in D.C. – and I definitely didn't want to totally switch topics (what if Sophie's dad came expecting to hear about Mingus?) – but I would need to come up with something new and interesting.

I was thinking about my conversation with Sophie, and about Joni Mitchell. It's before my time, obviously, but still it surprised me to see that it would have been thought acceptable – if mildly controversial (what a wag!) – for her to go blackface on the cover of her 1977 album *Don Juan's Reckless Daughter*.

Does it surprise you to hear this as well? Take a look: that's her in triptych, on the left in the guise of her pimp alter ego she called 'Art Nouveau'.

I was sitting on the bed in my room with the laptop on my knees, stripped to the waist as I struggled to acclimate to the summer heat that seemed to accelerate as the days wore on. I placed it to the side and looked up into the ceiling fan making a pathetic journey round and round with barely arced wooden blades, providing almost no respite despite its insistent effort. As I let my eyes glaze over, focusing past the ceiling as I if was gazing towards the unobstructed sky, I tried to remove my twenty-first century sensibilities and see the decision from the point of view of Joni, someone who was, presumably, not actually a racist. What did it mean to a white young Canadian woman to present herself as a 'streetwise' American black man? Was it drag at its most authentic? Or authenticity at its most drag?

The album had caught Mingus's eye, that much is known. And as if to repudiate this uncertain caricature of hers, he suggested they collaborate on a sonic reimagining of Eliot's *Four Quartets*. But to this she demurred, so he approached her with less allusive material he wanted lyrical vocal lines over, and both were left unhappy with what was finally recorded, two vibrant but uneven personas clashing against the weights of style, artistry, and commercial opportunity.

As a white Scottish man, I wasn't the one to probe at the historical injustices at the heart of their racial/sexual dynamics, this much I knew, but I could nevertheless recognise something poignant about the juxtaposition on display: Mingus spent a lifetime alternately indulging in and rebelling against a received image of himself as domineering, violent, and confrontational; Joni had made a conscious choice to dabble in pastiche of the same. Without lauding or criticising either, there was space here for disentangling the double-bind of the artist. While we as an audience desire works that can speak to our common experiences, we can't help but feel drawn to its most characterful representations: to the outlandish, the playful, and the lurid. Was there a better metaphor for this than jazz, with its ever-shifting textures composed by excessively eccentric personalities? Perhaps this was something Auster himself might be interested in.

The question, then, became how to best represent this in the prescriptive form of the fifteen-minute paper, a misnomer if there ever was, given just how many speakers seemed to rely on slideshows which, in my opinion, rarely had much power or point. (A bad joke I scribbled down while I pretended to listen to one once.) Pondering this it occurred to me that maybe I didn't need to change my brief at all; that, by approaching the same topic from the obverse vantage, I could demonstrate why metrical analysis would be so lacking in this context, precisely by appearing to deploy one. I'd refer to Mingus and Joni only as Person A and Person B. I'd cobble together something so mind-numbingly dull, so devoid of humanity, the questions would naturally raise themselves. I'd short-circuit the stuffy panel and force them to drop their pretence of highfalutin detachment from our baser instincts to consume and to be entertained.

In short, I would have something to write home about.

XI

SHE EVEN HELPED me write it over the next few weeks. Not Sophie, my friend from the library. The day before I was due to leave we were in her sitting room, resting after another day in the archives, our routine now firmly established. I had spent most of it continuing to pore over the piano-vocal score of one of their collaborations, approaching each side like how I imagined a computer would, reducing every element to the ineluctable sequence of an algorithm. She was documenting the displacing effects of irony and humour in the narratorial strategy of Roth's *The Professor of Desire*, part of a chapter on something she was calling the reader's experience of 'disillusion and collusion' with an author. The late afternoon light was streaming in through her venetian blinds, casting slatted shadows against a hastily-painted lilac wall. As she sat down and handed me a bottle of beer, the shadows fell against her face, and the poise she exhibited sitting there in the luxury of her own space, also a sublet, only exacerbated the butterflies I would feel in such proximity to her. I was at school all over again, stuck in a Formica desk to punishingly face my most fervent crush.

(I'm not going to say I was ever in love with her. I don't believe it's possible to love someone who you don't really know, who doesn't really know you. But I was infatuated, and I had started to feel slightly more attuned to masculine figures of an American society I'd only read about, with their preferred prostitutes stationed overseas, or very young secretaries stashed away at the office, or even secret families installed in the next town over.)

I'm thinking of starting with a joke, I told her.

I coughed.

Today, I started, for my contribution to the panel I am going to attempt an *Elizabeth Costello* thing. But I'm afraid it's likely to end up more of a Lou Costello thing.

Initially she frowned and scrunched her forehead up, then seemed to laugh in spite of herself. I was blushing deeply.

Finally she responded verbally, saying, That's a terrible joke and no one is going to get it. How long did you spend on that?

Not long, I lied. And you get it, right?

I really don't, she said, wiping a tear from her eye.

I coughed again. Um, Co-ett-zee? I asked, struggling suddenly as I realised I had never actually heard anyone say his name aloud. And Abbott and Costello?

No, no, I get the references, she clarified. I don't get the joke.

Well, it's just, like, I'm saying that I'm going to do something kind of performative but there's also possibility that it's going to fall flat.

Abbott and Costello were extremely accomplished comedians, she replied. Why would anything they do fall flat? And you're not really preparing anything like Coetzee's Tanner lectures, are you? He conducts multiple dialectics under the veil of fiction to subvert the very notion of 'human values' he'd been asked to speak on. Whereas you're exploring almost precisely the opposite; your points will only cut through if you're presenting them as Miles Beard, Early Career Researcher. If you strip away that ambiguity from the very start you'll end up on the very same fault line you say that you want to expose, likely appearing as calculated and clinical as the mode you're seeking to satirise. I'm not trying to be harsh or anything – do whatever you think is best – but I really believe you risk obscuring your true motivations if you drown everything in a self-conscious self-referentiality. What you're attempting is really ambitious. Inspiring, even. Don't ruin it by backing down from all that before you can even get going.

I'm Scottish, I said. You don't know what it's like. We don't have your people's innate sense of confidence and self-importance. But thank you for using the preferred term for PhD student, I joked. It's very kind of everyone to assume I have a long career ahead of me, although possibly damaging in its own way.

You're changing the subject, she said. C'mon, I'm being serious. Commit to the bit! What did you say the song you're analysing is called? 'Sweet Sucker Dance'? They're the suckers, now do the dance.

All right, all right, I said. I see your point. But the joke wasn't half as bad as you're making out.

I will concede that you might be the first person in existence to attempt that pun, regardless of the fact that it was straining to create a disclaimer that would ruin your paper. But that's all that I'll concede.

We kissed, my butterflies beside themselves now as I reached to grope her breast.

She pulled back. Do you really think Americans are arrogant?

Absolutely, I deadpanned. No, I'm just kidding. Well, no, I'm not kidding, but it's not your fault. It's like you've had this completely different education from us, one that teaches you how to express yourselves and to be really articulate all the time. It can be a little dazzling, in both senses of the word. We're in awe of it at the same time as being suspicious. There were these two Ivy League guys who studied abroad at my uni during undergrad and you'd think they ran the seminars, the amount they spoke. The tutors appreciated it, of course, especially because – as I now know through experience – they'd often not prepared anything themselves. But these guys talked a lot of rubbish, too. In my opinion, anyway. No one ever bothered to call them out on it because they were so competitive – with us, as well as with each other – that they'd jump on whatever anyone had to say in response, so we had to content ourselves with just rolling our eyes whenever their hands shot up. (That's not something we really do, by the way.)

I began to laugh at my own transparent jealousy. And then, I kept going, and then they'd leave for the gym – which they were already dressed for! – and complain about its paucity of, like, adequate free weights, or whatever. You know, really shocking stuff, I said, still laughing.

Well, I wouldn't let two frat bros colour your opinion of the rest of us! she huffed. I hope no one thought that about me when I was at Oxford. I would always raise my hand…

Aw, I'm sorry, I said. You're right, it's not fair. And I'm sure you'd've fit right in there, anyway. You have to understand we feel this way with each other, too. It's an implicit outgrowth of this thing we call the Scottish cringe, a real scourge on our society. We're just not comfortable with ourselves. When someone asks how we're doing we have to say 'not bad' because anything more positive than that and you'll get the shit ripped out you for being so up yourself. It's an inferiority complex borne out of feeling like we don't matter. Throw the ravages of the upper echelons of academia into the mix and it's a recipe for all the bitterness you're presently witnessing. When I was a teenager, I got caught with some pals shooting fireworks from this derelict plot in the city. The police took us down to the station and everything and our parents had to come get us. Mind you, mine didn't really care but you know what my dad says as we're leaving? He goes, So you've got a police record now, have you? What is it, like – 'Walking on the Moon'? It's a dumb joke, a play on the song by Sting, you know. But I didn't realise that at the time so all I took from it was the second layer of meaning that's embedded within it, a layer that I think remains even if you do happen to get the reference. It's the sarcastic suggestion that you've got your chest puffed out. It's telling you not to get big-headed over the fact that you were paid this level of attention, even if it was only the negative attention of the carceral state. My parents don't know how to talk about the fact that I'm doing a PhD, for instance, because the fundamental elitism of it makes them uncomfortable. I'm sure they're proud of me in their own way, but they'll feel some pressure to do it down outwardly with their friends and family. I have the same impulse. Whereas Americans seem much more comfortable in their own skin to us, which we resent.

I don't know, she said. Maybe we are, but it doesn't necessarily come from an abundance of confidence, like you say. I see what you're describing as a general ignorance that affects every level of our society. Americans feel like they're the centre of the world, because, to a large extent, we are. Geopolitically, of course. But culturally as well. You're here and you understand, or at least recognise, all the basic functions of our society. You've seen our films, you've read our books. Even that one semester in England demonstrated to me how much there is out there that I don't know, even within the Anglosphere. Or at least can't immediately identify. I never stayed long enough to start to fill in some of those gaps, but at least I was aware of them. Most of us here don't ever get that opportunity. Or, like those guys in your class, they don't care to take the opportunity even when it's handed to them. Because they don't need to. I just realised I can't even name a single contemporary Scottish author! Who are they?

Well actually, I said, you're not missing very much there. We're in the midst of a prolonged period of artistic stasis.

She laughed. Wow, the cringe is real!

We kissed again.

I looked over to the notes I had been taking during our discussion. Do you think anyone is going to get this? I asked. I mean, really.

That's the risk, she said. But yes, I think they will understand it. Even if they don't know at the conscious level that they understand it.

You're saying not to expect any rapturous applause.

Let's just say I'm looking forward to hearing how it goes. It'll partly depend on your performance of it, of course.

Do you think Coe—, I started, stumbling over his name again. Do you think the Tanner lectures would have gone over as well if he wasn't already famous for his extensive intertextuality with the self?

Probably not, but even Coetzee had to begin somewhere. Just look at *Dusklands*. He doesn't introduce it. It just *is*. I think you'll need to define for yourself what the success of this looks like though. If it's to risk antagonising the audience into dimly acknowledging their own fascination with the lives of artists, I think you're all set. If it's for the plaudits of senior academics you can network with over a cheese cube during the break…

In either case, it's not like anyone will remember it.

Maybe that's true! So why not? And one day I can be a character witness when you conduct a hoax on a grander scale. You're still early in your career, right? she said, winking at me.

We worked on it some more together and then moved into her bedroom to engage in what I, personally, would consider nearly perfect sex. And when her flatmate's key dropped into a glass bowl on a table in the entryway, our passions, rather than abate, seemed only to intensify. After, while she towelled herself off in the bathroom, I sent Sarah a quick text to say goodnight.

What do you want to do now? I asked. I've got the evening free.

Of course you do, she said. I'm the only person you know.

Okay, you got me. Regardless. We could watch a film?

Sure. What did you have in mind? *Brigadoon*? You seem homesick.

Very funny, I said, grinning. But I came across a folder today that had some production files for *All Night Long*… It's an adaptation of Othello set in the '60s London jazz scene. I don't know if it's any good, but Mingus is supposed to be in it. Dave Brubeck, too. Any interest?

I quickly signed into Sarah's account so we could stream the film through the browser. I didn't take notice of any prompt to indicate what I think must have happened, but I don't know how else she could have discovered Sarah's name and details: the password had to have saved itself somehow.

Her laptop purred between us as we lay there on the bed, still naked with only a light, perfumed sheet wrapped around us in the decadent warmth and stillness of a Georgetown summer's evening. No longer at school, I was now a panting undergrad on the cusp of learning to express myself and my desires. What I'm trying to say is that our once-insignificant liaison was beginning to grow there into something more, brief though it would ever be, and that I was utterly beguiled by her at every movement, the perpetual sense of bohemian transience backdropping our relationship seeming only to heighten my tingling fascination with the unfamiliarity of the situation, like I had been given the rare but ubiquitously craved opportunity to not only entertain a second life but to live it, to test it, with the coveted knowledge that I would only ever need to reset the system again in order to go back to where I had first started. And I shouldn't speak for her, but I think she must've felt something close to the same. She never indicated otherwise, anyway. As I've said, I never asked her about her other relationships or suggested that we should be exclusive, the hypocrisy of such a suggestion too much even for an academician who prides himself on his ability to hold multiple contradictory thoughts at the same time. I know there are those who would use these details to cast doubt on the consenuality of the time we spent together but I would ask that you take up such concerns with the myriad tales of delusive romance that have helped to shape our literary traditions, rather than me personally. (Off the top of my head: Salter; Carver; Theroux, even. So if you want to 'throw the whole man away' or whatever, I would humbly suggest you start with them first.)

When the film had concluded, we looked at each other.

Not brilliant from a research perspective, I said, since Mingus had only featured in a few scattered shots. But I liked it.

I liked it until the last five seconds, she said.

The closing shot of the Othello character putting his arm around Desdemona? Why? Because it wasn't faithful to the play? Or don't you acquiesce to Hollywood's need for redemption?

Redemption for a man who would hit his wife over his own petty jealousies and insecurities? she replied. No.

The next day, on the train ride to New York City, the words came to me unbidden: *Go on, Maggot Brain! Go ON, Maggot Brain!*

XII

I WAS FEELING a little apprehensive when the train pulled into Penn Station. I had tried to make it easy for myself with as little requirement for direct communication with actual, live New Yorkers as possible on that first day because I couldn't bear the thought of stumbling around a metropolis of such a scale rolling a bag around like a yokel who's only three hours away from prostituting himself for a roof over his head. But I was worried I wouldn't be able to ensconce myself easily without a smartphone. And, once speaking became necessary, I knew embarrassment was sure to follow.

I'd been to London a handful of times, mostly to visit friends who'd gone to university there, and was never left very impressed. It is very wide, that much I'll grant. But its width is precisely what makes it not New York. Your artists, your playwrights, your sex workers, they're all pushed further and further out towards the post-war terraced exurbs where proud salarymen once raised their idyllic families before giving in and actually moving to Bedminster, leaving nothing left even within walking distance of the centre but a hollowness filled, superficially, with bankers in darling three-bed homes, international students in alternatingly beggarly and ostentatious dormitories, and publishers huddled in damp flat-shares. Whereas New York seemed like a terrarium that the more you crammed into it, the more everything within would have to find a way to move up, or perish entirely. In Scotland we have no such pretences. No claim to Edinburgh other than its outlandish, volcanic beauty; to Glasgow, it being simply a place where a lot of people seem to live. Sarah always said that one day we'd move to the village on the coast where she grew up. I would teach; she would write; our children...

So I'd booked a room at the Hotel Pennsylvania, which I knew to be very near to the station. But when I walked out, expecting to see it right across the road, formidable with a spare intensity as in the photos I had seen online, I found instead a quite ugly theatre. Though I know it now to have been Madison Square Garden, which – contrary to my assumptions – isn't a garden by any stretch of the imagination, to me it was just a curved, cautious reminder that I was in a real city, that I could become lost without ever leaving the same block. I circled around, reading above the Corinthian columns of the grand building I'd exited from a cryptic prayer of some kind. *Neither snow nor rain nor heat nor gloom of night stays these couriers from the swift completion of their appointed rounds.* The words were familiar to me, though distant, as if I'd encountered them before but within a totally different context, and their phrasing only exacerbated my sense of unease. (Why bring up the 'gloom of night' at all?)

After I'd made it to the diametric point of the block to where I'd started, I saw the hotel, not nearly so prodigiously placed as I'd expected, lost as it was amongst a sea of similarly cut wedges of thick cement. The first thing I noticed as I wandered into the vestibule was a door off to the side leading directly into a diner. Who's in there today? I wondered, thinking to all the stories I had heard of where the great artists of their generation would meet to drink black coffee and eat Reuben sandwiches. It was only on leaving later that evening that I realised that the restaurant was in fact closed, permanently.

But the lobby itself was sparkling exactly as I'd imagined, as if the house lights of a small but well-funded theatre were falling onto and reflecting off the marbled floor to welcome us into the warm and inviting glow of a virtuosic performance. Mirrors had been carefully placed to enhance this sensation, and as I walked by one, I caught sight of myself looking slightly slouched. Wanting to meet with the stage presence I'd come to feel would be demanded of me, I rolled my shoulders back to elongate my spine, and approached the long desk with a local's bravado. In a crowd of other repertory players, I stood patiently for my turn.

Yeah? said the guy sitting there, scrolling through something on his phone as I walked up.

I have a booking, I announced.

Name?

Beard-comma-Miles, I replied.

Without so much as a glance towards me he turned to the computer next to him and typed a few keystrokes.

Say again, he commanded, staring at the screen.

Beard.

He continued typing.

Bird? he asked, looking up at me now, reluctantly acknowledging my corporeality for the first time.

Beard, I replied. Beard. Like the hair on your face. B-E-A-R-D. Beard. Be-ard.

More typing.

Okay, found it. Here you go, he said, handing me the key, and then, so quickly I couldn't follow, recited his prepared spiel about the available amenities and fire exit locations.

While I waited for the lift to arrive, I sent Sophie a text, saying something like, New Yorkers appreciate when you stop them to ask for directions to a hotel that you're literally standing in front of, right?

It wasn't true to suggest that this had happened, but I was trying to sound jocular as I reconnected with her, and perhaps play up the foreignness of the setting I was finding myself in, as if I was in need of shepherding.

Hackneyed though it may sound, my room really was on the 13th floor, an obvious but even more insidious portent than I realised at the time, for I have reason to believe it was Frank Olson's room that I stayed in. And though it may make me sound like a complete unsophisticate, I couldn't be sure that I'd ever been so high off the ground, unless you counted hillwalking. I had suggested once to some friends that we go on the London Eye and, when they all burst out laughing, I played it off like it was the joke they clearly thought it was.

The room itself seemed to convey that the hotel had checked its pretences on the ground floor, and that it'd be wise if I did the same. As I put my bags down, the first thing I noticed was the television remote chained to the bed, and, when I went into the bathroom, the showerhead covered in black mould.[6] But it didn't occur to me to say anything. This

---

6 Even as I reread this I can't help but picture Olson's body tossed from the window and smashing against the pavement. Still alive, just, when the night porter rushed to him; his brief, incoherent mumblings fluttering into the air as he crossed the threshold into death's ungainly embrace.

was New York, baby! Once I was clean (relatively) I checked my phone to see that Sophie had texted me back to say that she wasn't going to make it to my conference presentation in the morning (fair enough) but that she'd be up for grabbing a drink when I was finished. In truth, this was far preferable to me. Suggesting that she might be interested in my paper had only been a gambit to open a friendly dialogue with her, and now that I was planning to go down the precarious, so-boring-it-becomes-exciting route, I had dreaded to think she might attend and bear witness to something that the audience would find outrageous, or, even worse, as dull as it would initially seem.

I texted back in agreement and suggested that we meet in the early afternoon as I was planning to quietly escape during the lunch break, before anyone would have a chance to question my routine informally, when the façade would inevitably shatter. An evening to myself in the Big City lay ahead. I looked at the navy suit I was planning to wear the next day. It would seem a shame to have brought it all the way from Scotland, and then D.C., only to don it for one brief occasion. I put it on and fixed my hair in the too-white light of the bathroom. I wished then that I'd had my smartphone with me so I could snap a pic and filter it down to the warm atmosphere of a candlelit ristorante: so that I could send it; so that someone would see it; waiting for those three little dots to announce that a reply is rapidly forthcoming; my pulse quickening; a ding in my brain. Look at me! look at me! look at me!

Outside, under the hotel's grand, fluorescent awning, a doorman I'd somehow missed upon entering appeared to ask if I wanted a cab. I told him that what I really wanted was to see Times Square, and if he could please point out the direction I'd be very grateful. He struck his arm out far along towards one direction of the street.

Just keep going? I asked.

Just keep going, he answered.

I don't know what I was expecting to see, but whatever it was, I know that I didn't see it. It was a bustling evening, as I suppose nearly every evening is in that part of town. I was already feeling dizzy at the momentum of the streets, at the extent to which my senses tingled, and it was difficult to fathom how many people were within a 100-metre radius of me at any given time, though most were probably tourists, as I was. The air smelt like a food rubbish bin left in a sunny window and the sheer magnitude of my surroundings was overwhelming. But the commercialism was also extreme in ways I hadn't anticipated. Most of the restaurants and shopfronts I saw were recognisable to me, or at least imparted a familiarity through their intentional genericism, and I guess I'd wanted to see something I had created in my head that I can only term now as 'real New York'. Any New Yorker reading this will guffaw at the idea that whatever authenticity that I thought I was looking for I'd find in Times Square, but you have to understand that what I don't mean is that I wanted to go to, like, a trendy bar in Williamsburg that doubles as a crazy golf course. (Believe it or not, we have hipsters in Scotland, too.) The Times Square of my imagination had peep shows, whacked-out beat poets doing their best takes on the military industrial complex, and, with a little luck, some Jean Genet-like figure standing on a dark corner with a haunted look, beckoning me towards all manner of vice and debauchery. This was a glorified Piccadilly Circus.

What did I find besides the aforementioned chain restaurants? Investment firms whose names I associated only with the crash, the same fast fashion outlets I knew from home, and way too many absurd motive billboards for crap films I couldn't imagine anyone actively desiring to see or for luxury consumer products that traded on their perceived (by distinct segments of the global population) brand value over any practical functionality or aestheticism. I knew I wouldn't find an original Joe Camel hoisting his robotic arm to puff it up or anything but the idea that what I'd stepped into was just more of the same shite I was used to at home, only somehow hastened towards the next moment of market implosion under its own untenable weight, disturbed my preconceived notions of what I thought was supposed to be a shared yet distinctly vibrant culture. Was such a crushing sense of disappointment naïve of me? Yes, of course. Was the desire to find myself surrounded by totems of American sleaze pure? Also yes. And for want of a better way of putting it, this seemed to pose some issues for me, psychically. For instance, I almost lost it when I saw the U.S. Armed Forces Recruiting Station – ironic, it turns out, as I later learned it's actually one of the oldest institutions in the area – situated across from an NYPD station that looked more like a tourist's office and indeed appeared to be used as one. But, in any case, I could feel myself starting to get worked up – mutterings becoming tremulous, gestures less and less confined to my person – so I decided I needed a drink, and, for the most part, it seemed to work. Temporarily, anyway.

Inside a tenuously Cuban-themed restaurant that at least had an original, if kitsch, approach to design, with plastic palm trees and an abundance of tropically-patterned flourishes, I sat at the bar and ordered their signature drink. At first, I found the waitstaff's demeanour palliative. I enjoyed their reflexive use of honorifics (can I refill that for you, sir?) and the polite detachment they would exhibit from my own obvious misery. But when I threw my hand out to order what was probably my fifth or sixth, the veneer began to crack.

Another classic mojito, huh, sir?

Is that a problem? I growled.

Not at all, the moustachioed bartender said. In fact, seeing as you're a man who clearly appreciates a fine rum, why don't I mix up a couple of shooters for the two of us? With the top-shelf stuff.

Fine, I said.

I suspected this was simply a ploy he implemented regularly to increase his tips which I knew servers in the U.S. to rely upon. He sneaks a bit away from management, finagling a drink for himself in the process, and I make up the difference with him directly at a discounted rate to compensate for the risk he's taking. I respected the hustle, as they say, and, I knew, if he tried to get cheeky with me again, I could always decline to acknowledge the gesture he'd made and simply pay the tab exactly as written when it was handed to me.

So you'll imagine my incredulity when, after he'd spent several minutes carefully pouring various liquids to produce something as thin and pale yellow as the sun at home, I knocked it back and then sat there, looking at him, waiting for it to knock *me* back.

You fuckin' serious? I said.

What's wrong? he asked, too wide-eyed, like he thought he was in pantomime for the visually impaired.

Think you forgot to put the rum in there, mate, I said. I may seem like a drunk tourist to you but I know when I'm being had.

I really don't know what you mean, he said, furrowing his brow into an expression of bemused indignance. You watched me make it.

I wasn't watching anything, I said, and you bloody well know it as well. Guess I'm the rube, eh? Serves me right coming here. How many drinks am I going to find on my bill, I wonder? At least twelve, I reckon. Because they were all double-shots, aye, and in America that means you pay twice what's on the menu. That'll be the excuse if I notice. Ooh, don't forget the tax, too! And, like a numpty, I'll just pay up, right? Or maybe I'll pay without even bothering to look at it, 'cause maybe I can't even read English, yeah?

I was standing up now, jabbing my finger towards his stupid face, the wide wooden bar between us preventing any real contact.

Look, he said, I'm sorry if—

Oh! I exclaimed. Sorry! Sorry! Sorry, sorry, sorry. You know who's sorry is me; I'm sorry for coming into such a shite place as this.

Still jabbering, I was backing away towards the entrance as the realisation dawned on me that an excuse to not pay for any of my drinks was now dangling out before me. If I could ramp up the level of offence I was taking just a bit more, act a touch more righteous, and thereby create a bigger scene, he might just as well be happy to see the back of me, and I'd save a fair amount of my travel budget in the process.

What a funny joke, I said, raising my voice while continuing my retreat. Really, really great stuff. Truly. You should be a comedian with patter like that. But, hmm, you know what, I wonder if it's *illegal*, actually, to discriminate like this against a—

I was halfway to the door when I felt the worn-smooth soles of my leather shoes lose their traction with the shiny lino floor. For a moment I was able to hold my balance and flailed my arms wildly at my sides to try and keep it. But as I felt myself begin to tip over, my hands jutted out behind me to prevent any fall onto my back, and my eyes squinted shut in anticipation of the impact to come.

Whoops! I heard myself yelp once I'd begun my inevitable descent.

But I wasn't able to grasp anything and, instead of falling onto my back, I fell on my arse, the response to which was gasping and cackles. I then felt my head smack onto a hard wooden surface behind me, and, after a moment or two of sitting there mumbling incoherently, like I thought I was Rab C. Nesbitt or something, I turned around to see that a dining chair awkwardly situated by the door had partially broken my fall, while the edge of its seat had just made contact with the apex of my occipital bone.

The bartender loomed above me, extending the bill.

You'll be hearing my lawyer, I managed, before turning away to flee into the night.

As the door closed behind me, I could hear the dining room burst into applause.

XIII

THE WHOLE THING was a guddle and I think it was made worse by the fact that my injuries weren't visible. If I'd showed up with a bleeding gash, walking on crutches, icing a bruised eye, the excuses for my behaviour would announce themselves, or, at least, solicit a modicum of sympathy for me. I couldn't very well stand there in my unmarked suit, visibly hungover, smelling distinctly of alcohol, and tell everyone that I'd been the victim of a classic New York mugging, to say nothing of admitting the truth, which was more like I'd connived to cheat a bar tab, somehow mugging myself in the process. It would only have provoked more questions.

Though I maintained – and still do, to some extent, although I've learnt to distrust some of my memories from this period – that it was the bartender who'd committed the original sin, I couldn't argue with who had paid the bigger price. I would have given several times the figure I'd saved to not have to deal with myself experiencing a head injury.

By the time I reached my room, I was sufficiently sober to log onto the hotel's Wi-Fi (at an expense of $29.95 per night) and look up the signs and symptoms of concussions. This meant I not only spent several hours reading increasingly incredible webpages offering either apocalyptic prognoses for my mental capabilities going forward or promising remedies to salvage the probable damage through herbal supplements, available here, now, and at a discount for a limited time only, I was also very scared to sleep.

When I posted about my predicament in a forum (board/notadoctorbut) most of the users told me not to worry, but I just couldn't make myself believe them. All I could see was my academic future slipping away from me as my memory closed-circuited on itself, relegated to only its most basic and literal functions, while I would grow more erratic, dyspeptic, or morose with each passing day. My awareness that these feelings were almost entirely psychological in nature only made my experience of them worse. Jung may have overcome his own fainting episodes after such an incident in childhood, but I knew I just wasn't as strong as he was. Any phobic reaction I'd develop to dense journal articles from this point on would surely last the rest of my career, and I doubted whether it'd pass muster on a disability disclosure form for any job demanding that I read and write them.

When dawn started to break, I was starving and desperate. I took another shower beneath the poisonous fixture and put my suit back on. I was still committed to my delivering my paper, but I wanted to get checked out first. And I needed to eat, preferably something with turmeric or high in Omega-3 fatty acids. I grabbed my conference handouts and a roughly sketched map I'd made of my subway journey to the university campus and the walk from there to their healthcare services.

Though my route to Columbia was only a straight shot, and helpfully labelled with its own discrete stop, still I found the system fascinating and bewildering. This is how I'd wanted to feel. Local, express, numbers, letters; it was all unfamiliar to me. At home, there's one underground with two duelling circular tracks. You were either going one way or the other, and you'd always reach your destination, eventually. Whereas in New York it was like I could hop onto the wrong line, fall asleep, and wake up transported to another world, Coney Island.

On arrival to the clinic, I had to wrangle with a functionary who wouldn't listen to me as I tried to explain that I didn't have a university ID card or number. He continually directed me to log in at a bank of computers where students were accessing a waitlist for appointments, but it was clear I wouldn't be able to get past the first screen, so I sat there looking at him petulantly, waiting for him to notice me.

Finally, after several cycles of students had successfully moved through to the waiting room, I clutched my head, saying, Ow, ow, ow, ow.

Now that I had made this his problem as well, he deigned to take notice of me again.

Is this an emergency? he asked.

I don't know, I replied. No, I don't think so. Maybe. I hit my head.

Come here, he said, waving me to his desk. So you're not on the college's health plan?

I'm not a Columbia student!

Okay, okay. Show me your insurance card?

Ow, ow.

All right, malingerer, follow me and fill these out. But you'll be charged whatever the no health fee rate is for your treatment, got it?

I nodded, not quite catching that word he'd just used, *malingerer*.

I waited for the doctor for forty minutes who then saw me for five. After I explained all that had happened to me – well, just that I had lost my balance and fallen backwards onto a chair – she did the torch thing with my eyes and then put her hands onto my skull.

I can't feel anything, she said. Are you sure you really smacked it? There aren't any bumps. You probably just have whiplash.

Whiplash? I repeated. Is that serious?

Very rarely, she said. You might want to get it checked out further if your pain lasts for more than a week but my guess is that it'll be gone in a couple of days. In the meantime, have tried taking any over-the-counter painkillers?

Knowing that if I'd truly been in serious pain this would have been the obvious first port of call, I lied and said yes but that it was still killing me. And when she then wrote me a prescription for an oral diazepam, I accepted it with no intention of filling it. She had a gentle way about her, and a wave of satisfaction had run through my body while she looked into my eyes and held my head. I didn't want to reveal my neurosis, not to her.

But, back in the lobby, where a bill for $100 even, printed with coloured ink onto what felt like a premium cardstock, was handed to me, I knew that Sarah wouldn't stand for this, that she'd tear it up in front of them, say that they were barbaric, or begin to bawl in frustration, tears running like mustangs, as she wedged the natural into the mechanical, bewildering them, disarming them, deftly subverting their vicious inhumanity. Nevertheless, I paid what I owed, resolving never to mention the whole debacle, to anyone. But it occurred to me then that I'd never even asked Sarah to join me on this trip. She'd had work, that much was true, but here I was in this city, *our* city, and we weren't even able to experience it for the first time together. In truth, of my time in the U.S., it was this that felt like the greatest betrayal.

I overestimated my audience. Or perhaps it would be more accurate to say that I severely *under*estimated them and was left humiliated by the experience.

It was 09:45 by the time I made it to the impressively collegiate Dodge Hall, with its red brick and cement columns, low steps, and campus novel grandeur. I followed some 72-point font signs to the Center for Ethnomusicology and installed myself next to an enormous urn of coffee and a tray of pastries labelled Danishes. One bite turned my stomach and I retched quietly into my plastic cup, locking eyes above it with the reproachful glare of a man I would've said resembled Jonathan Culler, if I'd had any idea of what Jonathan Culler looked like. *You are now my referent*, I thought in the dregs of my drink-soaked panic. *My name is Metaphor.*

I picked up a programme and retreated with a sense of resigned purpose into the classroom where the first batch of papers was to be delivered, mine included. I would be first to present amongst four. Pondering this, I was nevertheless surprised to hear someone speak my name, though it wasn't actually to me.

I never received any materials from Miles Beard, somebody said. Is Miles here? Miles, is there anything that you need to project?

Miles wasn't at the conference dinner last night, somebody else replied. We waited for him for a little while, because he'd RSVP'd. But he never showed.

I thought about standing then and simply walking out. I probably should have done. But I was too afraid. Afraid that they'd realise it'd been me the whole time, slouched there like a goon. I took a deep breath.

That's me, I said, brightly, turning to them, smiling ingratiatingly. I'm terribly sorry about the dinner. I spent all last night tweaking my paper and it completely slipped my mind. I hope you didn't wait too long. And, no, thank you, I've brought my own materials, which I'll distribute.

Everyone in the room had fallen silent during this exchange and was looking over to us.

The one who was first to have spoken, who I presumed to be the chair of our panel, responded after a brief pause, saying only, Okay, then, and walked away.

But I needed more reassurance than this and so turned to the other. I really am sorry about last night, I said.

A beat passed. Then, Don't be! was the reply that was shouted back to me. The food was awful!

A few people laughed at this and then began to speak about the evening before. Truthfully, I couldn't recall signing up for such an excursion, though it sounded like something I might, and I unsettled myself further by wondering if this was but the first of many instances to come of a memory that my fall had dislodged. But, in any case the topic had moved on, so I looked away and down towards my script. *Just be fast and shut up*, I thought to myself. *You don't want them to think you're a complete nimrod.*

I sat there shifting in my seat with a look I hoped suggested arch, knowing amusement as the typical preamble was conducted about how, really, it's a quite informal event yet all the same important that the schedule be maintained and therefore the chair of each panel will discretely snap their fingers to alert the final two minutes of each allotment of speaking time.

Suddenly, I heard myself being introduced, and something like an indulgent smile crept onto my face when the chair referenced my fellowship at the Library of Congress. No matter what they might think, I considered, they'd have to contend with the fact somebody, somewhere, at some point, thought that my research was worthwhile. I passed around photocopies of the marked up musical score.

You'll notice, I began, that for clarity's sake, Charles Mingus's original score is reproduced here in dark grey and the final version that Joni Mitchell produced after his death is notated over it in a light grey.

I expected a titter of laughter at this. Even though I'd agreed that opening with an excusatory joke wouldn't be conducive to my aims, I couldn't resist breaking the tension for myself in some way; at my own expense, if necessary. But instead of breaking any tension, I only seemed to create more of it. I watched as they glanced through what I'd handed to them, trading judgey looks with each other. *I do have eyes*, I thought. *I am standing right here in front of you.*

Nevertheless, throughout, I tried to do my best impression of a machine reporting on one machine talking to another, and, when I'd concluded, I raised my eyes from the paper I was reading from to gauge the expressions of my fellow presenters and conference-goers. They did seem rather bored but not unusually so. When they realised I'd finished, there was some polite applause and I sat down on the front row to watch the rest of the panel. Out of the corner of my eye I'd seen the appointed discussant taking notes while I spoke, so I pinned my hopes on her giving me some kind of reaction that I could manipulate towards my goals, though it has to be said that even I was beginning to lose sight of them. What was I expecting? Someone to leap to the floor shouting, These are people, man? Senior academics aren't exactly famous for their demonstrative approach to their subjects.

I was too full of post-public speaking adrenaline and anticipation to pay much attention to the other papers but the topics were obscure to me anyway: what the historical popularity of Wagner's *Ring* cycle could tell us about the present political moment; sonorance in/of 'Thoreau's Flute'; and David Foster Wallace as a fundamentally polyphonic author. When each had concluded, we were asked to move our chairs to front of the small room and to turn them around to face the audience for the question-and-answer portion. The discussant seemed to move in reverse order, and the youngish man – bearded, bespectacled, sporting a bolo tie tied tightly around his neck – became visibly agitated when she mentioned that someone called Mary Car(?) had recently alleged that Wallace lifted much of *Infinite Jest* straight from AA meetings and their mutual friends and would he like to comment on how Bakhtin's belief in a plurality of voices in the novel could be complicated by this introduction of an ethical grey area in the writing process?

I crossed my legs and cocked an eyebrow, feigning an eager interest in the conversation that took place next to me as I pretended to scribble relevant notes onto the back of a page from my own handout. Instead, I was jotting down a smattering of unrelated keywords that I was hearing, words like *shame, digression,* and *found objects.*

But I couldn't keep up with the charade for very long. As it became clear that the discussant was indeed proceeding in reverse order, and had some carefully considered remarks to make in response to each paper in turn, I could feel my legs start to wobble, and it took a considerable amount of weight from my body to stop this from being clear for all to see. I sat up in the chair and bore down on my soles as though I might be about to jump out of my seat, like a squatting exercise from the one gym class Sarah and I had ever taken together, when she'd turned to me and said, Why are you good at this? You just lie around all day, and then walked out midway through.

It was now the person who'd gone after me's turn and I could feel my heart pulsating rapidly inside my chest. I closed my eyes to recite the mantra an NHS hypnotherapist and I had devised together after one too many appointments with my GP regarding something the pamphlet I was given had referred to as 'burning mouth syndrome'. Though the recording we'd made was on the smartphone I'd left back home, still I knew the affirmations by heart. Placing the thumb and forefinger of my right hand together, closing my eyes and taking three deep breaths, I quickly entered into a meditative state while I hoped the audience's attentions would remain diverted. I allowed a sensation like peacefulness or solitude – fragile and momentary – to engulf me.

You are as brilliant as Nabokov, my inner voice recited dutifully. *And as handsome as Obama.*

There was a cough. I opened my eyes to see that the discussant had already started her question for me and was reading it from the pad in her hand.

...a mode of analysis that would sit more comfortably in the previous century than—

I didn't know what had already been said, so I cut her off and reinhabited my guise of detached, ever so slightly effete politesse.

I think I can see where this is going, and I suppose I can only apologise. Did you find it very difficult to follow?

Well, yes, I did. The methodology—

I expect you had trouble distinguishing the two versions, I interjected.

No, no, she said, waving the suggestion away with her hand. It's clearly not ideal but, believe me, we all know first-hand how much more expensive colour copies can be, and I appreciate you bringing something in for our reference in any case. What I would like to hear more about is your thinking process behind the bodily erasure of a man of colour who faced persistent racism throughout his career and a woman who faced equally persistent misogynistic attitudes throughout hers. I assume the choice to reduce them to such a static form was deliberate and so I was wondering if you could speak more to that.

Um, I started, gazing out the window like I was plotting an escape, or my suicide.

This wasn't a contingency I had planned for, and I suspect my friend hadn't considered it either when we were working together, probably because she herself was unlikely to face the same criticisms directly. But I recognised that an important point was being made, and, in fact, the calm presentation of that point was precisely what made it so difficult to respond to. No undue emphasis was being given to the sociological milieu surrounding what I had to say; it was simply asking to be acknowledged. I was backed into a corner where either I'd double down and become the worst possible version of myself: someone who'd argue that one's identity is an inherently neutral concept and that it was those who would argue otherwise that are actually the ones most threatening to the harmony of our society; or I'd put my hands in the air and disavow everything I'd stood up and said for fifteen minutes to try and painstakingly explain that in some ways my point was being made for me by her as I had intended, a prospect that would, more than anything else, appear like a hasty attempt to retroactively come out good in a debate that, I knew now, I'd really had no business trying to instigate in the first place.

She pressed her advantage while I panicked.

I'm sure you're aware, for instance, that Mingus is a Scottish name? An Anglicised and, then, to a greater extent, Americanised form of Menzies, I believe. And I'm sure we don't need to get into how black man could end up with a name like that here in this country.

I looked to the audience helplessly for a cue that someone was ready to come to my defence, but they remained placidly seated and apparently only faintly curious about my predicament.

If I could go back to this moment I think I would say something like, Yes, absolutely, thank you for raising that, and then I might have gone on to relate a bit of dialogue from *All Night Long* that had stuck with me, a neatly distilled exemplar of the myriad contradictions laden in the appreciation of black-constructed works by white audiences during this period, about how the groups that seem to enjoy jazz the most are 'negroes, adolescents, and intellectuals'. I would have said that there is little doubt that these contradictory impulses continue to have bearing today but it was promising nonetheless that we'd found a better grammar for describing them, imperfect though it may still be, and that I was sensitive to the notion that the ideological and artistic landscape remains vastly unequal for wide swathes of the population, not least women.

Instead I said, Th-that's possible but, um, far from definitive, I think. Menzies is pronounced Ming-us in Scotland, not Min-gus, and, at the end of the day, his parentage and racial background is in fact far from certain.

If I'd ever had any of them, they were lost after such defensive and unhelpfully ambivalent remarks. I knew that as a result of being ambitious in my choice of conferences I was often the youngest person in the room, but, for perhaps the first time, I really felt it, too. The heat exploded onto my neck and face.

An embarrassed silence followed and after allowing me to stew for a moment the chair concluded the proceedings.

In the stairwell, plonking myself between two floors above, I held it back until I could no longer do so and then vomited between my legs. I needed to speak to Sarah. I needed to know that someone was standing by me, even if it was from a distance; that there was nothing that could happen which would ever change her opinion of me; that even at my most worthless, I still had some worth yet. But she was at work and I knew I wouldn't hear from her for hours.

I fled to the toilet and, for a time, was near inconsolable. Then, suddenly, an idea innervated me. I asked a student where I could find the nearest chemist, although I'd had to clarify 'pharmacy'.

XIV

THERE'S SOMETHING OF a melancholic irony to the fact of my health anxiety. Namely, that I don't actually care very much about living. I've never been particularly prone to thoughts of topping myself but nor have I ever felt much biological imperative to keep going either. So keep that in mind during this next part as I think it'll make much more sense to you if you do.

My dad told me he thought that they gave you a hard time, was what she said.

Oh my god, I replied. He wasn't there. Please tell me Paul Auster wasn't there.

Sophie had decided that we should meet at this tiny bar hidden in the back of an art gallery in the Bowery, the caricature of a speakeasy. I was a little disappointed. I had suggested several places I knew from books, film, and music, but somehow it seemed like they didn't exist any more, or that if they did she didn't know of them. Not Café des Artistes, not Elaine's, not Max's Kansas City, not even Mr Cacciatore's. I think she thought I was doing a bit so when she texted the name of this favourite haunt of hers, I played along and gave the impression of wearied acquiescence, saying it would be fine so long as it would be a place for us to see the great New York artists of the day. When she responded to say, I am an artist, I replied with, Visibly? and she said that she'd do

126

her best. My heart fluttered at her use of ellipsis and a static cartoon face smiling coyly. (I admit this all sounds rather flirtatious but I swear none of it's going the way that you're thinking. To be sure, despite activities which would suggest the contrary, our evening together was anhedonic in every way except perhaps its self-indulgence.)

He said it sounded really interesting! she reassured me. A little over his head, maybe, but he thought if the questions had been fairer he could've understood it better. He tried to find you after to tell you that but you were already gone.

Hearing this only makes me feel more foolish but tell him I'm sorry I missed him and that I appreciate him coming to see it. I'm really surprised! And aghast, obviously.

He has *a lot* of free time. He just finished the novel he'd been working on for years so he's exhausted. Of course, it's a compliment because he wouldn't have gone if he didn't want to. But equally don't feel like it was a huge deal to him. Any excuse to visit the *alma mater*, you know. Anyway, it's not far from them. He's probably still there, bothering people!

I became aware that continuing to talk about her father would eventually take its toll on our afternoon for her, and I truly hadn't lured her out for that reason. I'd simply seen the opening and wedged my foot in; she was annoyed at me and I'd tried to undo it. That was a different Miles than the one who was here, sitting in front of her, and I'd needed to prove to myself that I could still be charming. Plus, I wanted a friend.

So is meeting strange men from the internet something you do often? I asked.

The bartender was setting our cocktails down right at this moment – mine mezcal-based and hers a Manhattan. If I'd clocked his approach I wouldn't have said this, so poorly worded and clumsily clichéd. But because he'd heard me, I blushed for what felt like the millionth time that day.

Not that I'm strange, I added quickly, looking now to the expressionless bartender's face as he turned away from us.

You're a little strange, replied Sophie. But then, who isn't?

I took a gulp from my glass of exotic smoke, rich and perverted like a tampered whisky, and said, Just so you know, I'm not really much of a drinker.

Oh, well, we didn't need to meet in a bar in that case, said Sophie. I'm just happy to be out of the house for a little while. Would you rather we go somewhere else instead? We can check out the art here. Or a friend of mine has an exhibition around the corner.

No, it's fine, I said. I like this place. Do you ever take pills?

Pills? she asked. What kind of pills?

Don't worry, I replied. They're prescription!

I handed the bottle towards her.

I think I'm okay, she said. But knock yourself out. Actually, don't knock yourself out. That would be annoying.

I took one.

What's a 'co-pay', by the way? I asked.

I finished my drink quickly and then ordered another. It was probably only a psychosomatic effect at this point, but I felt myself finally relax in her presence and next thing I knew we were engaged in an intense conversation about the nature of photography I was only able to keep up on through my superficial knowledge of Nadar and his contemporaries.

At some point she returned from the toilet, looking all, you know, super hot and sexy and stuff, and she said to me, as she sat down, Why, hello, Dr Beard.

I almost melted into the floor.

But I began to find myself having difficulty focusing on her, and the words with which I responded felt distant and disembodied, The doctoral degree shall be conferred upon completion of 48 credits and the successful defence of the thesis before the examination committee.

Oh, so you haven't had your defence yet? she asked. When will that be? Are you nervous?

I tried to look her straight in the eye and respond adequately, but my attention span kept shifting, like it was on an off-kilter axis that was falling this way and now that, reminiscent of this ride we'd gone on at a travelling fair that was held near Sarah's village each year, The Gravitron.

In the future, I said, slurring ever so slightly, packages will be sent to distant lands through beams of light.

Sophie looked at me somewhat curiously, then laughed. Well, I guess you could say that they already are…, she replied. In a manner of speaking, I mean.

Undaunted, I began again. In the future—

Wait a minute, she said, I recognise that. Where is that from? Is that… Disney World? Are you saying something that they used to say at Disney World? At the Place of Tomorrow, or whatever? I remember going there with my dad and—

I cut her off. Paul Auster at Disney World, I said.

Look, she said, I know he's Paul Auster to you but to me he's just my goofy old dad.

Paul Auster, I repeated. At Disney World.

Hey, are you feeling okay? she asked. You look kind of green.

Caffe Cino, I replied mischievously, knowing that it'd be misinterpreted.

Um, you want to get some coffee? Okay, sure. I know a place that's over—

La MaMa! La MaMa, La MaMa, La MaMa.

Huh? Your mom? Do you need to call your mom?

A play! I exclaimed. We should go see a play. You're totally gorgeous, by the way. I think I'm wasted. Are you?

Sophie smiled nervously. Miles, you're crazy.

When I told everyone that I knew I'd get Lyme disease from the tall grass on the pitch as we walked towards the circus tents, they had laughed at me. But it was true, and, because I remained so vigilant, I was able to get the antibiotics I needed very soon after. I'd had the bullseye rash and everything. Served me right trying to wear shorts in Scotland though, that's what Sarah's dad had said. *Who does he think he is, Mickey Mouse?*

Wait, what was I talking about? I asked, stopping suddenly.

Something about a bloodsucking parasite, I think, Sophie said. I'm not really sure, to be perfectly honest.

Oh, please be perfectly honest, I replied. It's a contradiction in terms for us sinners. I was with them at the kirk this one time and the preacher or minister – dunno what they call 'em up there – gave this big spiel about how to attain a state of 'divine grace', that sort of thing. Meanwhile, the tenets we're supposed to be living by – don't lie! – are just totally incompatible with anything resembling what the laypeople would consider a graceful life. On the way back to the house, he's breenging round a hairpin turn on single-track road so I say to him, Stuart, you're going sixty miles an hour – where's the lie? – and he was in a huff for the rest of the afternoon. Was I supposed to be praying instead? Sorry. I'm not sure if any of that made sense. Did it?

Should we get out of here? Sophie asked. I feel like we're getting dangerously close to the point where you're going to need to lie down. Where's your hotel?

Don't make me go back there! I countered. They'll toss me out the window, I just know it. I wonder why they never got married.

Huh? Who?

Mickey and Minnie.

Why do they have to get married?

I don't know, I responded, a little dejected now. I like being married.

You're married? she asked.

I don't wear a ring because I might go into dentistry, I sighed.

What's she like? Or he?

Sarah, I said. Oh god, Sarah. She's gorgeous as well. Should we call her?

Do you really want to?

Well, we don't have to, I replied huffily.

We sat there looking at each other for a moment, my head starting to loll a bit.

Do you think this could be a play? I asked.

What, us? Like, right now, you mean? I guess. Three actors, she said, gesturing to ourselves and the bartender, plus a simple set. Okay, yeah, why not? Off-broadway, obviously.

Off-off, I corrected. Do you want to write it together? Maybe I'd even ask you if it was a play in it too. Totes po-mo.

Hmm, she shrugged. But why?

I dunno. Is that stupid?

Not if you have a reason for it. If you do it just to do it, then yeah, it's probably a little gimmicky.

It's kind of what your dad does, I said. No?

Uh...

You know, I said, digging myself deeper, 'and then the book that the guy was writing this whole time is the book you're reading right now!' That kind of thing. 'Oh, wow!' I flicked my fingers out from the side of my head while widening my eyes, suggesting, quite meanly, that my mind had not, in actuality, been blown as intended.

Okay, Sophie said, I don't think you're trying to be offensive right now but you're really reminding me of this loser on that forum where we met who was a complete jerk to me about him. So cool it, please. God, I'm sick of people trying to involve me in his shit. This is why I don't live in Brooklyn! I prefer my mom's stuff to be honest but guess what? No one ever says anything to me about *her*.

You're right, you're right. I don't know why I said that. I'm sorry. I'm jealous, that's all. No one gets to be 'Paul Auster' any more. Or even, you know, um, your mum. Everything has become so fragmented, and you know they've changed the Booker Prize, right? You don't even have to have a connection to the U.K. or Commonwealth now. Chalk up another win for globalisation! Woo-hoo.

Are you a writer? she asked. I didn't realise.

Yes, I said. Well, no, but I would like for it to be an option. Fuck, Sophie, I'm really sorry. I shouldn't have said that about your dad. I wish you lived in Scotland. You have to come visit us. I mean it. This part isn't going in the play, by the way. We'll just leave it out, I said, waving my hand.

No, she said, looking down. I think it should stay. I can tell that you're sweet but I do think you're a little strange, Miles.

Well, I think you're lovely, I replied.

And then – I'm not sure why – I began to weep, there at the table.

This trip hasn't been what I expected, I said. I don't know what I expected but this isn't it. I'm sorry. I'm so sorry.

The bartender – witnessing this, I assume – came around to inquire after us.

Can we just get some water? Sophie asked.

I can't believe you're still here, I said to her.

Hey, what do you mean? she asked. It seems like you're really going through something. And maybe trying to 'medicate' it wasn't the best idea, but that's okay too. We've all been there. Do you want me to call your wife?

You're so nice. When our play premieres, whoever portrays you is definitely getting an Obie, I said, sniffing.

An Obie, huh, Sophie said, smiling. They don't have their own theatre awards in Britain? You know, for British people?

You got me, I said. And I'm not xenophobic or anything but I don't see why we have to let Americans compete for our prizes. I guess I shouldn't care. I'm Scottish, anyway, and we're only allowed to win every couple generations or so.

This all does sound kinda nationalistic, if I'm perfectly honest. Oops, I forgot there's no such thing, she said, winking.

Scotland can afford to be less nationalistic once it runs its own nation, I replied.

I feel like you're not the typical jazz fan, Sophie replied. They're usually *less* neurotic than the musicians themselves.

Oh, I'm not really. Okay, I am, but it's more of a professional interest at this point. You know why I like it though? Or why it fascinates me, should I say? It's, like, antithetical to the way in which we govern our lives. The improvisation, I mean. We're all so rehearsed. Quite literally, if you're religious and you're hoping to reach some measure of 'divine grace', or whatever. But even if you're not, in the choices we make, our interactions. I must have played some version of this conversation in my head fifty times on the way to meet you here. I'm planning the things I'll say before I've even said them. Where is the spontaneity? Is it in literature? Is it fuck. Because if a character were to do something overtly spontaneous we'd all go, 'Oh, well, that's not very believable.'

I pulled out another pill and popped it into mouth.

Do you know what I mean? I asked, swallowing. It's like—

Miles…, I could hear Sophie cautioning. And then soon after I must have blacked out. When I came to sometime the next day, only bits and pieces of the rest of our evening together returned to me, and they were all hideous. Sophie in distress, me making a nuisance. Why did you do this to yourself? I would ask myself later. And why would you do this to her?

Had I really demanded to be checked into Bellevue hospital, specifically? After dragging us to the Hotel Chelsea? What significance did these places even hold for me? Why was it that I couldn't seem to stop seeking to enact my literary fantasies? Why did I seem drawn only towards that which had already been drawn for me? What was I trying to prove? Or disprove? Why wasn't being Sarah's husband good enough for me…

I found myself strapped to a gurney.

You must understand, I was nearly shouting to the young nurse wheeling me through a brightly lit corridor, I'm not deranged!

'Deranged' she repeated in an accent, *my* accent. What d'ya mean 'deranged'? Who talks like that?

Why, you're Scottish! I exclaimed.

Aye, a Musselburgh lass born and bred—

Then you have to help me, I interjected. You must know I won't be able to afford this. The American healthcare system is an abomi—

Och, away! she said, cutting me off. We know who yoo are.

What do you mean? I asked, now with some horror. Who... who am I?

She stopped pushing to turn and look menacingly into my face, obscuring the lights above like an angel of darkness. You're a research fellow of the Library of Congress on a grant in collaboration wi' the SRGSAH, of course.

You... You're mocking me, I said.

Look, Dr Beard—

I'm not a doctor! I said, this time actually shouting.

Fine, whatever! Jeez-o. Whit I mean is, yoo have insurance. We've been in touch wi' your university.

About my concussion, you mean?

Uh, no, not exactly. You're no concussed... Anyway, it's all sorted noo.

Do my supervisors know? I asked.

How should I know? If I was to guess, I would say that they'll be aware something has happened tae ye but even if they were tae learn that yoo'd been hospitalised they would never be able tae acknowledge it in front of ye or to put it inte writin' unless yoo mentioned it first, personal data protections being whit they are these days. The extent tae which that'll make a material difference in your studies I couldn'e say. Gossip is gossip, ken. Anyway, yo're safe. Tha's all that matters tae anyone.

Was I given electroshock therapy? I asked, rubbing my temples.

She stopped again to look at me.

Yoo bein' serious? she said. How lang do ye think yoo've been in here? No shock treatment this time, I'm afraid. We've just pumped your stomach, lad. Everything's okay noo.

And Sophie?

The lassie 't brought ye here? She stayed fir a couple hoours but I believe she's gone the noo. Affy bonnie wee thing, eh? Whit's she doing wi' the likes of yoo?

I snorted.

The nurse kept pushing me down the corridor. I couldn't move. The rows of fluorescent lighting I tracked with unfocused eyes, one after another after another after another after another. I wasn't going anywhere; I had already been everywhere.

Do'y'know yoo never gave an emergency contact tae the university? she asked. We didn't know who tae call. Do yoo have any family?

I myself am hell, I mumbled.

She didn't respond.

At the automatic door I was released, but not before I could confirm, after several attempts, the fake address that I had apparently given to them: *Revolutionary Road*.

XV

THERE'S LITTLE POINT in pretending as if that I wasn't in the midst of some sort of breakdown. For days I lived like a vagrant. Only when a New York official, after providing me with a shower, clean clothes, and a hot meal, offered to pay for a one-way bus fare out of the state did it occur to me that perhaps something wasn't right with me. But nor will I pretend as if the detour I subsequently took didn't follow its own disturbed logic, or that the Sun Valley's most famous resident, memorialised now with a bust of himself standing on a stone pillar atop an altar of rocks like a secular, rum-soaked Golgotha, didn't impel me towards what otherwise could be mistaken (by me, anyway) for a random dot on a section of a map which I had to admit to myself I couldn't fully appreciate, with only vague understandings of the American geography and its civic structures. But this doesn't mean I'm a delusional person, generally. I'm not. But the dramatic landscape that I recognised I would encounter there was the salutary environment I felt impelled towards by the now-wild, hill-drawn eye of my Scottish forbears which had become simply repulsed by the stagnated vistas at the end of each treelined street in Georgetown; no matter how pretty, no matter how clean. I couldn't bear the thought of returning to there. For as much as I admired its nonchalant but erudite vibe, its milquetoast, status-chasing inhabitants, the good restaurants, the safe bars, and, above all, the (surely misguided) feeling of a seat at the table of world power, or at least as close witness to it, that it prompted within me, a part of me hated myself for admiring it, because I knew how quickly I could submerse myself in its milieu, and how totally I would then fall from my purported values of unassuming disobedience that resisted every pathetic entreaty to the noblesse that seemed to so often surround me there. Call it manifest destiny, call it something without all the imperialist overtones; the young man was going West, like his crofter brethren had before him. And, as with much of the preceding, I can only say that I'm fortunate that the true nature of these events is being disclosed by me, now, at a time in which I am able to take command of my own story. Because if they'd dug it up it would have been blown completely out of proportion. It would have been all wrong.

So many of the scenes that I saw on those first few legs of the bus journey to Ketchum, Idaho frustrated rather than reified any of my understandings of the American way of life and its relationship to the land. The tiny towns we stopped in, the great grain elevators in the distance, it was all deserted, or, worse, besieged by implausibly innumerable cuisines of fast food, depressed cheque cashing and wire transfer shops, or massive, simply outrageous superstores. Was this a country that was out of ideas? All I could see was a bloated parallelism of monotonous sublimity not capable of conveying anything with so much as a semblance of real meaning: there was neither stoicism nor passion, not leisure, not bustle – certainly not community – and not even the suggestion of an honest day's pay for an honest day's work. It was as if someone looking down on us from a godlike isometric perspective had created a simulation of the mid-century institutions and ideals that everyone had in their own way cherished (even if not everyone could partake) and which had once enjoyed a proper context and, slowly at first but then more quickly, stripped that context away, replacing it only with a greater tolerance for absurdity in the populace and a reduced sense of their collective awareness of how far from those ideals that they had fallen, turning some dials higher while others lower. I was vaguely disgusted by the scenes from those highways, and, for the people that traversed them, felt only an intolerable pity. Every now and then a glade of wildflowers blooming spasmodically on some verdant, unattended verge, or bursting, even, between the lanes of traffic, would catch me by surprise and draw me deep into their overridden weeds and ivies. But, a moment later, they were gone again, only to be replaced in my vision by yet another cop car with nothing better to do than to harass and harangue its own citizenry.

I didn't get it. Who wants to live like this? Speaking to the other passengers, I realised that the answer was basically nobody. When word passed around that I was from abroad and had a funny – and, to some, indecipherable – way of talking, it seemed they were keen to get my impression of the States and would prod me with questions and hypotheticals. Whenever I ventured that some aspects painted a somewhat bleak picture to me they would roar with laughter and tell me it was terrible, worse than I realised. As I grew more comfortable in their obvious warmth to me (I was truly touched) I started to tell them about the standard of living we were able to expect in Scotland and how, truth be told, quite a lot about America seemed barbaric to us, from the neo-monarchal power of their presidency on down.[7] This [expletive] gets it, an older man said to his young companion, slapping him on the back all the while as I extolled the sense of competitiveness I saw at the centre of their society, forcing everyone to scrabble amongst the wreckage left by those at the top, almost invariably having been born at least within touching distance of their lofty positions. These points of view weren't original, and I wasn't saying anything they didn't already know much more viscerally than myself. But they all seemed hungry to have their perspectives validated, to have an external party verify, if not actually mediate, their daily struggle.

Or so I thought. After making myself a bit of a celebrity at the back of that bus, buoyed by my audience's graciousness into taking more and more extreme positions (I think at some point I said that whenever we saw a clip of them doing their pledge of allegiance it made us snicker) I realised not everyone had been totally on board, and that a few within earshot further up had started to grumble, calling me arrogant, a know-nothing, and, though not in these words, essentially insensitive to the only lifestyle they knew.

Eventually, someone approached to put me back in my place.

Hey chickenshit, he said, do you know where I just came from? A hospice facility to visit my father. You wanna know how I pay for that?

---

7 It's worth reiterating that this was just before the Brexit vote. I wouldn't be nearly so pious about the structures of our government now, though I do think parliamentary systems in general must be superior to whatever the fuck has been happening in America. Can you imagine identifying as a Republican? Or as a Democrat for that matter?? Pathetic. Although there are similar allegiances in England, I suppose. Anyway, quite weird.

He held his finger out to count on.

Work all day doing maintenance for a college that doesn't recognise our union,

Next finger.

Deliver food at night to the same people who try to convince us that our lives are better for it,

Next finger.

Refinance my house,

Next finger.

Sell blood, he said, elongating the words, holding stare with me all the while,

The final finger.

and the bank's trying to take that house away now because even after that I'm struggling with the payments. You think this is theoretical for us? Why don't you and me turn this bus around and we'll go tell Dad (who was drafted to Vietnam when he was eighteen years old, by the way) that the government doesn't care about his needs. I'm sure it'll come as a big shock to him and he'll feel a lot better once he's heard you say it. What do you think?

We're on the same side, I said, feebly.

Are you a student? he asked.

I nodded.

You going to join me on the picket line? Watch my kids when I'm out driving all night? Speak to my father on the telephone? None of that would cost you anything.

I looked away.

Huh? he prodded. Well?

I gave a few false starts and then trailed off, unsure of what I was about to say, unsure if he was looking for literal answers or just a figurative one. I shrugged.

Then we're not on the same side, he said. And he returned to his seat.

I was left chastened, didn't dare to speak again. He'd proved that I too was an individualist, and, worse, one who affected not to realise it.

I hadn't asked to be born in Scotland any more than he in America. I might have voted for the right things, on occasion, but what had I done to effect any real change, even in the most minor way? In fact, I was sat there in receipt of grants from both of our respective governments. The most radical thing I'd ever done was to squander both, courses of action I knew to have no true political motive. I could consume as much of the alternatingly biting and righteous content online as could fill a day, forming reasoned, passionate opinions beyond impeachment or correction in the process. All they would ever lead me to was a comment someone had fatuously left beneath one of my erotic narratives, a comment that has stayed with me since, an unpunctuated *non sequitur* that simply asked, without reference to any of the panting orgasms I had detailed above, wheres the praxis. Presently, I had just been asked this same question, only now I was actually expected to answer. But I'd ignored it all the same. That I was capable of boxing myself into such a rhetorical corner seemed only to bolster the implication that I had some duty to make good on what I said I knew to be right. Instead, I surrounded myself in ever greater layers of ambivalence and turpitude, as though I thought holding an idea in your mind had an equal, if not greater, value to acting on it.

There were no fewer than seventy hours left until I reached my destination, such that it was one, and more than five until

I would need to transfer. It remained very quiet on the bus for much of this time, and I fell again to thinking of Sarah: my heart, my conscience.

Towards the end of our module on American Fiction 1945-1995 that we'd inadvertently, to mutual humiliation, both signed up for – though Sarah did give me a hand job under the table one day (not to completion) – our seminar leader asked us to look across the various novels we'd read to identify their common themes. Not the various themes that we'd discussed explicitly throughout the term but any that we could see now in retrospect at the end of our reading. She said that it would be useful as we prepared our final papers but could also form the basis of a dissertation for those of us doing honours degrees who were intending to write on the period.

We were given a few minutes to look through our notepads, to cast our minds back through the syllabus. I started to jot down a few talking points about cultural values, something about how the implementation of the G.I. Bill had rebuilt their societal aspirations around collegiate life. This wasn't a wholly original idea: I'd skimmed an article a senior lecturer in the department had written on the recent deprecation of novels as a medium which had seemed to argue that its pride of place during this period was more of a blip than a natural state from which we'd somehow fallen. Connecting this now to the G.I. Bill and its expansion of access to higher education was an extrapolation I was making because I remembered it as a key term from our reading, and because it'd seemed to me that 'English majors' were a kind of totem for middle-class, middlebrow intellectualism throughout this time. Decades later, on the other side of the sea, when I told people I taught English they appeared quizzical, asking, You mean as a foreign language?

It was our final year, and everyone was only halfway present. No one would want to be the first to speak in any class, as if we'd regressed to being first years again, only it wasn't due to shyness now but weariness. Leaving the cocoon of education in the middle of a recession was hardly what we'd been promised, and we were all jumpy at the thought of graduating, to say the least of it. Several of my friends had suggested they might join the army as officers.

So I took one for the team, I felt, and began to read aloud from my notes, expounding as I went in a rather circular fashion, since no one was bothering to cut me off. When I had finally run out of steam the seminar leader looked as though she was thinking carefully about what I'd said and then asked, Can you give us an example? Of what would fall under what it sounds like you're terming as 'collegiate values'?

I thought for a moment. Uh, well, everyone's shagging, like, I said, partly as a joke and partly because I didn't have a real answer.

The class chuckled. Without much mirth, I must admit.

The seminar leader – who I can now recognise as probably a PhD student, perhaps not many years older than ourselves – did well to take what I'd said on face value. It'd had a kind of blurted truth to it after all.

Okay, she replied. Though I think for many students you're really talking about media portrayals of university life rather than their lived experience of it, let's just accept that premise for now. What do you see as actually tying the texts together?

What do they say about society then that we don't also say about ourselves now?

I tried to explain how it seemed like the extramarital affairs so commonly portrayed in these narratives had mostly evaporated from our lives, rarely were they even plot devices any more, except in the most derivative crime fiction. The internet's ubiquitous presence in our lives might have increased the opportunity to conduct such affairs at a distance, but it contained alongside it the increased possibility of being caught as well. There was no one I knew who was sneaking around behind their partner's back or indeed at their side as so many writers before me had seemed to do. Maybe they were still swapping photos with ex-partners, maybe they would check out their options on dating sites every now and again, but no one was properly involved with multiple people at once when they were supposed to be exclusive. Not anyone that I aware of, anyway.

It was common knowledge that Sarah and I were properly together now. And as I'd been speaking, many of our classmates had looked to check her expression, to gauge how acceptable it was for me to even reference the possibility of infidelity in front of her. But anyone who thought it might turn into a spat would be sorely disappointed. She took it all much less literally than they – or, for that matter, I – did, and, as a result, she could see the fuller picture, the palimpsestic relationship between art and life in which nothing was ever just one thing or another, in which nothing ever appeared, disappeared, or reappeared, but was only emphasised to a greater or lesser extent at any particular moment in time, a continuum *ad infinitum*, sketched onto a canvas of unyielding proportions.

Whether more affairs are actually happening compared to now is totally immaterial, I remember her saying. Their treatment in these novels is an obvious literary response not only to the cultural values of the period but the cultural upheavals as well, all of which challenged the notion and conflation of individual and national innocence. The Atomic Bomb, Watergate, the AIDS crisis – infidelity, as an idea, is uniquely able to negotiate the boundaries of what's private and what's public. Our responsibilities to the self and our responsibilities to each other. These are issues that neoliberalism eventually settles, at least until the next upheaval, but were still in high contention then. It surprises me that Miles doesn't seem to recognise that.

I knew she was right but wouldn't allow myself to be so easily outwitted without a fight. But it has to be economic, too, I countered.

Can you expand on that? the seminar leader asked. Because it wouldn't necessarily refute Sarah's point but you might be adding some valuable context here. In what way is it economic?

I'd sighed, feeling like my answer was more of an instinctual response than a deduced and vindicable one as Sarah's was. I groped for an explanation of why my mind had strayed in such a direction to begin with. Was it the mention of neoliberalism? Then I had something.

Single income households, I voiced triumphantly. Every book we've read this term has had a single income household. By the time you get to 9/11 – probably the next big event such as Sarah's describing – the system has been reshaped to such an extent that they're much less common. It's cultural, too, of course, but in either case a trajectory is set into motion that by the time you reach to today, sneaking around with your neighbours – if you even know them – really can't be done unless one of you is a very high earner.

Or if you don't have children, Sarah interjected. Can I change the subject? (This had seemed generous of her, but her own theory would go on to put mine to shame.)

Go ahead, the seminar leader replied.

Sarah went on to talk about the parallax of narrative, how the introduction of distance between what the reader is told has happened and what the characters seem to experience as having happened had undermined not just our ability to tell stories with any objective understanding of what we wanted them to be about, but to tell stories even about ourselves in good faith. It has always been the case, of course, that narrative is a multifaceted thing. But the postmodern turn had submerged us beneath ever greater depths of doubt, she said, and, like our expulsion from the Garden of Eden, it was irrevocable. We'd have to learn how to negotiate our lives in this new world now: there was no going back.

Unfortunately, I can no longer recall anything from the rest of that day.

As I trudged off the bus to wait in a downtrodden terminal for the next one, it was difficult convince myself that the merits of the mission to which I'd assigned myself, whatever they were, held any scope for personal or even professional improvement, and I was becoming acutely aware of the ever-greater distance I was putting between Sarah and me. Emotional, even more so than physical, as each action I seemed to take was in its own way unspeakable to her. What did I even know about Hemingway? 'For sale: baby shoes'?

Is that why I'd felt the need to visit the site of his self-inflicted death? Because of fucking 'For sale: baby shoes'? Was it to witness how misery begets misery, and to provide for myself a much-needed warning of misery's most logical conclusion? Or was it to confront the deleterious effects that books would continue to have on my relationships for as long as I remained committed to fetishising their provenance?

I didn't know how to take myself. At that moment, I didn't know how to get home.

Out of the window, America was unfurling itself before me. I gazed at it impassively. To see the mountains, it seemed I was to first endure the flattest landscape I'd ever seen. I thought of Sarah again; her mum, actually. What was it that she'd said? That our miscarriages were a blessing from God? That the fruits of our union had passed the ultimate test before it'd even started, that He'd loved them so much He wanted them back straight away?

It struck me then, not for the first time, that perhaps heaven is a prison.

XVI

NIGHTS OF THE DOOMED MOTEL.

That's what I told myself this section of my life would be titled were I to ever transpose it into literature. I could picture its place amongst the tradition of analeptic road trips as I made my own voyage through the bright days and chilly nights of a country that would, in an alternating fashion, entrance and bewilder me. A poetic cycle, perhaps, or a series of experiments in very short prose that would suspend the boundaries of the critical and creative. Something on the end of Americana, the refusal of isolation we each, inevitably, must eventually make, and a paean to those uncompromising literary stalwarts like Jim Harrison who would seem to genuinely write as if it was a compulsive habit, or a sweeping act of humanitarianism he was bestowing upon a voracious public. Of course, I never even started the damnable thing.

I knew the kinds of stories my readers were interested in, if that isn't too grandiose of a phrase for them, 'my readers'. In the beginning, there was only truth: a painful, exquisite kind of truth; bleeding, with fatty slivers of the gristle and pus showing. I'd return from a night out and the first thing I did – if I hadn't already saved all the relevant details onto my phone in the taxi home – was fire up my laptop and begin to narrativise the whole ordeal for myself, and then, with some edits, for them, my online audience. I'd start with her – always.

No one wanted to know my height, my hair, what I had been wearing. Not really. If these attributes became relevant, they might get a mention here or there (I remember, as an example, that once it was necessary to explain what would provoke the woman I'd met, after we had both been kicked out of one of the university bars, to moan, You're so much bigger than my boyfriend, to me, over and over, on a park bench near the flat where they stayed) but otherwise I would remain merely a shadow for the experiences I would describe; an everyman that every man might reasonably inhabit.[8]

As the years went on, and my sex life with Sarah became routine (and in many ways more rewarding for that), I started to exercise my imagination a touch, lifting certain acts or scenarios from the realm of fantasy, and lacing them within our real encounters. I also tried my hand at being more descriptive, writing flowery impressions of our bodies, of our noises, and of our exclamations.

But I learnt quickly that their need for the immersive experience was so great that they refused to tolerate anything which resembled the fictive, no matter how slight. It's the details that are important, but – and this is crucial – not too many of them, or else an otherwise generic story could be interpreted

---

8 That being said, there's this entire other side to the endeavour that might not cross your mind unless you were to participate on these kinds of forums yourself, which is that being a man writing about sex with a woman seems to invite a lot of messages from other women. I'm sure it cannot possibly compare with the deluge that women who post their own stories receive, but I think it's worth mentioning that there's a cyclical gratification schema which accompanies the public, digital diary. It's not so surprising: my stories give the impression that I've already been vouched for; that I'm a safe, satisfying fuck. Often, they want to chat or trade photos.

as a bespoke experience designed to deceive, rather than a truthful account that happens to have been rendered with precision and the occasional flourish. Beneath my posts from this period was but one damning leitmotif, 'fake'. I noticed that even aspects which had really occurred between us could be called into question, either due to the manner in which I had included them, or because they had, in the aggregate, seemed too incredible to be considered an accurate depiction of our encounters. Perhaps that time that we had, essentially, conspired to seduce this shy lass on our course whom we'd both admitted to fancying was redeemable as a concept in and of itself, but the entirely factual moment in which she'd told us, mid-ecstasy, that she couldn't believe it was really happening when she was 'just that girl from English class', was, taken together with my boastful, lascivious descriptions – despite their equally formal veracity – simply too much, taken for a kind of gestalt theatre, where character was, above all, transcending any psychological realism, my lusty imagination serving only to break down the desired patterns of ordinariness found elsewhere on the forums. Like cheap performance, a kind of clickbait. But I never intended for it to be read so.[9]

I still couldn't tell the therapist about any of this. Not the real trajectory of my research trip or the true nature of my online profile. Instead, at my subliminal behest, we seemed

---

9 The truth is, even at such a distance, I still think of Sarah in this way, nearly every morning in the shower. Do you know what it's like to jerk off to a ghost? To observe your miserable selves struggle valiantly against the drain, seeking their only instinctual purpose? Have you ever felt your brain pull you deeper and deeper into the glacial crevasse of your own misbegotten sexual psyche, when all that you have ever wished is to escalate to an escape from it?

only to turn over the same feelings of panicked desperation again and again, usually prompted by my recurring dreams of Sarah shutting down or my occasional admissions to certain, it must be admitted, obsessively circular patterns of thinking. I could tell that this frustrated her at times. Despite the new appearance of forthrightness I gave since we had reached common ground on exactly how I fitted into the Scottish media landscape – to some a criminal, to others an activist – I think she could sense that my resolution to keep us at a restrained superficiality remained rather undiminished.

One particular stalemate of ours was noteworthy. She said that sometimes after the death of someone close – especially if that death happened to occur during a period of acrimony – there can remain, with the survivors, amongst the pain and devastation, a confused set of feelings. Feelings like satisfaction, relief, and anticipation for what in life still lies ahead for them.

Naturally, what follows from this, she said, is an immense sense of guilt. Guilt, as well as dread.

Dread? I asked.

Dread that you'll be found out. That your hidden acceptance – like a secret wish that's finally coming true – is plain for all to see. That it's repulsive to them. That *you* are repulsive to them.

I didn't respond for a moment, unsure if this was fair way to describe me. If, indeed, it was meant to describe me.

The little room in which we were situated felt very small then, very insignificant. The natural light of day was fading away in the threat of an oncoming storm, and there was the sound of traffic piling up on the thoroughfare abutting her normally quiet residential avenue. I looked to the clock. Only ten minutes had passed since we'd sat down.

Miles, she said, it's okay. Everything is over now.

I pursed my lips. What is it you're trying to get me to say, exactly? I asked.

Say whatever you need to, she said. You can let go here. This is your space.

I think for some reason she thought I would begin to cry there, but I just couldn't be moved in her presence. Alone, I was, for the most part, content with doing nearly anything I wanted, or at least anything which I could admit to myself that I wanted. I could stay in bed all day, my room like a jail cell, rising only to use the toilet as my stomach demanded the food that I would unthinkingly neglect to provide it. I could doom-scroll through old messages with Sarah for hours on end. I could even toy with downloading a dating app. But, in the company of someone who actually knew of Sarah, even this much time after the fact, I instead felt compelled to default to a morassy, stagnant stoicism that was as inscrutable to me as it would seem to others, given that I could actually feel myself withholding the spontaneous comments or emotions that would have been considerably more palatable than my suspect demeanour that was so readily viewed as too calm, too collected.

But it was never my intention to frustrate her efforts, and I didn't want to keep coming all the way here only to not give any of what I was expected to. So I tried opening up.

The cruellest month.

It was my birthday and something rather sad happened. Sarah had planned the day for us and in the morning gave to me these headphones, really fancy ones. Like really, really fancy, and I was overwhelmed by her thoughtfulness, by her generosity. I didn't know what to say. In fact, I started to well up as soon as I saw the logo peeking out at me from behind the torn paper; she had remembered a conversation from months prior in which I'd extolled the virtues of this particular brand for its wide frequency range. In fact, I'd confidently stated that they'd be my first purchase once I landed a real job. (What job this might be was mercifully allowed to remain undefined.)

She was so sweet as she looked to me and asked if they were the right ones (she knew that they were) and if it was okay that she had got them for me even though I'd said I wanted to buy them for myself (she knew that it was). I couldn't wait to put them on and she sat there at the breakfast table watching me as I connected them to our amplifier and then switch on a favourite song of ours: one of those deceptively poignant soul songs, melodic and doleful, the trio's plainspoken expression of romantic love masking a tale of heartache and disbelief that is, at bottom, really about the experience of rejection and humiliation.

I listened very intently to this track while Sarah smiled at me. The drum break had a rich quality to it and, as the vaguely menacing strings and punchy electric bass kicked in, I started to laugh, because the tapestry of sound they created in my ears was so pleasurable. When the vocals – plaintive and yearning – were added to this, I felt slightly overwhelmed, as I always would playing in the band we'd had at university whenever the little riffs I'd bring in suddenly started to become actual songs, a giddiness coming on me that bordered on hysteria, that unreal sense of what it means to be a human in the act of spontaneous, collaborative creation, so primal and possessing. The funny thing was that after a couple of gigs a local label got in touch to ask if we'd be interested in doing an album for them and then we all seemed to lose interest. It was the natural next step (wouldn't we like to have something to sell? they'd asked) and yet, being partially improvisational, the knowledge that we'd have to determine static versions for all our songs was too intimidating to us. Plus, the truth of it was that none of us had very strong musicianship. I know I would have struggled in a studio setting given I mostly assumed my guitar was in tune rather than ever holding an expert opinion on the matter.

I kissed Sarah while the enchanting sounds of a doo-wop harmony continued to flood round my ears.

Are you planning on leaving me, baby?

Did you find another while I was away?

You're acting strange and it's been a real long day!

Later, when she was in the shower, I put on some other tunes I liked, ones I'd not heard before in any genuine high fidelity. What I began to notice was that, going from the crap pair I'd had for years to these new ones, on many there was this whole other layer of filled atmosphere coming through that I'd never been able to detect before. This could make for a rewarding listen for most pop but on some of the junkier music I liked – irregular genres that defined themselves by their enthusiasm for dissonance, harmonic distortion, or intentionally muddy recording environments – I felt like I was looking into something I was never supposed to see, like I was a grubby voyeur whose own barrenness is laid bare to himself by his witness to tender acts he knows he has no hope to ever achieve for himself. And when I turned on one our band's rehearsals, I nearly threw them off. There we were clamping onto our effect boards, adjusting their dials mid-performance. There was me laughing to myself when I struck a bum note. Most pertinently, I could hear exactly how the song came together. My riff, though catchy, is incessant, my vocals barely rising above the rhythm guitarist who's busy saturating the background with errant but dimly on-key noise; the bass player is basically walking the line; and the drummer does the fast beat for the fast parts and then the slow one for the slow parts. Intellectually, I knew that this was how we wrote our songs. How, in fact, nearly every song in the modern Western canon is written. And yet, and yet. Where was the magic? I wanted to go back to when I could listen in wonder: to my own hamstrung efforts; to my friends who'd pass their handmade tapes around; to my teen idols with their cool photoshoots and doomed, laconic minor-celebrity statuses – how did we all do it? Was it really so simple? I had always been especially fond of repetitious music, the kind that dared to stretch on for seven minutes or more with a click track, subtly changing electronic melodies, lyrics that, drawn out, were mysterious and affecting but written on a page would seem vacuous and juvenile. How difficult would it be, really, to do all this myself? I thought of the software that was sitting there on my phone, cloyingly suggesting that I too could become someone's teen idol. I wasn't even sure if I had downloaded it especially or if it had just come pre-installed. Again, was it really so simple?

Sarah came in to tell me it was my turn to shower.

What's wrong? she asked.

Nothing, I said.

Are you okay? she asked.

Yes, I said.

Are you sure? she asked. You're not angry I got those for you, are you?

No, I said. Of course not.

When you have the money, you can still buy that daft cassette deck you were coveting in the shop.

I love you, I replied, giving her a kiss, trying to stem the pit now plunging through my stomach.

In the shower, all I felt was a deep remorse. Sarah had expended a lot of money, a lot of thought, on getting me the perfect present, and here I was regretting ever mentioning it, regretting assuming that what I'd wanted was the latest thing, 'the best'.

When I was dressed, we left to go for lunch at a pub we both liked but didn't visit often because we preferred to save it for special occasions.

Into the second beer – I had been thinking about this too much – I decided to at least broach the topic.

The headphones, I started. I wonder if they're actually *too* good.

What do you mean? Like, you stepped up in the world too quickly? she said, laughing.

I smiled appreciatively to show I was a good sport and then said, Well, no, I mean, I'm just hearing some things with them I'd never really noticed before. In the music, like.

Do you wish you'd had them earlier? That could have been good for your module on minimalism. Think of how many C notes you might have missed in *In C*!

So many, I deadpanned.

Man, was I glad when you'd finished with that. That music made me – as my parents would say – feel like I should check myself into the State Hospital. But now you have decent headphones! Yas!

She reached over and tickled me to convey her excitement for me to have something I had wanted for so long.

The thing is, I said after she'd stopped, I was listening to some stuff earlier and some of it I felt wasn't really meant to be heard in that way, if that makes sense. As in it wasn't recorded in a way that could have anticipated all the capabilities we'd have now.

If you're trying to tell me that, next, you're going to want alternate wee devices for whatever you decide you want to listen to that day, that's fine, but *you're* paying for the storage unit. Also, I'm probably moving out.

She grinned and raised her eyebrows.

I tried again. It's not that, I said. The thing is, I'm so grateful to you. For remembering, for going out of your way to find them, spending that much money, all of that. But I feel bad, too. I only want you to have got them for me if I know I'm going to appreciate them as much as they should be. And, earlier, something about the listening experience while I was wearing them just felt off to me. It was kind of uncanny.

Wait, she said. Are you actually being serious right now?

What do you mean? I asked.

Oh my god. This is just like the TV.

TV? What are you talking about? I don't remember anything to do with the TV.

Uncanny. That's how you described it when you made me turn down the rate of streaming because you didn't like how it looked in HD. You said it looked 'too real'.

That's different, I said.

Is it? she asked. It sounds very similar to me.

Okay, it was actually *you* who first pointed out how the fixtures on film sets and the clothes of most wardrobes are always way too pristine to ever be realistic. Ultra HD exacerbates those kinds of thing. I like that old sheen of fuzz our screens used to have, so what? Sometimes, I think the TV looks more real to me than real life, and I find that disconcerting.

But you don't have to fixate on those things! You can just ignore them!

Well, sorry, I said. It's not that easy for me, okay?

You're impossible, she replied. I can't do anything right because no one in your eyes can ever do anything right. You just want things to stay the same, forever. For most people that would become a nightmare. For you, I think you'd truly appreciate it.

I sulked, looking down into my drink. Why did she have to be right about this as well?

Hey, she said, I'm sorry. They're yours, you can do whatever you like with them. If you want to return them, it's no big deal. I'll get you something else.

No, I replied, I do like them. I love them. Really. I just need to get used to them. I wanted to tell you how they made me feel. I don't know why. I should've kept my mouth shut.

It's okay, she said. You know you can tell me anything. Doesn't mean I won't have something to say back, though!

We laughed, and she went to buy us another round.

In the end, I kept the headphones but rarely used them: the worst of both worlds.

Miles, the therapist said when I'd finished, can I ask why you've chosen to tell me this story?

I don't know. I thought that's what you wanted me to do? I intoned as if I was asking a question.

I'm not being critical, she replied. Merely curious. You could have said anything. You could have said nothing. Why this? Why tell this story to me now?

I just felt like I needed to say something and that's what came out, I replied.

Had it been on your mind recently?

No. Well, yes, I guess so. I always think back to times when we fought and then made up. I don't know why.

You weren't on good terms with her. When she died, I mean. Isn't that right?

We hadn't spoken in a while by that point, I said.

Was that the longest you'd ever gone? Without speaking?

Pretty much. There were a couple weeks while I was abroad that we couldn't talk very often, but she understood it was a busy time for me.

Right, she said, writing something down. I remember now.

And at the end we hadn't split up or anything, I said very definitively.

You've told me that, she said, looking into my eyes now. I do believe you.

Okay, I replied. It's just there's some people who say we had, and that's just not true. We wanted to figure things out.

I understand. And these dreams you've been having: Sarah always goes away in them but she never comes back again, is that right?

Yes, I said, choking on the word slightly.

And the valetudinary episodes you've been having, they're also about not letting go, aren't they? Not succumbing to movement of life in which one might take ill and then get better again. Or not, as the case sometimes is.

I guess, I said.

After you left last week, I was thinking about what the role in our society is of the person with health anxiety. Boswell, our first national critic, used 'The Hypochondriak' as a pseudonym. And Kant calls the hypochondriac a 'crank-brackets-visionary'. Aren't you a kind of critic, in truest sense of the word? Don't you try to hold onto things because you're able to see what's on the other side? This new technology you're talking about, where does it lead us? You're questioning something most of us would take for granted as inevitable. That won't always make you friends, but it's equipped you for what you want out of life. You teach at a university, you contribute to the existing knowledge of how we read literature.

This is all flattery, I said. Don't get me wrong, I appreciate it. But I don't deserve it. And you missed a bit of the Kant line. Kant says the hypochondriac is a crank-brackets-visionary 'of the most pitiful sort'.

'He stubbornly refuses to be talked out of his imaginings…' she finished.

That's right, I said.

It was time again. In this instance I stood first and gestured us towards the door.

Have you been working on your journal? she asked.

I'm trying to, I replied, emphasising that clumsy word, *trying*.

Good, she replied, accepting the tawdry banknotes from my outstretched hand.

At home, dark now, the roads choked with cars splashing through the flooding rain, I turned her phrase – Kant's phrase, actually – over again in my mind. Why had she said it? *He stubbornly refuses to be talked out of his imaginings…* Was she wanting to prove that she knew more of the quotation than I did? Or was she trying – there's that word again, listen to the way it curdles in the back of your throat – to tell me something?

XVII

TINSELTOWN IN THE RAIN – that could have been cinematic. Alas, it was a muggy, sweltering yet overcast day, pollution just on the edge of choking me as I walked across the La Cienega Boulevard where a pickup truck had dropped me, the driver carrying on somewhere further out; into Irvine, I think he said. The threat of wildfires played dramatically on the talk radio I could hear through his open window as we cruised through West Hollywood, past the vaunted Chateau Marmont suites.

The stop in Ketchum had been a mistake, obviously. It was weird and discursive, not in keeping with any way in which I liked to think of myself: rational; dispassionate; in control. I never even liked Hemingway's books and couldn't stand to see myself as others would see, part of a long queue of pathetic pilgrimages to pay homage to the Master. There wasn't anything to see there anyway, not really. Some skiing infrastructure abandoned for the summer, a few sites of impressive natural beauty; his grave; and a couple of stupid cans of beer some had felt fit to leave on top of it. I was alone when I saw him there, wandering through the graveyard when I came upon him, his name and the dates of his birth and death apparently the only information considered worth imparting, taken for granted that everyone would know the rest of his story, forever. I stole one of his tributes and retreated to a patch of grass under a tree within in eyesight, to watch those who would visit under more genuine auspices than I was able. I needed a drink, and I'd wanted to distinguish myself from them, if only in my own mind.

The thing is, I've never been a 'troll'. It's not a term that's ever made much sense to me, and though many would-be commentators often sought to portray some of the legal manoeuvres made on my behalf as 'trollish' – questioning how many of the religious beliefs invoked were truly believed in springs to mind; challenging them to come up with a biblical alternative to the Glasgow Coma Scale – what they miss is that 1) I had very little control over the strategy to defend myself for doing what I had decided was right and 2) I have very little interest in drawing attention to myself, generally.[10]

The first time I ever came across the term was perhaps a decade or more ago on social media – don't look for me there now, I'm long gone – when I thought I could contribute to the burgeoning independence debate after the SNP had won their first ever majority in the restoration of the Scottish Parliament. I dropped into a politics group I often lurked in and wrote something to the effect of, It's well funny that the only attack you lads can come up with is that it'll turn our country into a 'disaster' – by what measure are determining that it isn't a disaster at the moment? You're just like all these weirdos who bang on about how uniquely awful communism would be without stopping to ask yourselves if maybe capitalism isn't exactly all it's cracked up to be either.

---

10 It still shocks me to see how many people continue to believe that the injunction Sarah's parents filed was against me personally. It was against the NHS. No matter whatever else you might think, she was still my wife and I loved her. It's only right that I was consulted.

I was pounced for this, for being somehow purposefully inflammatory, or at the very least unserious in the point I was making. (The invocation of Marx in particular seems to have this effect. To borrow some of his phrasing, such worn-out creatures become so consumed by their own worries that they have severe difficulty even countenancing the sorry fates they must endure each day, let alone evincing a critique of those fates.) I made my apologies and exited the exchange. What difference did it make? In their minds, and in their words as well, I was only trying to get a rise out of them, someone whose opinion could be discarded, a mere sower of division.

Ironically, I had actually attempted a spate of agitprop at one time, and, to my own disbelief, was rumbled quite quickly. During the call-in morning programmes on the national radio channel I played the role of Gary from Greenock, someone who'd definitely seen some things and implied (without ever stating) that he was a Thatcher-era shipbuilder with some particularly strong opinions concerning the devious Conservative rule *vis-à-vis* the British government and their cruel austerity measures. Through texts, emails, and even one actual phone call in which I attempted a Billy Connolly-like accent – stifling my nervous giggles all the while in an emphysemic cough – I threw Gary onto his high horse, ignoring the presenter's attempts at 'balance' as Gary really went off on one, my inspiration being the often-unhinged right-wing invective by the seemingly quite elderly or just uninformed who I thought were given too easy a time, too ably allowed to disseminate their messages of arrant bitterness with impunity. Would someone equally radical from the left be permitted to make such assertions, to exhibit such flagrant refusal to find common ground that most of us feel compelled to at least be seen to attempt? It seemed not to be. Maybe they just suspected my underhandedness, my inhabiting of a character, but after only a few fevered attempts at inclusion, I was de-platformed. I felt bad for Gary, but I think he knew that's how things usually went for us. At least I stopped paying attention to drivel that probably never changed anyone's minds anyhow – they were all only talking to and for themselves. Yet I was trying to speak for someone who was too jaded to ever make the effort: the platonic ideal of Red Clydeside, an apparition.

After only a couple of days I knew I needed to leave Ketchum. It felt as though I was coming to my senses again there, like the change in altitude had awoken me from a *fin de siècle* fugue state, alert and alarmed. I was so far from anything I understood. I had crossed beyond a place I'd created from my imagination to somewhere that was now specific and defined, and I found myself at a loss as to how I'd get back, how I could ever explain it. I asked around town for a ride to the next city over and was directed to saloon that many, I was told, stopped at when they were passing through.

After I'd ordered a drink, dropping one of the last of my five-dollar bills quickly onto the bar (I was a sworn ally to all waitstaff now) I asked if she knew anyone who was trying to get out of Ketchum in a hurry.

You in trouble or something? she asked.

No, I said. Well, kind of, maybe. It'll only be with my wife, though.

She laughed.

Ah, so you're one of those.

I can't say that I'm entirely sure what you mean by that, I replied. But probably, yes, I am one of those, I said and lifted my drink towards her.

She wasn't my normal type at all, or, a more precise way of putting it might be to say that she was exactly the type I'd always denied myself, knowing deep in my fibre that I wasn't nearly adventurous enough to hang out with someone with so many tattoos, piercings, and, I presumed, hidden chambers of leather outfits, swings, and extraneous appendages. Our life in Scotland was fairly quiet, my greatest vice a thesis-driven dependency on coffee that would've made Balzac blush. I was a Janissary of the educated class, someone who could as easily go criminal as straight so long as they felt unremarkable in their surroundings. Distant destinations like the New Hebrides called to me; Guyana. All I needed was a context. All I ever wanted was to be transported through the volition of another into an environment I could one day learn to live in. I had the wanderlust of the missionary with none of the belief; the drive of the explorer without any of the cartography.

Whatcha reading there? she asked, disappointingly placing the substantial bill into a pitcher alongside countless others without appearing to have looked at it.

Couples, I answered. John Updike. I just picked it up from the charity shop over there.

Charity shop... Oh, do you mean the thrift store? she said. The only charity that place performs is for the people who go there. It's just good stuff cheap, isn't it? The couple who run it are real friendly though. I think they're hanging on for the sake of it.

I thought about this. It was an interesting way to put it. The book had been very cheap, 75¢. At home, the largest international charity bookshop would have sold it for at least £3.99. Not much regard there for providing the widest access to reading material possible. And let's not even get into the relative good that these charities purportedly provide. (One of them gives out supermarket loyalty points for donations, for God's sake.)

I like Updike, she said.

This startled me, for two reasons: I wasn't expecting her to keep talking to me; and Updike seemed especially incongruent to her alternative style of dress. But I shouldn't paint people in such broad strokes. She was cool. I was naturally drawn to anyone with a curious nature, and I could sense some of that in her. Slamming body, too.

I prefer his poetry, I said. (Not because this was a statement I could in any way justify, having read so little of his corpus, but because I thought it would make me sound interesting and knowledgeable. And I appreciated that his commitment to the everyday was so strong that even in the most metaphysical realm of writing he still confined himself to topics like doorknobs and breakfast cereal; truly, a phenomenologist of the suburbs.)

His novels *are* poetry, she gamely replied.

He's a tease, I said. All this about his cock and he died before any of us could get a look at it. Can you imagine him sliding into your DMs?

Don't be such a prude, she replied, still dancing this dance with me.

I'm only joking, I said. *The Centaur* blew my mind when I was a kid. I didn't know you were allowed to write books like that.

A kid? she said. Why did you read that as kid?

What do you mean? I asked. Why does anyone read anything?

No, no. It's, um, just surprising, that's all. My fave back in the day was *Anne of Green Gables*. A classic, sure, but – hey, do you want another beer? – still within the bounds of appropriately moralistic children's literature.

I nodded, taking out my wallet, and said, I started out with whatever was around. My parents were part of that newly educated class who put a lot of stock in the value of reading as having some intrinsic good for the person. I mean, they never said this, probably never consciously thought it either. But from what I remember there was a time when the trip to the corner shop for the literary supplements on Sunday was the most important part of their week. They read airport paperbacks now.

That's cool, she said.

There was a lull.

Anyway, it was either this or Bradbury, I said.

She lit up. Oh, I *love* Bradbury.

I laughed and said, See, that makes more sense to me.

But I forgot she couldn't read my thoughts and couldn't have known what I meant by this. She turned away.

Because, I started, looking for an excuse/explanation, not knowing exactly where I was going with it, you know, Updike isn't very fashionable at the moment, is he.

Lol, she said, walking back towards me. That's either a compliment or an insult.

Definitely an insult, I deadpanned.

You're a real charmer, aren't you? she returned. Seriously though, they're not so different. Updike and Bradbury, I mean. Do you know about Mr Electrico?

Mister Who?

It's Bradbury's origin story.

Go on, I replied.

She told me the story, a yarn Bradbury had spun throughout the years about a childhood experience. On the way back from the funeral of a relative he was inexplicably drawn to a circus where he met a performer called Mr Electrico. Mr Electrico introduced him to the others, took him for a walk on the beach, and told Bradbury that he was the reincarnated soul of his friend who had died in the Battle of the Ardennes. At points she was running out of breath for overexcitement and pulled out her phone to make sure she was repeating all of the details that made his vignette so compelling correctly for me. When they parted, Mr Electrico left Bradbury with one dictum, one raison d'être: *Live forever*.

That's a good story, I said. Doesn't Bradbury also remember the moment he was born?

Yeah, you don't? she asked.

I laughed. No, I said, but I can remember the day I gained consciousness.

Shut up, she said. Really?

Yes, I replied. I was sitting on a little step in the back garden of my grandparents' house. We were having lunch. I was holding a little paper plate with roast lamb, mint sauce, and a Yorkshire pudding. (My granny was English.) A random thought was brought to the forefront of my mind as I sat there, a slightly scary one. I tried to vocalise it to the family around me but I couldn't get anyone to take notice. I thought, everything that's happened in my life up to now I've had no choice in. I couldn't recall, until that very moment, a single instance of taking any deliberate action, my memories as unreal to me as those from a storybook. I was dimly aware of all the events that had taken place, but only as if I had been a passive witness to them. Now I knew – and here's what I found scary – that from this point of time, until the end, until my death,

I was an active participant. From here on I would have to shape myself.

How old were you? she asked.

I said, About four, I think.

Whoa. That's nuts. Me, I feel like I just got older. One day I was this age, the next day I was that age, and so on. Everything that grew from that grew alongside me.

Mr Electrico, I said. Was he real?

That's the thing, she said, nobody knows. It's otherworldly, of course. Almost like it's an old movie. But not it's so otherworldly that it's impossible. Bradbury was very clever or very lucky. However you want to think of it.

You said you think he's similar to Updike. How?

Forget their generic differences, she said. That's meaningless. (Bradbury didn't like the term 'science fiction' anyway.) Every act of writing, of good writing, is an act of fantasy, you know? That ability to manifest it, to bring it into a place where it's a legible, tangible thing for others to take part in, that's rare. That's the difference between literature and all those beach reads, the kind of books you said your parents read now. Formulaic thrillers, murder mysteries, romance novels, those are the idle daydreams. 'What would happen if this happened', domino setpieces. Updike and Bradbury, they might have had quite different aims – who cares, I get it, death of the author and all that dumb shit – but their ability to fill in the space between the world as it is and the world as they imagine it to be, as they imagine it *could* be, well, what's the purpose of fiction, if not that? Everything else is imitative of that experience. That we're able to come together as a species and share these fantasies with each other, it's pretty incredible, don't you think?

And fantasy is a neutral concept. That's why it holds our fascination. It doesn't have to be good, it doesn't have to be acceptable. It just has to be real for us, as real as it can be.

Here I was going to say I thought Mr Electrico was just a particularly vivid metaphor for the artistic impulse. But what she was getting at felt right. What is a metaphor but a word for other words? Like my own name, they're all just words.

The bar area was presently filling up and we weren't able to speak again until closer to the end of the night. I ordered some food and sat there looking at my book. Not reading it. But looking at it. Turning it over and around, thumbing through its pages. *To Mary*.

Listen, she said. So I'm in a band. We're playing here later tonight and then heading to Boise, Portland, and San Francisco. Does that take you anywhere you want to go?

What do you want me to say? We fucked all the way to California. Sarah thought it was funny (It's just so typically Miles, I've heard she told her friends) that I'd try to get 'discovered' while I was out there, and I was ambiguous about the fact that they were a girl group mostly interested in my willingness to help them unload and stage their instruments, suggestively implying that I'd been brushing up on my guitar skills. Sarah knew the date on my return ticket would remain the same. Sarah didn't care what I did, her support for me too total to judge. In her slipstream, I was allowed to become myself, whoever that self might end up being. Whether this was an equitable arrangement is something that has continued to haunt me. Did Sarah get to become herself?

We were so young, so stupidly, maddeningly young.

XVIII

HELLO?

Hey, it's me. I'm calling from a payphone. Did I come up on your phone as spam? I got your voicemail a couple of times. I had to stop and look around for more change to try again.

Miles? Where are you? I haven't heard from you since the conference… I guess it didn't go too well, huh? I was sorry to hear that.

I'm in Los Angeles.

Is that right? Have you been having a good time?

It's fine, I said. I'm, I'm better now. I'm doing some research on Mingus's childhood. I wanted to tell you that I'll be coming back to D.C. soon. How are you?

I gotta say I'm a little pissed off, she said. I've been worried about you. You send me this crazy message saying you're in a shelter in New York, and then you ghost me. This whole time I've been like, is this guy serious? I keep thinking I'll see you at the library but another day goes by. Did you block my number?

Of course not! I wouldn't do that.

You know you're in a bunch of photos, right?

What kind of photos?

One of my friends, she's like a superfan of the band you've been doing whatever it is you're doing with them.

She showed them to me. It seems like you know the singer, maybe? It's fine, I don't mind about that as much as you thinking you can just randomly get in touch with me whenever you feel like it. But I'm trying to understand what the deal is. What happened? I thought you had a return ticket on the train.

It's been a crazy couple of weeks, and I am sorry about that message I sent you. That was a bad joke I was making, and I can see why it might've worried you. I should've explained. My phone broke a while back, and, yeah, so that band was giving me a ride out West. They're gone now. I never told you I needed to come out to Cali for my research?

No. Well, I don't remember you saying that. Are you okay? You sound kind of different. Like you're trying to do an American accent or something.

Very funny. I'm surrounded by you people and your lazy, indeterminate way of speaking is infectious.

So why did you say that you're calling, again?

I'm checking in, Christ. It's not your fault about the conference. I can tell you all about it when I'm back in D.C.

Why would anything that's happened to you since you left here be my fault?

It wouldn't. I mean, it isn't. I'm just saying, if you thought I was mad at you about something.

Uh, okay. Thanks. I think I'm the one who is angry though. Angry and confused.

I shouldn't have called, I guess. My bad.

'Your bad'. Awesome. Answer me this, why do you think that you're so special?

If you are actually asking, I was often told in school that I am.

Stop being a prick for one second and please listen to what I'm saying. Why do you get to go in and out of people's lives like they're nothing more than symbolically definable elements of your life's story? I'm not going to act like those couple of weeks that we spent at my place was, like, the most meaningful thing that's ever happened to me. It wasn't.

Ouch.

I said listen to me.

I am listening.

But we made plans together. You go away for what's only supposed to be a couple of days – no big deal – but you write me this batshit screed about how much you hate New York and you don't know how to get back. Weird, but okay. I respond, with sympathy and concern for you. And then I don't hear from you again. At all. I tried your phone multiple times. My friends are all telling me that they were right about you, that you were too perfect and just came out of nowhere, and how I'd dodged a bullet because you're probably a serial killer and everything. So, whatever, fine, I guess I've been dropped by this guy I liked. I'll get over it. Then, *now*, you call me out of the blue, acting like I'm just some secondary character you need to re-establish contact with to keep the plot of your own hero's journey going. Do you see how unfair that is? To me? Do you see how unfair that is to me? You're not saying anything. I'm legit asking you this question; it's not rhetorical. Do you see how that is unfair to me?

If you wanted to put it that way, then, yes, I can see how it would be unfair to you.

I *am* putting it that way.

Okay, yes, it is unfair. I think maybe things moved too fast for us and I played an equal role in that, I know.

Too fast? What? No, I don't care about that. You're not getting what I'm saying at all. I enjoyed the time we spent together. If you had kept in touch, if you hadn't humiliated me and made me worry about you, I would be excited to see you again, in a normal I'm-not-sure-where-this-is-going-but-I'm-looking-forward-to-finding-out way. But for you to call up – there's a time difference if you didn't realise, by the way; it's really late here – from a *payphone* and – what was it you said when I answered? – 'It's me'? Are you kidding me with that shit? 'Me' who? The level of entitlement you must have, it's embarrassing, dude. Like, seriously.

PLEASE INSERT ONE DOLLAR OR THIS LINE WILL BE DISCONNECTED.

Sounds like I gotta go.

Oh my god, I can't believe this is for real. What year is it?

Look, when I'm back I'll call you again and we can meet up and I'll make it up to you. Okay?

I don't know. Maybe. But you're going to have to explain yourself more, especially to–

THIS LINE HAS BEEN DISCONNECTED. GOODBYE.

XIX

ONE DAY, not long after all of this was over, and I was back home, my worst fears started to come true. Sarah had seemed to become suspicious of me, in a generalised sort of way. It was such a happy occasion when we reunited (we both cried at the airport when she picked me up) but it was also somewhat awkward to be in each other's presence after so much time had passed, to be in each other's way. I knew we just needed to get used to each other again but, for Sarah, I'm not altogether sure. She said she had grown while we were apart. I told her at the time that I knew what she meant, but it was a statement I would ponder over long after, that I have continued to ponder over. What was this feeling, of growing? I could agree with Heraclitus that we existed in a permanent state of flux. How could I not? The response to any given problem being only a matter of time isn't just good advice, it's also an observable fact of science, if only from the widest possible vantage. And 'It is not possible to step into the same river twice' is essentially an unfalsifiable statement. Perhaps I didn't speak in the ways that I used to, didn't have the same patterns of thought, of anxiety, of fear. Only, as I surveyed the events that had transpired over the past six weeks that I was away, over the past six years that Sarah and I had been married, I wasn't totally convinced. Growth, to me, suggested a linear trajectory and an idealised state of being, two concepts I struggled with, in either the abstract or the material sense. Whose consciousness could we rely upon to make these distinctions, if that consciousness was, indeed, always changing with us? And by whose judgement should we then stand? For Heraclitus the answer to these questions was simply that we were ruled by fire. But, like the Milesians before him, I figured there had to be a firmer sense of stability to undergird the chaos, and that this stability would not be able to accommodate movement in any true sense. We were trapped in this state of flux, as in a snow globe being shaken by an overexcited child. And all I am was who I could ever only be. No religious or civic basis is necessary in this respect; rather, as logic establishes illogic, only the intellectual recognition that the experience of being human is itself timeless, bound and drawn together so we are by our unrelenting need for each other. Sarah would of course challenge me on something like this, would first patiently wait for me to finish my prolonged, insufficient meanderings and then, like an incision, remove the organ of the thought that proved to not be so vital after all and had in fact risked exploding into sepsis for as long as it remained. *I suppose the way I look at it is...* But her mind died with her, and all I am able to perform now is my best imitation of her, an imitation that worsens line by line as it grasps only for an image that continues to pull further and further away from its object with every attempt that is made at any representation.

As you might expect, I found Sarah's newly invigorated sense of distrust unsettling, to say the least. Where had it come from? If she knew of something, she wasn't letting on, beyond a few pointed questions about whether I had kept in touch at all with anyone from the library or conference, which

I could just as easily take for vexation that I wasn't placing enough emphasis on my future career during my research and doing more to partake in the drudgery of networking and goal-setting, preparing for the next steps. Balancing the elation and paranoia of my extramarital attentions hadn't exactly been easy while I was away, but, I mean, really, I didn't see these things as very much connected to what happened in Scotland. I'm not going to conduct some, you know, historical analysis of the social practices of monogamy through the ages for you here, or something. (Besides, I think this is a topic that has already been well covered, probably much better than I ever could.) But any kind of critical endeavour, like a doctoral thesis, that inculcates scepticism for the very idea of ideas is likely to lend one an unusually heightened toleration for rationalisation, compartmentalisation, and depersonalisation.[11]

Eventually, I started to realise what was going on. See, since coming in off the road, I'd developed certain aversions to aspects of homelife that I had previously taken little notice of, like the ex-con wary now of his newly deregulated surroundings. Mould, chemical cleaning products, microplastics. Sometimes it felt like my body was positively humming with toxins, surfactants, and E numbers. And I think I was probably acting a little differently as a result. For instance, I had been abruptly leaving our kitchen when we were together at what would have seemed like strange, irregular intervals. What Sarah didn't notice – I couldn't face telling her it was getting this bad – is that this was

---

11 It sounds like I'm blaming Foucault here – I'm not. But I do wish to be read in the widest possible context, as it were. I think everyone deserves at least that. Don't you?

only whenever she put the microwave on, because I'd decided that I was afraid of the radiation. As a result – and, again, this is just one example – sometimes she would call across the house to ask if I was checking my computer, if it was because I waiting to hear from someone. I was mostly bemused by this suggestion. She knew the last thing I ever wanted was for someone from the university to get in touch when all that would mean was one of my supervisors expected the next chapter from me or an administrator was trying to rope me into joining another useless committee. I told her as much but this didn't seem to allay her doubts. So what happens next is coming at an unusually fractious period for us.

he's lying to you sarah, the message read completely out of nowhere. That's all it said.

It was after dinner and we were just settling in with a glass of wine, a necessary measure of fortitude for the next episode of a series we'd tacitly agreed to endure for no real reason. Sarah called me over to where she was on the couch. I was jotting down a thought I had just had: how, by titling his book *Beneath the Underdog*, Mingus was positioning himself at the furthest possible bottom of society, a lowlife *ne plus ultra*.

She kept hold of her phone but thrust it in my direction, resisting my attempt to reach for it. I couldn't see who the sender was.

Uh, that's weird. That was all I could muster in that moment. Then, Who is it from? I managed in a brutal staccato.

Sarah didn't respond. Instead, she reached out for my heart and held her hand against my chest, gently but deliberately. She had done this once before, a half-joke I'd presumed. I looked into her eyes, somewhere between them, almost like I was seeing past her to the window with the construction site in the distance – the last days of our view of the water plainly numbered – and held her gaze.

I don't know who it's from, she said. Do you? Are you lying to me?

No, I replied, breathing deeply, steadying myself under her mock-reproach.

Okay, good. And she started to type a response, seemingly satisfied.

Over her shoulder I could just make out her simple but effective phrase, piss off.

Our conversation soon turned to scams and phishing and everyone's own private fantasy of turning someone's entire life around through the landing of the perfect lucky guess. Walking up to a stranger on the street, maybe, whispering something innocuous but potentially freighted with a meaning and significance for them that you'd never know yourself. Something like: *It's over.*

But a few minutes passed and her phone issued another terrible noise of excitement.

he lied to me and he's lying to you too

Sarah showed it to me and watched my face carefully. I shrugged and tried to take a drink of my wine without gulping it but I happened to inhale at the same time and started to choke. I coughed and I coughed, blood rushing to my embarrassed face, tears filling my haunted eyes.

She stared at me. Recovering, I returned her stare with a studied insouciance.

She must have written a response that asked for clarification as to the subject of the message because it was clear now that Sarah was no longer convinced that this was an act of random, exploitative spam.

And as we sat there, in silence, I began to grow very weary. It was like a wave of exhaustion was flooding over me but still I endeavoured to maintain a credible benefit of the doubt, by neither confirming nor disavowing Sarah's suspicions, by sitting there with an ambiguous display of curiosity and amusement, and a posture that was neither particularly worried nor overly relaxed either. Yet beneath the sleeve of my cashmere jumper I could feel those two red itchy hives I knew so well start to rise on my forearm: a stress reaction, my GP had told me.

After a moment or two, like a death knell, her phone chirruped yet again. Sarah glanced towards me and then unlocked it with her thumb. Her face at first registering confusion and then her fingers on the screen opened and closed between themselves like she was zooming in and out on something. Finally, she turned the phone onto its side as a picture popped into frame, and with her other hand she began to gnaw at her nails.

I'm not happy about this, Miles, she said.

What is it? I asked a bit pathetically. I knew by this point what it was she was looking at but I had no idea how it could be explained, how I could explain it without explaining everything.

She held it out to me, though I didn't need for her to. I knew it so well and knew it held no additional information to impart to me. She would have known this, too, because handing it to me wasn't for my benefit at all. It was for me to identify, like a corpse. Before it was even in my hands I recognised my face, my good shirt. My false, TV presenter smile.

It was my Reader Identification Card.

One thing Sarah and bonded over the morning after we first met (during fresher's week, very late at night) was that we were both only-children. We talked about having to learn to entertain yourself, keep your own company, and establish your own sense of taste and discretion. When we did play with other children, occasionally we found it difficult to relate to them. Why wouldn't they want to do what we wanted to? Why were their moods and emotions so difficult to understand? And how could anyone say no to an idea as good as hanging from the washing line to see who was best at *Gladiators*? But as the weeks went on during that early period of finding each other endlessly fascinating, more differences in our upbringings began to reveal themselves and it soon became clear that despite a superficially similar family dynamic, we'd been given substantially different roles to fill.

Basically, Sarah's parents were just very involved with her and exceptionally keen to ensure she'd end up where they believed was best for her. What this translated into was a presence in her life I couldn't fathom myself, a presence that seemed in preparation for some fairy-tale future for her I never got the impression they had even wanted for themselves. I'd never heard of anyone taking seven highers (all A's, except for a B in drama) or having their pupils checked when they came home at night. When she was old enough to date, boys had to meet her at the door and were introduced to her father.

For my part I got into university through clearing, stayed out most of the weekend, and did my best to give the impression that girls were an irrelevance to me, an image belied only by my obnoxious pubescent preening before school and evident unease when my parents asked if I was planning to invite anyone to the discos.

They had actually wanted her to study divinity and to become ordained. This was, by the end of our degrees, pretty hilarious to us. But I had to admit that I could also see some of what they would have seen in her: a quickness and depth of understanding for catechism; a patient and engaging way of speaking for prayer. I tried to explain. First, respectfully, and when that didn't work, disrespectfully. But they just wouldn't hear that she didn't consider herself a Christian. (Nobody wants to admit that they don't know their own children.)

What this left us with was a quite divergent approach to conflict resolution. I was more likely to blow up and to then as quickly apologise. I couldn't stand rows and would do whatever I thought in the moment might make them pass. Sarah was different, and in some ways this was her contemplative nature getting the best of her. She would retreat into herself, dwell upon things, tell me she wasn't ready to speak to me yet, shut away in the bedroom for hours, even days, then emerge tearfully, still hurt, but ready to offer or accept forgiveness. There were times I didn't know how to deal with someone who took everything so personally, so I'd leave the house, go for a walk in an aimless fashion, only to, within a few minutes, find myself in desperate need of the toilet, the diarrhoea like an abortion of whatever pain or shame that I had caused her.

I didn't know what to say. The thing was, as far as I could remember, I hadn't actually told a lie to anyone. Not directly, anyway. It was like the photo of the card and cryptic messages before it were designed to produce just such conditions; I was being boxed in, compelled to present the evidence with which I'd convict myself.

Whatever this is, tell me, she said.

I think someone is playing a trick on us, I tried.

Really? That's what you're going with? she asked.

What do you mean?

Miles, you're sweating.

Was I going to do it? Was I going to tell her? If so, how much? I think what's been misunderestimated is the extent to which I would have needed to share myself if I was going to be fully open with her.[12] I'm not saying we weren't close. Of course we were. Closer than I've ever been with anyone. We had an intimacy and fondness for each other that could make my skin prickle, my sides ache with laughter. But how could this have ever been my whole self, when it was revealing my whole self that would have destroyed me, destroyed us? For years I'd had this fantasy, a fantasy so outlandish, so unacceptable that, even if she would have been willing to listen to it, to help me act on it in some way, I would have still exploded before a single word of it could be uttered to her. It's only now, through this distanced medium to a – let's face it – by now mostly disinterested audience, that I can even begin to sketch it out.

Each day, as I walked around the city, I imagined that I was carrying a number of business cards. On these business cards, it would explain, to the couple that received them, that I would like to watch them have sex, in their room, and

---

12 The word just feels right. Whatever else you might think about the gut-wrenching slaughter of several hundred thousand Iraqis, this was a genuine contribution to the English language by Bush.

that I would pay them for the privilege of doing so. In their confusion, their anger, or their sniggering, I would walk away, back into the crowd from whence I'd appeared.

The fantasy didn't make sense. I was roughly the same age as those I'd actually be interested in watching (was I really interested at all?) and I had a long-term partner I was hopelessly attracted to. It was like something a sad old man would do, a genuine pervert. And yet, day in and day out, I thought, *They won't call*, or, *Those ones might*. It was unconscionable and it felt wrong. Was this the sort of thing Sarah would have wanted to know about me? I didn't think so.

I slept with someone when I was away, I said. I think she must be who sent that to you. I'm so, so sorry Sarah. I don't have an excuse, and I know this is just, like, what people say in films and stuff, but it didn't mean anything. It really didn't.

Sarah put her head into her hands.

Why are you telling me this, she said quietly.

What? But you asked. I'm telling you the truth.

You couldn't make something up? You had to actually say it?

Tears began to spring from her eyes.

I don't know, I said. I mean, what… Why…

You're a piss-poor liar, you know. But you could have tried a bit harder.

It was a one-time thing, I said. I was still angry about that party last year, and I wanted to get back at you. That was childish, I know.

Why did she have your ID?

I left it at her place, I said. I felt so guilty in the morning I ran out as quickly as I could and I left it there. I had to go back the next day and get it from her. I'd hurt her feelings by leaving without saying goodbye, and I think this is her revenge. When—

I don't want to hear any more! she shouted.

All right, whatever, fucking hell. What do you want me to say, then? Tell me what to say and I'll say it.

Can you just go away, please?

I stood, looked at her there, knees pulled into her body like a wee girl, hunched over and crying silently. When I opened the door into the hall, she cleared her throat.

You forgot something, she said.

What did I forget?

You forgot to explain how she has my name and number.

When I got home Sarah was gone. She called my mum, who called me, to say that she was staying at her parents' and that she was coming back for some things later in the week and would need for me to be away.

If only she'd been able to stay pregnant, I thought. *If we'd had our child.*

XX

I KNEW I had been ruined by literature because the nexus of the film industry meant nothing to me except as the vaguely sinister milieu for characters like Philip Marlowe and Lew Archer to inhabit. Two ciphers to the human condition, they seemed to represent, in the first instance, the struggle to conduct ourselves in ways we can later regard as honourable, and, in the second, the struggle to recognise those around us for who they were, which was an irredeemable set of a million others just like us engaged in a never-ending series of decisions that comprised the first struggle. I wondered if either could have found Weldon Kees, a writer beset by his inability to reconcile the two struggles who disappeared at the Golden Gate Bridge on 19 July 1955, exactly sixty-one years prior to the date I saw it after I said goodbye to the band. But perhaps San Francisco was too far out of their jurisdiction.

I made my way to a self-consciously retro diner with a copy of the *L.A. Times* and ordered a cup of coffee. The shock of Brexit had penetrated even this far, into the provinces of actors, agents, and all their underlings who keep the show running. I was grimly fascinated by this as it seemed to turn the 'special relationship' with the U.S. on its head. Is this what the English had always wanted? A little bit of recognition for their own propensity to toss petrol onto fires they decide could burn with greater expediency under less caution and technocratic stage-management?

I thought then about how Sarah would be pleased with the result. Outwardly, she would lament the fatalistic determination that it must go ahead and the democratic deficit of only two nations of the United Kingdom voting in favour of it at the heart of the folly, especially. But I was confident that what she believed this represented for Scotland's future, would, with me, when we were alone, if she'd had a drink or two, shine through her eyes as we discussed the future. She died before she could witness just how long the process of carving our own path again might take, but the optimism she held for the place she loved more than any other couldn't have abated and she'd have been cheered to see how implacably opposed to such small-mindedness our voting public has seemed to remain since.

I felt suddenly homesick but also hopeful that this homesickness meant that I was getting closer to being ready to go home, that I was on the precipice of finding whatever it was I had been looking for. In some ways this would prove to be more literal that I could have expected, in that what I was able to finally take away with me was in the form of a construction, something with a distinct image I could hold onto in my mind whenever I might feel myself gravitating towards nihilism's seductive orbit, the concentric rotations that would seem to tighten when Sarah and I fell out, and then all the other shite which happened after that as well. Like her dying, for one.

I'd asked the fellas behind the counter how I could get to Watts Towers, a place Mingus had expressed fascination for with an unmitigated sense of admiration not found much else in his autobiography as he often came across as jealous and petty even towards the influences he considered heroes, like Duke Ellington. But they hadn't heard of it, and I wasn't able to describe it very well, only going from what I could remember in Mingus's book. I wondered if it might be gone now and I could feel a short tingle start to develop in my head at the thought, towards the top on the right-hand side about six inches from my eye.

Hey man, one of them said, don't get aggressive with us. We've never been to this place you're talking about. It's not our fault. We can't give you directions to somewhere we've never been before.

I'm not being aggressive, I replied. I just know it's around here somewhere and I want to see it.

So go find it, why don't you? Whaddya staying around here for? Look it up on your phone or something.

I said glumly that I didn't have a phone and walked towards the door, apologising, thanking for them for the coffee, promising it was the best that I'd had on my entire trip to America, and that I would always treasure my memory of the place, Ray's Kitchen or whatever. (I couldn't locate it now to save my life, and the coffee was burnt.)

But when I got outside – sunshine piercing my retinas, oppressive heat enveloping me – a woman who seemed to be in her seventies or so came out behind me, saying, I know where it is you looking for.

Can you help me get to there? I asked.

My mama still lives near it, she said. Hop in the car if you want. I'll drop you off.

We didn't speak for most of the way, and, after about fifteen minutes had passed, I was no longer surprised that the short-order cooks at the diner hadn't known what I was on about. Los Angeles, I later learned, has nearly five hundred neighbourhoods, with only the occasional demarcation to differentiate them for the non-local. New York City had felt as if it was the biggest city in the world, but Los Angeles was another world entirely, unbuffeted by state lines or free flowing rivers, with a conurbation stretching beyond any conception of space that could have been conceived before the end of the previous century. The thought that I could get lost in it – wholly, existentially lost – gripped me like the footpath on the Golden Gate Bridge had, right there at the spot where she told me she thought she might be falling in love with me and I'd had to demure, daring myself to self-annihilate.

I really appreciate you giving me a lift, I said.

It's fine, she replied. I gotta go out there, anyway. Where did I hear you say you were from, baby? Sweden?

Scotland, I corrected.

Now what brings you out here to South Central?

I came to conduct research on Charles Mingus, the bassist. Are you familiar with him?

'Course I know Charlie, she said. I only met him a couple of times when I was little but my mama and him were friendly for a time in grammar school, I think it was. Maybe high school, too. What kind of research is it? Are you writing a book?

Sort of. I really just want to walk around where he lived. I remembered him saying he grew up in the shadow of those towers, and I felt like was something I could try to experience for myself.

She laughed and said, I got a feeling you don't know exactly what it is that you're about to see.

I considered what she might mean by this, all too aware that the legacies of our differences were vast, the contours staked much further out than I could ever expect to traverse on a short car ride. But I was grateful for her kindness, and as she pulled off the highway into a distinctly residential area, I said, I like this aesthetic. I mean all the bungalows with their own wee gardens out front. It reminds me of home, in a way.

Well, Watts has changed a lot, she said. But if you want to understand Charlie, you gotta remember one thing: Charlie *is* L.A. He might've moved and went out to New York. But that background he had, that upbringing, that stays with you. He was multiracial, sweet and mean, and he was an artist – that's Watts all over. That's *L.A.* all over. He never missed a chance to come home. This city made him in its image, and he made it in his. There's nowhere more important than where you come from.

Can I still see it? Where he came from?

His family house is gone if that's what you mean. They tore it down to build a new school. Charlie wouldn't have minded. That's not what he was about. What you probably want to see is the art centre they put up for him there. It's got free music lessons for kids; it's a place for seniors to go; and they got stuff for people with special needs, too. That's a better way to honour him than setting up a shrine where he'd had just as many bad times as he did good.

And the towers? I asked.

Again, she laughed. You'll have to judge those for yourself.

For the rest of our journey, she told me how Watts had transformed from a diverse, semi-rural train hub with a burgeoning industry due in large part to the Second World War into a segregated hotbed of racial tension and black oppression. Much of this was deliberate, traceable directly to various pernicious policies of the local and state governments, and in 1965 this culminated in the worst riot the city would see until the Rodney King riots nearly thirty years later.

With her emphasis on social history, I was able to see Mingus now as less of the icon I'd conjured for him and more of an actual person. A person like me. A person who had been shaped by the society around him, who responded to that society in ways that were both conscious and unconscious, locked into cycles of destruction and soothing. It was sometimes said that any dialogue with Mingus inevitably devolved to vain rants of how persecuted he was, for any number of reasons but especially due to his skin: too brown, too light; 'half-schitt coloured', someone once called him. This had seemed as much as a verbal or epistemological tic to me as a notion that could be practicably proven, yet our grievances are our grievances for a reason. That is to say that the essential unknowability stalking our daily interactions must contain, alongside their inscrutable or pathological patterns of action, certain germs of truth, a bacterial infection of reason that may or may not be in the process of spreading throughout the body, to the spine and then up the way. In other words, maggot brain, or, as has seemed to enter our lexicon over the last few years, brainworms.

As she made her approach to where she said she'd have to drop me off, I could make out some structures in the distance blotting out an otherwise empty sky of hazy blue.

There they are! she exclaimed. What do you think?

It's beautiful, I said.

You're pulling my leg, she replied. But it does my old lady heart good to hear you say that. I had to leave Watts but it's always in here, she said tapping her chest. I gotta go see my mama now but promise me you'll stop by the art centre.

Could I come with you and speak to your mum? I asked. Because she knew Mingus, I added quickly, to clarify my intentions.

She hesitated and then said, My mama's very fragile. I'm not sure you coming into her house is a good idea. It'd take me too long to explain who you are and then she'd tell me off for picking up a stranger. I know I'm ancient to you but I'm still her daughter, after all. I'm sorry, baby.

It's no bother, I said. Just thought I'd ask. Thanks very much, again, for the lift.

I think you're going to do well with your book, you know, she said as I climbed out her car and looked around me to get my bearings.

You do? I asked, glancing back.

Yes. You are a very polite young man and you kept me company on a ride that isn't always easy for me. To understand someone like Charlie you got to have soul. And that's what you have; you're soulful. Now, hang on just one second. I got something here I want to give you.

She reached into the glovebox and pulled out a what looked like a brochure that she leant over and passed to me through the open window.

It was an issue of *The Watchtower*, a magazine published by the evangelical Jehovah's Witnesses. On the cover was a crestfallen woman, covering her ears and closing her eyes on the steps of a walk-up brownstone, with a framed photograph of her and a man lain aside her. When a Loved One Dies, the strapline read.

Thanks, I said. I'll have a look through it.

When she'd driven away, I walked over to a rubbish bin and tossed it in. I felt bad about this, but what else was I going to do with it? The only scripture I thought I would ever need I already knew off the top of my head.

> I hate and I love. Maybe it puzzles you, why am I this way?
> But I am so anguished, and I cannot say.
> – Catullus

Trying to not take any close notice of the towers yet – they were surrounded by a fence with faded placards on their provenance that I wanted to understand first – I found myself watching the ground beneath me as it became cluttered with a pack of feral cats who would run through and about my legs. This was cute but mostly gross due to their manifold deformities, and the scene gave me an acute sensation of déjà vu, their mewling at me as if I might at any moment give in and distribute kibbles for them flustering me further for the abject desperation they exhibited in their affronted cries. I tried to shoo them away, but their zigzagging circle kept pace with me as I walked, forming a ragtag band of the diseased who seemed to act as though they were suddenly relying upon me for leadership. Eventually, only after I nudged several of them with my feet, did they disperse, off to find a more dupable mark. I watched as they scarpered down the street, spontaneously hop a fence together, and then disappear completely out of view. For a moment I wondered if it had really happened at all. *Not again...* was my silent prayer then. *Don't let this happen to me again, please. I'm right here. I'm okay.*

I still wasn't looking at the towers. Not properly, anyway. Instead, I was reading about the man who had created them at the site where he lived, an Italian immigrant Sabato Rodia, a man seemingly in need of a project following his divorce. I remembered Mingus writing that the local children would alternatingly taunt Rodia for his eccentricities and bring him new material for his creations: old bottles, remarkable seashells, broken pottery. Rodia approached his work without any formal design, making it up as he went, often tearing down something he'd just built if he decided it was no longer conducive to his entirely withheld aims. After more than thirty years had passed, he finished (no one knew what this meant, or how he'd determined its completion) and simply turned the deed of the property over to a neighbour only to disappear from town, not resurfacing until a decade later when a conference at Berkeley had decided he might be an artist of note. For most of the conference, he sat in the audience, unnoticed, watching the carousel slides of his own masterpiece, listening to their academic discussions of its merits. When the lights came up, he stood and made his presence known. The audience applauded. Now in his eighties, this was the only formal reception he would ever receive. He died not long after.

The towers have been threatened ever since, with several public campaigns necessary to preserve their integrity; most recently a bid to have them protected for all time as a UNESCO World Heritage site. It survived 10,000 pounds of hydraulic pressure applied by the city to bring it down. It survived the riot. Perhaps it can survive property developers, too.

I walked through the open gate and began to take in their resplendence all by myself there, thousands of miles away from anyone I knew, feeling both stilled and startlingly moved. Multiple chills ran down my spine, the physiological response to an epiphany, a visiting professor had told us in his inaugural lecture. The mosaics cresting every structure, the way the individual objects forming them were their own articles of a complicated history, buoyed by an often asymmetrical patterning that drew the eye across them, pulling you this way and that as you ambled amongst the seventeen heaps and pinnacles, inviting your hands, setting your imagination alight, bringing you to – yes, it's happening; it's really happening – tears, gave me a feeling of intense, pleasurable vertigo, like I was falling upward into their haphazard, coolly metallic protuberances. Nothing else could matter in that moment as I found myself wonderfully bereft of any of my puny humanly concerns. Sex was a biological process; love, by mistake or design, only the chemical created in its wake. We were, each of us, part of something so much greater than ourselves, and if a person who'd lost his family was still able to devote so many years of his life to providing such a captivating and intense experience for others, in such humble surroundings, there was reason, surely, to find faith that, despite everything constantly screaming to the contrary, there were still good things to come for us, if only we had the spiritual wherewithal to wait for them.

When asked to describe his motivations, Rodia would respond, 'Why a man make the shoes?' and the quotation often attributed to him in lieu of an artist's statement is, 'You gotta do something they never got 'em in the world,' presumably repeated for its humorously ungrammatical syntax and peculiar voice.

But there was another answer to this same question I found later which I thought seemed a closer insight to his impulses, the most direct expression of what he'd decided he was capable of, and why he had chosen his methods. 'I wanted to do something in the United States because I was raised here, you understand?' he said. 'I had it in my mind to do something big – and I did.' Not many of us accept that challenge, let alone rise to meet it.

He started with the bottles he'd been drinking day after day, wanting to repurpose their utility for his own redemption. Once he left Watts, Rodia never returned. 'No, I won't go back,' he said. 'I break my heart there.'

I began to climb the tallest tower, like the mast of a great ship, not stopping until I reached a view that stretched across an ocean of suburban houses and parkways. I didn't need to visit the art centre. Everything I'd wanted to see was around me, beneath me, or, perhaps most of all, right there, up above me.

When the sun had set, I climbed back down and found a bus that was heading directly to the airport. Finally, it was time to start making my way back home.

XXI

BACK IN D.C. I had several loose ends that I needed to tie up. Though I hadn't actually considered my friend there to be one of them. There was all my stuff in the house in Georgetown. The wince-inducing number of boxes of material waiting for me at the library. Whatever it was I was going to do about my thesis. And I had to find some money to pay Sarah back for the flight from L.A. which she'd bought for me, calling into the airline while I waited and giving them her credit card details. I knew this didn't matter very much to her as the chief drive in her perennially upward mobility was to provide for us and the children that we'd eventually raise, but I hadn't really explained how I'd ended up in L.A. without a plan for getting back, and I thought if I could reimburse her quickly, it wouldn't need to come up again. Another case of me being disorganised, a bit spendthrift; a 'waster' her dad would say.

So once I was able to get a new phone, I hit my friend up like I'd said I would, acknowledging that she had every right to still be angry with me, if that was indeed the case, but that I had a proposal for her. And when she dryly responded to say that the proposal better not be marriage, I knew that I could get back into her good graces, become someone whom she'd look forward to seeing again.

She was still quite guarded while we texted, but with my suggestion that this proposal could be to her benefit as much as to mine, she started to relent, and then, after I'd said that I would like to go out for drinks with her friends – if they would like to as well, that is – she finally invited me over to her place to discuss.

I grabbed the key from under the tile in front of the small townhome where it usually was and let myself in. She was round the back, sitting on the porch, drinking a beer that was neither pretentiously up itself nor doing itself down for the irony, and dutifully writing along the margins of a worn, dogeared copy of *Bech is Back*.

She didn't look over when I opened the glass-fronted door to her unkempt garden area, so I stood there, knocked on its frame and said, Hi.

Hi, she said, adding a touch of sarcasm to the greeting, still looking at her book, facing three-quarters away from me so that I could just make out the furrow of her brow as she scribbled another note. I wanted to push her hair back behind her ear.

Maybe she was feeling the same. Maybe she didn't know if we were supposed to kiss, hug, or shake hands.

You'll never guess what I'm reading, I said, opening my bag and flinging *Couples* onto the table, equally worn though no more so from my usage. The motion of my action nearly knocked her can over and she had to catch it before it toppled and fell onto the ground.

How *apropos*, she said.

Oops, sorry, I said.

The can fizzed. I stood there lamely, knowing I should fill the silence but unsure whether it was banter she was wanting, or an apology.

Hey, so did you want to talk about—

There's no point, she said. We weren't exclusive. I'm sure you always used protection. And, again, this was tinged with sarcasm, although I wasn't entirely sure why.

Then—

What is this proposition you have for me? she interrupted.

I think 'proposal' was the word I used, I replied.

Whatever. What is it?

You're still doing your tutoring, right? For mummy and daddy's very special boys and girls so they can do keg stands with the rest of the B-squad American elite at Dartmouth, right? I asked, mispronouncing it as 'dart mouth' to irritate her.

Uh-huh, she replied, ignoring this.

And you said that you wanted a break from it so that you could finish your monograph—

You want to take over, she interjected.

Just for the next two weeks, I replied. Before I leave. In the evenings, like you were doing. I'll be working in the library during the day, too. I need – I mean, I would like – to have U.S. dollars. To buy some books before I leave, the ones that are harder to get at home. More expensive, anyway. There's a first edition Exley at Second Story Books that I want. It's pretty cheap. For what it is, anyway. Have you read *A Fan's Notes*? It's brilliant.

And this is why you called me, she stated.

No, I said, moving closer to her. But it is something I'd hoped you might be interested in. I'm using it to worm my way back in, I said, waggling my finger at her.

Good luck with that, she returned, placidly.

Now that we were making eye contact, I could feel my whole body grow tense with nervousness.

Fuck it, I thought, and then leaned down to kiss her.

You're such an asshole, she said, as she kissed me back.

I know I am, I replied.

That's how I ended up helping high school students write their college application essays. And, no, I didn't try to sleep with any of them.

To be sure this was for the most part a fairly dull endeavour, though one lucrative beyond what I could have imagined which clarified for me how it was she had been able to live in the city for such an extended period of time. By virtue of her own pedigree, she provided a channel of access to circles that once weren't so difficult for anyone with right upbringing to find themselves in but had become increasingly competitive even for those with moneyed names, private tutors, and esoteric extracurriculars. For my part, I was the necessary stand-in while she was 'ill' and brought along some international credibility as well.[13] Had I been on one of those – what do you call 'em – gap years? If you were to ask my new benefactors, certainly. Through the Voluntary Service Office I was stationed at Punishment Island on Lake Bunyonyi in Uganda, and how marvellously that experience enhanced my interview to St Andrews! (This was the only university in Scotland they had heard of.)

I can remember on a train journey a friend and I made many years ago, I hadn't bought a ticket all the way to our destination, because, for some undisclosed reason, if I did, it would have meant I wasn't able to get an open return and would have had to buy two, separate, single tickets for there

---

13 Funny, isn't it, that this was the one instance in which they didn't mind a foreigner coming in for one stated purpose and surreptitiously offering a different service in exchange for cash?

and back at a higher cost. As we were going away for the weekend, I had no intention of doing myself out a few pounds because a rail company arbitrarily decided this particular route wasn't fit for my purposes. When the conductor came round and asked why I hadn't alighted where I was supposed to, I replied immediately that the ticket machine was broken, that it wouldn't let me go back a step to buy the correct one, and that an employee at the gate had said it would be okay just this once, so long as I promised to buy the correct ticket on my way back home. This mundane, needlessly long explanation satisfied the phlegmatic conductor and he moved on. But my friend was shocked, and he told me that it really freaked him out how quickly and saliently was I able to tell a lie like that. Don't you feel guilty? I remember him asking. Doesn't it make you feel bad?

This is something I've never understood. How could I feel guilty over something so inconsequential? Especially when it's to extract some of the profit back that they'd been making on me my entire life? And what was he going to do about it, really? The idea that you won't feel like you're lying 'if you believe it' has been promulgated by television, but an even more straightforward approach is to recognise that you simply don't have any reason to care. The same principle applied here: there was nothing to lose, so there was nothing to fear. Like a stripper, I was whoever the parents wanted me to be.

One of the families I took the bus out to the Palisades to meet at their mid-century brick home, modest in size by American standards (only three bedrooms and three-and-a-half bathrooms) but furnished exceptionally plushly, and on ample acreage with a basement and carport as well.

The daughter and I sat in a small conservatory at the back of the house, on two fashionably-worn Morris chairs facing each other. It was quite hot that evening and a standing fan oscillated between us, whirring at varying intervals which mainly directed noise towards you and then away. I took a sip of the iced tea I'd been offered (revolting) and, as I caught a warning shot of the girl's teenaged venom for going Mmmm! and sardonically smiling at her, I – without wishing to – began to laugh at the preposterous circumstances I was finding myself in.

What's so funny, she said, her vocal fry sizzling.

Oh, I don't know, I replied. What isn't funny?

Working in July on an application that isn't due until November, for one.

Fair enough, I said. What would you rather be doing?

Literally, anything, she responded.

Literally? I asked.

Another warning shot.

Right, I said. Well, we don't actually have a lot of time, so why don't we make the most of it and then you can go do literally anything else when it's over. What have you been working on?

We've done the personal essay. But I have to write a separate statement explaining why I want to study English.

Why do you want to study English? I asked.

Dunno. My parents said it would be easier to get accepted if I picked something unpopular and then, if I wanted to, I could change it when I got there.

Interesting, I said, as I tend to whenever someone says something I find uninteresting.

Plus, I like books.

Now we're getting somewhere, I replied, sitting up as I said this, as if I really believed it. What kind of books do you like?

I just like whatever.

I sat back again.

Hmm. But is there something about reading that you like?

Um... She looked away, beyond the fence, to an adjoining residence where two boys and a girl could be seen playing basketball, teasing each other boisterously.

What's different about it from seeing a film for you?

You mean watching a movie? she asked.

Or anything else, I said. Why is reading different?

You have to put effort in, she said. It's not something that happens to you. You have to happen to it.

And why is that important to you?

Because it's what makes it distinct from entertainment. My friends all read before bed because it helps them fall asleep. I can't do that. Because if I do, I'll stay up all night reading.

Okay, now we're *actually* getting somewhere, I said, opening up my laptop and writing down what she was saying, so that I could visualise the progression of our conversation and hopefully reach the germ of an idea for her to expound upon in the statement.

Tell me about a time when you couldn't stop reading, I said.

I guess the last time it happened was *Save Me the Waltz*, she said.

I'm not familiar with that, I said. Who is it by?

Zelda Fitzgerald, she replied.

Oh, is it, like, a companion to *The Great Gatsby*? I asked.

She rolled her eyes.

No, Zelda wrote it several years after that. From an insane asylum. It actually pre-empts *Tender is the Night*. Scott was furious that she'd taken the same material from their lives, material that he was also planning to use.

Is it good? I asked.

Would you ask me that if I'd said a book by her husband?

Maybe, I said, if it was one I hadn't read. But I take your point. And it really doesn't matter, now that I think about it, if it's any good. Not for our purposes, anyway. I was just curious.

I cleared my throat.

But something about it gripped you, I prompted.

All right, so, I read the introduction first which I normally never do. Big mistake.

Why? I asked, typing this.

It was a pretty old copy, and it was basically this guy going okay it sucks but mayyyybe it's worth reading if you're interested in her husband. I just thought that was unfair. The last couple pages of his thing were *literally* only about Scott, like that's the only prism that matters.

It's a sexist attitude, I said.

Totally! she exclaimed. But. honestly, it made me more interested in her. And maybe it's just because *The Great Gatsby* is so – I don't know if cliché is the right word – but let's go with overdone or something since everybody here is basically forced read it at some point during school, but I preferred *Save Me the Waltz*. It's as much about the psychosexual dynamics of flawed relationships as her husband's was except it's coming at you without all the pretence, technical showiness, or grand, novelistic ambitions. The books ends with the main character unable to find fulfilment in anything going on in her life. Shocking that a man would want to believe that's it's just the published version of one crazy woman's private diary! Otherwise, he might have to admit her words have just as much resonance as the masculine version and maybe his own wife isn't as satisfied as he thinks she is. but there's something in her book that you never find in her husband's ones, in my opinion. Not at the tangible, granular level of the writing. It's her pain, I guess. And the way that the story makes you a part of that. This guy says it isn't well written as *Tender is the Night*. But that's a weird bar to set when you think about it and why is he the one who gets to decide that anyway? I loved *Save Me the Waltz*. Because it's real. Do you get what I'm saying?

I do, I do, I said. And I don't want to come across as patronising but it's a very mature way to think about it. I'm surprised you're still in high school if that's how you're approaching your reading, rather than regurgitating what your teacher or the material says. Was this for an assignment at school?

She blushed. Um, it was for a national essay contest. On anything in American Studies. I didn't win. My mom thinks it was probably too bitchy for them.

It doesn't sound bitchy, I said. It sounds like you're taking the novel for what it is, instead of getting bitchy about it not being something it isn't, like that no-name did.

We were quiet for a moment while I typed out my interpretations of what she had been saying. When I had finished, I held my fingers to the keyboard, steadying it on my lap, absently looking at her while my mind drifted away from me.

What's wrong? she asked. Is there something on my face?

No, I said. It's nothing. Sorry. Being here with you reminded me of someone for some reason.

Uh, that's fine. Can I ask who?

It doesn't make much sense, I said. I can't remember what she looked like, and I didn't really know her to be honest. She'd be much older than you, anyway. She'd be my age, I suppose. I never really thought of that until now. I only knew her first name and sometimes I wonder if I made her up.

Oh.

Come on, I said, snapping my fingers. Let's get this into a statement. For your parents – I mean, for the university.

She shrugged. What do I say?

You're basically referencing about a mode of criticism (or post-criticism, rather – but that doesn't matter) that's sometimes called 'reparative reading', I said. I don't think you should use that term because it could come across a bit try-hard or as if someone like me wrote it for you, but one way we could approach this is to…

That was one my last sessions tutoring, and it was good to have the experience to take home with me as I soon needed to find a way to start paying for a place by myself. Who knows if any of my efforts were helpful to them. Maybe she came along later and changed it all. But when I left I had more than enough to pay Sarah back, and now it wouldn't be like I had wasted all of my research stipends either, even though I knew I really had.

After I'd packed up my room, said goodbye to a guy I stumbled upon in the kitchen who I think was the same one as before, I went to the library. They were confused that I hadn't told them I'd be away but they didn't seem upset by it, maybe just a little frustrated that all the boxes had stayed out for me when they could have been put away again to make space for other requests. I tried to explain that I had been writing the whole time and that I kept think-ing I might need more material but, in the end, it turned out that I already had everything I needed. They politely congratulated me for this and that was it. The same excuse wouldn't work for my supervisors, I knew.

But that night, on the flights home, stopping first in Heathrow where I walked the lengths of the terminal in broad, purposeful steps, I drafted the chapter still missing from my thesis, the one that would basically complete it, provide its overall shape, and, I think, offer a vibrant commentary on how we read memoirs of artists, why we read them, while raising some provocative questions as to whether it's always a loser's game to ever take what anyone says about themselves at face value in the process. Nadar called his book *When I **Was** a Photographer*. Tennessee Williams called his *Memoirs*. And Mingus opted for a literary title that wasn't even subtitled with 'an autobiography'. Weren't they all, from the very outset, undermining for us the idea that we would ever be given a definitive account of their lives? This isn't such a bad thing, nor is it a puzzle. In fact, as I went on to argue in the conclusion, wasn't it a framework that could stretch beyond literature, into an understanding of how we can better relate to one another? With a greater tolerance for, in others, the wildness we all privately admit to exist within ourselves? You're not the only unreasonable person guided by their unexamined whims, pathologies, and obsessions. It's me, too. It's all of us.

And the reason I never said goodbye to her is because I didn't know what to say. That was selfish of me, and, absolutely, the thought of it can still make me sick to my stomach.

I wonder. Are you out there right now, somewhere far away from me, reading this?

If so, then this part is for you, and only you: I'm sorry.

XXII

YOU'VE PROBABLY HEARD me say that telling our landlord we were getting a divorce had been my idea. That's 100% true. And it worked exactly as intended, although I couldn't have predicted its farther-reaching consequences.

I had a hunch that Sarah would be sceptical, and, more than this, that she wouldn't have wanted to be the one to be dishonest. But after she hadn't come home for several weeks and the rent was soon due, again, I told her I didn't think it made sense for us to keep paying for a three-bedroom house that only one of us was living in. But that, also, I had thought of something that might allow us to break the lease without penalty, but it would require her to take the lead.

See, our landlord was herself a recidivist divorcée, and, based on what I often heard from Sarah whenever they ran into each other at the supermarket, a rather embittered one, full of grievance and recrimination for the most recent 'two-faced bastart' to leave her. (I have no doubt that she had good reason for this chronic bitterness. I only mention it because that was the detail that this plan sought to exploit.)

I said to Sarah that I thought if she could give the impression that they were in similar situations (Sarah was also the breadwinner, after all) our landlord might take pity on her, and then we could walk away, giving ourselves as much time as we needed to work everything out. I further thought that since we had, for a while now, been discussing buying a place outwith the city, maybe this could speed that process up, once Sarah forgave me, that is.

Sarah agreed to the plan surprisingly quickly. I had to think this was to save herself the expense, as I was never actually on the lease and couldn't be held responsible if I were to abscond. Although I think she must have recognised that I'd sooner prostrate myself before the ghastly Temple to Bezos in Dunfermline, if that's what it took, than face the shame of sticking her with the bill.[14] But I hoped I hadn't been rubbing off on her with my – what my parents only somewhat playfully referred to as – criminal nature. I loved her for her principles; for her complicated, befuddling adherence to an ethical code that was hers and hers alone.

But I wasn't surprised that our landlord agreed so readily. I knew that once Sarah turned on the charm it would be game over. Why this matters is that when Sarah's parents became aware they seized upon it as a means of restricting me from having anything to do with what happened at the end. They got our landlord to sign an affidavit to this effect and everything; and I had to admit it was, on the page, pretty persuasive. Sarah had gone into more detail with her than I would have expected, and I could see that, since we'd only discussed my plan by phone, there wasn't any proof that it was actually any plan at all. Of course, this attempt to throw me out of the considerations was quickly dismissed by the courts – case law has firmly established that even the most explicit intention to separate cannot be considered a *de facto* separation due to one party's death – but it nevertheless

---

14 It's useful as a landmark when you're driving, which is probably how the Romans thought of the Colossus of Nero.

muddied the waters of our relationship, if nowhere else then in the public's imagination as I presume was their aim at least in part.

The truth is that they had always been suspicious of our marriage, and our elopement was only one part of that. While we'd decided that getting hitched was the best course of action for us (we were young and nervous, but pragmatic as well as smitten, and knew that it was probably the only way to get Sarah's parents off her back about our living situation short of moving abroad) we weren't convinced that going through an engagement was something we had any interest in doing, especially when it would have necessarily prolonged our presentation of chasteness. On the other side, we were mindful of not needlessly hurting anyone. I could be very open with my parents about these intentions of ours, and they were supportive in their own ironical manner, not kicking up much real fuss at the thought of not bearing witness to their only child's wedding while making a show otherwise. But for Sarah, with clandestinity paramount, giving the impression of doing it spur of the moment somewhere in Scotland not only carried its own risks (it doesn't make much sense in retrospect but getting caught during the notice period was something that would have kept us up at night) it also had the capacity to make the transition more difficult for them, because they would have felt left out by not being invited.

For all these reasons, we looked abroad. And you've probably heard this part before as well, but I'll touch on it briefly for anyone who, miraculously, didn't find the minutiae as thrilling as the press seemed to.

Sarah was spending her lunch breaks researching the easiest places to get married. As during the last year of our undergrad I'd won the scholarship a major publisher had recently endowed the other university in the city where we lived which covered my fees and offered a part-time, minimally paid internship, I was in the middle of a Masters (in Art Writing, if that matters), so it made sense that she'd take the lead on this, because she'd be footing most of the bill and because it was her family we were plotting against. Gretna Green was out, but we discussed the other obvious ones: Las Vegas, Paris, Blackpool. Each of those carried significant drawbacks, however. Las Vegas was too far; Paris was too bureaucratic; and Blackpool was in Blackpool. Then she came home one day while I was poring over Duchamp's 'Texticles'.

Hello, I said as she walked over to the couch where I sat. What do you think of Philadelphia? Maybe they'd let us hold the ceremony inside the *Étant donnés*.

I opened a book of his artworks that was next to me and showed her the view through the cracks in the false door that displayed the woman's splayed body against a forested backdrop.

Her eyes squinted as she took in the image. Is that her fanny? What am I looking at here?

Funny you should ask, I said. It's a lot more complicated than it seems. I turned the page to show her a scaled model replica of the artwork on its side that demonstrated how many various lights and effects were needed to create the experience of scopophilia.

Isn't this the opposite of what we want? she asked. I thought we were trying to *avoid* people looking at us.

Good point, I said.

But I have a better idea, she nearly squealed in exultation.

Oh? I asked. Let's hear it.

First, she said, a trivia question. Where did John and Yoko get married?

I don't know, I replied. Liverpool. In a submarine. Neither of those is very enticing, I have to say.

Gibraltar!

Gibraltar, I repeated. Okay, I'm listening.

She told me there were direct flights every week and how they didn't have any formal requirements other than our birth certificates, and, best of all, only required two days' notice.

How soon can we leave? I asked.

But we thought it prudent to leave it for a little while, to give ourselves time to plant the seeds of our going away so that we could plausibly justify that it hadn't all been planned in advance, that we had unexpectedly become swept up in the moment. Sarah also wanted to include her parents in our very fraught decision to book a hotel room together. All this might seem a little extreme now but, until her death, these measures kept the peace with great assurance. You know, they had speculated that something like this might happen but were glad we'd had to foresight to consecrate our vows before anything went too far – that kind of thing. And, just to elicit such a response, we'd told them we had it done at the only Church of Scotland on The Rock. Even this was a compromise for them as Presbyterians were much too wishy-washy, but at least we hadn't gone to one of the many cathedrals which would have been a grave sacrilege.

Where we actually had it done was in the Garrison Library, a gorgeously functional and historic building, in a largeish room they'd arranged for such a purpose, with a Registrar who walked us through the process. One thing we'd forgotten was witnesses. I hadn't realise this was a real requirement; I thought it was an outdated feature of weddings that persisted for the sake of a narrative device in television dramas. But we soon found two Spanish researchers who happily agreed to a play part in the occasion.[15] It was a deliberately secular affair, and this was as much at Sarah's behest as it was mine. In fact, in the end, her parents' disbelief served only to harm their argument. Because once conclusive proof was provided (I'm not sure why our marriage certificate wasn't enough but locating the booking of the venue in Sarah's email ended any further speculation) it became clear that she wasn't in lockstep with their values, which only bolstered my claim that it was me who knew her wishes the better.

When she finally died, I tried to give to them a picture of us one of the researchers had taken on their phone, for the obituary. But they weren't having it. You wouldn't believe how happy we look in it. A little scared as well, sure. Maybe slightly manic. But that smile on her face. The thing is, of course one of the reasons – the main reason – we did it is because we felt like we had to, like it was the only way for us to live our lives comfortably. But we'd wanted to do it, too. It was odd, for a while, being the first members of friendship groups to get married, being introduced by our mates as 'the

15 I sometimes think about them and wonder if they ever think about us. There's no way they could've predicted how everything turned out. No one could.

one I was telling you about who got married'. But it was also like we were in our own little a club, a club no one else understood but envied for its secrecy, its rituals they didn't yet understand. A small gesture – the index and middle fingers held together then splitting away – to the other at a party meant just that, it was time to split. Subtly widening eyes across the table in a restaurant: *Did you hear that?* And the recognition that one fight would never be able to untie the knot we'd formed, as if between us, though we'd chosen to have the ceremony away from Scotland, was the traditional handfasting that only with strong, concerted effort could we ever leave behind. The time during which we were – I'm reluctant to write it because it sounds more formal than it was – separated, all I could think about was the promise we had made to each other, even before we were married, that we wouldn't let the other go without a fight, that we'd never give up on us.

In the end, they chose an hideously lit selfie of her taken against a bare background they'd manipulated to make her look more youthful, the same one they'd distributed for all the papers, plastered atop every story that was published it was, a photograph I eventually stopped associating with her through its overfamiliarity as it became merely a symbol of their campaign, a campaign that didn't even advance their cause when it was all said and done, only heightening a debate I'd never even wanted to partake in, didn't instigate or invite.

People sometimes ask me if I hate them. I don't. They can't help what they believe. Maybe none of us can.

XXIII

I'M NOT GOING to go into all that Norman Mailer or William S. Burroughs kind of crap and say I was trying to fix her, or that I didn't mean to, or that I don't at all resemble the person that I was portrayed as by those most willing to denigrate me after the fact. Of course I resemble him. I'm a man who was in a relationship with a woman when she died. I am also a pseudointellectual neurasthenic prone to compulsive tendencies who looks a lot like the person in the photographs that were taken in front of the court buildings. Although, typically, I wear glasses. I was told it was contacts-only for the duration of the proceedings: something about not alienating the media by giving the impression that I think I'm smarter than them.

I killed her. Okay? It was me. I did it. It would just be semantics to suggest otherwise, or the subject of the kind of literati word-play game my colleagues in the university's Interdisciplinary Café might engage in over a particularly stale coffee break. In fact, with the amount of publicity it generated for a period of time, they almost certainly have. (I wouldn't know, I haven't been back since.) The point – and this I always tried to get my PR team to stress – is the circumstances in which I killed her.

I did think it was pretty funny – at first, anyway – the way some elements of my chapter drafts were misconstrued when

216

my records were eventually overturned by the university, especially the section on 'Life, Death, and the Resurrection of the Author'. As if that had anything to do with what I was concerned with, which was dignity, responsibility, and faithfulness.

Do you know Derrida's *The Post Card*? It's a remarkable work. Most of it isn't meant to be read in a linear fashion but instead savoured passage by passage as you skip about its many pages. Ostensibly about Freud and Socrates, it's a series of one-sided missives full of yearning and piety for the passions of a hidden lover, all the while the narrator is preoccupied with the spectre of death, the only partially returned requitals we're ever likely receive in this life, and the impossibility of language to mediate between the two. It's entirely serious and yet calls itself a satire of the epistolary mode. It's clearly autobiographical but claims the details have been 'abused'. Essentially, you're never quite sure what to do with it but find yourself nonetheless gaining something as you go. The problem I created for myself was to consciously draw upon this methodology of analysis. My supervisors had first been concerned that I wasn't expansive enough, that, after building a strict vocabulary of appraisement in the blogposts I had been writing during my internship, my instincts were now overly journalistic without the theoretical heft I would need to push me into a new space of criticism. Perhaps I swung too far, into what most would probably consider obscure, though to my mind this was supposed to be generative rather than restrictive. It's not really for me to say. I remain proud of the work I did and if my words left me too open to interpretation, too open to accusations of abuse, this, to me, would only conclusively prove how correct Derrida and I were; how our utterances derive value not from their murky, ephemeral intent but, latterly, their reductive interpretation, a recipient act we could only ever play the smallest of parts in shaping, mainly by attempting to precogitate that reductivity in the first place.

I can't go much further into the legal nuances because the fact of the matter is I rarely understood them by half. They've all become public records now, anyway, so you can find everything for yourself if you really wanted to. There were so many tribunals, and appeals, and then the Lord Advocate had to get involved. At one point it looked like they were going to take it to the Supreme Court, or even the European Court of Human Rights. (Some of the less melodramatic newspapers correctly ascertained that I would have relished the latter for how upset me winning in Strasbourg was likely to make my adversaries.)

But I can try to describe what the experience was like. I can try to tell you how it felt to hear Sarah's parents say all those awful things about me, to hear them say, contrary to any legitimate medical opinion, that Sarah was still alive, as if she was a martyr on her way to beatification, if only we could find the patience to wait for her. At the end of the day, miserable people not recognising how miserable they are has always made me feel miserable, and that's how I felt about her parents. I was miserable, too, of course. But at least I always knew that I was miserable. Their denial was so total that their lashings couldn't be confined to just me, the obvious villain of the story. I was too small and lacking in authority, too monochromatic an enemy. To demonise only me would make their spiritual adversary seem so negligible and deficient that their warfare was grotesque, if not immoral. So they had to bring in our beloved NHS, the admirably restrained Scottish Government, and any pressure group rallying to a cause they'd crusaded for longer than it had ever been on our radars as a potential cause, all to soothe themselves that what had happened wasn't simply a personal tragedy of fairly ordinary circumstances but the opening battle of an almighty struggle against evil itself.

One thing that this attitude of theirs disallowed me was the opportunity to grieve. You can't grieve when you're constantly mounting a defence. For them, it was like they didn't want to believe it was happening at all, like a coma was something we all needed to slip into from time to time. Just a wee rest, eh?

Did I find it easy to understand that she had suffered an injury to the brain from which she could never recover? To accept that she'd been epileptic this whole time and none of us had ever known it, seizures being, ironically, the disorder I was afraid of more so than any other, ever since I'd read it was possible to actually will yourself into one if you allowed your mind to enter such depths of darkness and trickery? How about that she was, apparently, on a date when it'd happened, if that's what you want to call it? That he had been the last one to see her before it was lights out? That he probably kissed her unconscious body? Or cuddled her and told her that everything was all right while he waited with her for the ambulance to arrive? Even stayed at the hospital overnight, from what I heard. Who could know what it was like to receive that information besides me? And what did they do? Well, you know what they did. You saw what they did to me. Raked me over the coals, they did. Went through every little thing I'd done wrong, brought people into it who had nothing to do with anything, made me out to be a monster, like our marriage was just some gob of shite we'd stepped into: dirty and unpleasant but just as easily fixed and forgotten. And for what? It set back their own cause![16] (Let's not even get into their refusal to acknowledge that she'd been smoking pot with him which was widely thought by her medical team to have precipitated her attack. What, so the toxicologist just made that up for a laugh? Also, oh yeah, I almost forgot: he fucking admitted it.)

Besides, it's not as if, when the doctors asked me what my feelings were, I was like, oh aye go on and pull the plug, then. I wrestled with it for days. I spoke with my parents, Sarah's friends. I even went to see a priest in our local area, for God's sake. Her undead state in hospital was the most unnerving sight I had ever witnessed. Alive, but not in any way I could understand. Speaking to her body, alone, for hours, not really convinced that she could hear me. Reading Proust (her favourite author) to her for want of the stamina to go through to motions of awkwardly telling her about my day (as if my days revolved around anything other than her own precarious state).

I had to wonder if they actually blamed her for what happened in some way, or perhaps themselves. The way it all transferred onto me first – and then onto everyone else in my wake – was noteworthy for its immediacy and resoluteness, whereas most people I knew asked what more we could have done: if we should have taken her not uncommon complaints

16 So that this kind of thing never has a chance at strangling the courts again, the LibDems have recently introduced a new bill, the Sarah McIntyre Dignity in Death Act. (Cheers for dropping the 'Beard' from her name, guys. Real classy.)

of headaches more seriously; if we should have pressed her to visit a doctor that time she became 'confused' and couldn't find her way out of a locked toilet at a party, instead of finding it hysterical that someone so clever could be so daft sometimes.

If they could have been more honest with themselves, they'd probably have recognised that, in many ways, the relative silence between Sarah and me in the few weeks leading to her accident in fact exculpates me more than anything else. While we were together, she'd always been safe. She'd always been cared for.

I suppose this is something I could have been more honest with myself about as well. Perhaps if I'd tried harder to patch things up between us. If I hadn't thought that letting her stew for a bit longer was going to teach her some kind of lesson (clearly futile as I hadn't realised that she'd started seeing other people, though some of her friends have kindly tried to assure me that wasn't really the case).

These are the thoughts I turned over while everyone waited for me to make my decision, and they weren't even the thoughts that mattered. Although, again, it has to be acknowledged that it can't actually be considered a decision at all – her doctors knew exactly what they wanted to do, and if I had gone against them as well everything likely would have turned out exactly the same, except they would have been made into an even bigger scapegoat by the frenzied tabloids, and I would have had to sit on the side-lines of the biggest event of my life; the only event of my life. I had to take the responsibility, and I accepted that responsibility as her next-of-kin. No one at the hospital pressured me, and, in fact, they went out of their way to give me as much medical information on the likelihood of recovery as was available.

But all I could really go by was what I thought Sarah would have wanted. I had to imagine her in her whole person. I had to inhabit her mind, become her, sink beneath her skin, and then ask myself questions only philosophers should ever have to ask. Questions like: what is the nature of being alive; what is it that makes life worth living; what is the process of death; and on whose timeline of it do we deserve to adhere. Undoubtedly, this was all the more complicated by the thought she might believe in souls, a remembrance I kept very much to myself during this time.

When her parents found out I was leaning towards ending it, that's when they got the probate involved, setting into motion everything else that followed. Our separation, the speculation that we were soon to divorce, my affair (she refused to participate and as she was in the U.S. they couldn't compel her to), the wedding, one single time someone saw me lose my temper, her meetings with the university chaplaincy, even my many forum posts.[17] All of that was considered up for grabs, and they stopped at nothing until they ran out of road. I showed up every damn day I was needed, to oppose them at every turn, condemning myself in the process, owning up to every accusation but refusing to be bullied or shamed into letting them keep her hooked up to a machine, to exist in a dependent state of nothingness like a figment.

Even though I knew the answer, before I told them of my decision, I asked a question that had been bothering me.

---

17 For a short period of time self-styled cyber-sleuths frenetically attempted to investigate my movements across the U.S. To what end, I have no idea. I think they forgot this isn't an elaborate conspiracy. Or maybe me violating their ethical code was enough justification to warrant harassing all the people I met along the way.

The only thing that could've changed my mind, irrational though it was.

It's not possible – I mean, you've checked, right – she isn't, there's no way that she's – this is so stupid, I'm sorry – but are you entirely sure that – I know you would have said if she was – but could she be pregnant?

Because of her parents, it took nearly four months for Sarah to die. She couldn't use the toilet. She had to be bathed. I watched her nurse cry on several occasions, saying to me that it wasn't fair to Sarah, and that it wasn't fair to her either. There were so many more people involved than any of us realised. I could feel sorry for myself, and I knew that if all I truly cared about was Sarah's own wellbeing then I would have been able to accept the situation for what it was with more grace, regretful mainly that she hadn't been able to stay with us longer, for her own sake. But I had never known the capacity for selfishness in the human psyche until I was faced with a braying mob calling me a murderer, for no reason other than their own inability to face that this is all we got. It's one shot and then it's over.

It's sad for them, really. For each of us.

XXIV

ALL I HAVE to offer are the confessions of a mask. Whatever you choose to do with them has never been in my gift.

Once I had reached the part in my journal that was almost like the present, as if I had worked my way up to the point at which my circumstances stopped changing (though admittedly, there was a significant amount of time before this moment, as after so much had happened by comparison the days just plodded along endlessly) I emailed it to her in advance of our next appointment, as I would with dreams, or any stray thoughts and images that recurred like 'a cold coming we had of it' or one of Picasso's many *L'étreinte*s.

A (separate) suit to return Sarah's personal effects to me had recently come to an end so I was busy that week sorting through her things, refamiliarising myself with her trinkets and articles of clothing I hadn't seen for more than a year. At a certain point it'd become more of a matter of principle rather than any fervent wish to have these around me again, but when I'd finally worked up the courage to begin opening the boxes, I felt like they had come home, like she had been waiting for me to liberate them from her parents.

The clothes I mostly looked through, smelled, and then folded to put away again. Eventually, I knew, I would donate them, as Sarah would have wanted, but felt I could hold onto them for a bit longer if I kept the moths at bay. Her various books (she read very widely) joined mine on our shelves again. And then I hung her framed photos of us around the house, because my girlfriend understood, and frankly, anything like that to do with Sarah she knew was a potential dealbreaker for me.[18]

Getting my words onto the page had maybe helped illuminate some of my own hidden thoughts and desires. In fact, had helped me to see how plagued by desire I truly was. But connecting this to my health anxiety still seemed a bit fanciful. I suppose it was true that that time devoted each day to writing had steadied me in some way, possibly stemmed a worry or two through distraction. I now had a routine and consistent outlet for my compulsions, so much more salubrious than my previous habits online, where it was a perversely unregulated yet nonetheless tightly controlled space governed by a mass shared dopamine addiction and erratic, megalomaniacal moderators. And having this document, this 300KB computer file, where I could pour the tender influence of my restless heart made me grapple, for the first time, really, with how stories don't just appear, but are structured, restructured, and soon ripped from their individual contexts for a wider audience. My therapist, in this case.

But even the knowledge that I might, in several years' time, write about the difficulty of opening that particular box of Sarah's, and that the passage of writing it would spawn could be poignant not just for me as a newly vivid personal memory but for others as well, in their own despair, perhaps, didn't make the actual act any easier. I saved it for the last and then couldn't find the strength, so resolved to tackle it on another

18 Yes, I have a girlfriend. And, no, I don't wear a black veil each day either.

day. But I awoke in the night and knew I wouldn't get back to sleep until I had confronted it in all its base cruelty. She had kept it all to the end; this, I was sure, was proof that she hadn't believed it was through between us either. Sarah hated clutter, hated waste. And she was never particularly sentimental. Everything in here would've been the first to go when she had moved out, if it was true that we had split up, that she had any intention of planning to initiate divorce proceedings.

I cut into the tape, tried to ignore Sarah's mum's handwriting on the side that in its smallness and joined-up formality seemed to convey her steadfast refusal to back down to me, even after they'd lost everything that they initiated.[19]

It was quite dark. Only the light of one small lamp on a table in the corner casting pale hues onto the garden-facing sitting room with its heavy curtains drawn against the cold dewy air.

I don't know why I needed to physically see them, to physically touch them. I knew what was in there. I could picture the sundry assemblage right in front of me, could visualise myself in my mind's eye rummaging through it all. And yet I felt compelled to literalise the painful process, for reasons I am still not able to articulate.

First, some knitted booties. This was Sarah all over: heaviest items on the bottom, the lightest on top. My hands were shaking as I laid them aside.

---

19 They've tried to give the impression otherwise but it's a cast-iron fact that they wanted to take the life insurance policy off me as well. I guess they thought it'd make them seem superior or magnanimous if they appeared to not care about such trivialities. But the truth is that the company, probably fearing a media backlash-to-the-backlash basically ignored them and paid out too quickly to me for anything to be done about it.

Then came the small wooden toys with their coloured, manoeuvrable attachments that I manipulated with my fingers, imagining myself rolling the horse along on the carpet for our 'us', the part of Sarah that could have kept going, could have stayed a part of me. I dried my eyes on a tiny blanket and then folded it neatly.

When I reached the children's books, I glanced through a few of them, not really paying attention to their content, just scanning the illustrations, some vivid, others spare and interpretive. Something about these seemed particularly cruel. They were not just anodyne objects. Our friends and family had picked these specially to mould our 'us', to impart certain values or to set alight their creativity, to give them a future attachment of nostalgia and wistfulness.

I repacked it all, carefully at first and then with frustration, finally tossing things in wherever they would fit. *What am I going to do with this now?* I thought. Unlike every other box, it contained no memories, held no specific significance for me except regret, futility, and remorse. Its continued existence was meaningful to me for what it suggested it had meant to Sarah, but that purpose was now expended, and all it had brought me was a shivery, unshakeable feeling of powerlessness. I found a similar roll of tape in our junk drawer, closed it up again, and then returned it to its place with the others, beneath her old university jotters. I didn't want my girlfriend to see that this was what had summoned me out of bed, and I knew I wouldn't want to see it still lying out in the morning myself.

I sat on the couch and in need of a distraction turned on the television very low. The only public channel still airing was the world news. After a few minutes I grew sick of it.

227

What did I need to know any of this for? What difference could this newfound awareness of a violent territorial dispute on another continent possibly make to my life, besides heightening my sense of doom? And not just for me, either. Brexit was taking up enough bandwidth, and even that, *especially* that, I knew I had no control over, not even minimally. My MP, and every MSP, were against it, so there wasn't even any point in writing to them. All most of us could do in Scotland was look on in horror. Sarah wouldn't have felt that way. She would have seen the seismic event for what it was, which was something very small, a blip in the wake of much greater forces. As always, Sarah.

In the afternoon I had my appointment, so I left the TV on but turned the sound all the way off, and then turned off the lamp. I looked at the presenters sideways, blurry, speaking their nothings, and then, after who knows how much time, fell to a rotten sleep.

I've started what you sent to me, she said when we had both sat down. But you're going to need to give me more time with it. It's much longer than I had expected – and bravo for that. I hope this is okay.

Um, sure, I replied. But I figured that's what we would talk about, so I don't have anything else planned for us to discuss.

Let's talk about you, she said with a slightly mischievous twinkle in her eye. How are you? How was your week?

It was okay, I said.

'Okay'? she repeated, looking pleased. You normally say 'not bad' or 'meh'. It must have been a good one.

How was your week? I asked, realising as I said it that this might have been a question that I'd never asked her. It seems like you're in a good mood. Not that you're ever in a bad mood, but, just, happier or something. More animated.

I'm always happy when my patients are happy, she said, smiling.

I made a show of looking around and behind me. You don't mean me, do you? I asked.

Of course I do, Miles. I won't take any credit for it, but you've seemed much more balanced these past few weeks. I think we're making real progress here.

All right, I said. I guess I have to tell you this now but I'm sorry if it disappoints you. In actual fact I had a terrible week.

Tell me about how it was terrible, she said.

I told her about Sarah's parents finally being instructed to hand over her things or risk jail time, the movers they sent seeming deliberately obtuse when they asked whose it was, and my girlfriend trying not to cry as I winced and swore every time they roughly set a box down, or threw down as the case often was. I said that now that I had it all, I wasn't sure if I wanted it. I mentioned looking through the baby stuff which – looking at the clock – I remembered had happened less than twelve hours beforehand.

When I had finished, she let my words hang there for a moment and then said, That does sound difficult.

I nodded and raised my eyebrows.

She continued, But what I mean when I say that you seem more balanced – or even that you've had a good week, for that matter – isn't that good things are happening to you. Rather that you're able to handle the things that happen to you better, good and bad. You're coping. That's what I like to see. You haven't mentioned struggling with your anxiety or feeling ill, for example.

Maybe so, I said. Last night, though. It wasn't a cakewalk, like.

You're still mourning Sarah's miscarriages. This is a way to mourn Sarah. Mourning Sarah is a way to mourn yourself. And that's okay. It's all connected. Do you see?

Maybe, I replied.

Let's speak more about last night. If you wish to. What did they mean to you, these things?

Well, nothing, really, I said. Maybe that was what bothered me.

You seemed to notice one book in particular, she said.

I did? I don't remember saying that.

The one you flicked through. You said, she looked down at the pad in front of her, it wasn't like the others because it didn't seem to have any story or message. What book was it? Can you remember?

Oh, that one, I said. *The Monster at the End of this Book*, I think it was called. Something to do with Sesame Street, which I don't have much familiarity with, I have to say. It's very American, isn't it?

My son loved that book! she exclaimed, almost in spite of herself it seemed. (I had no idea she had a son.)

The drawings were pretty cute, I admitted. But I didn't really understand what it was trying to convey. Maybe I took it too literally. Who is he was afraid of?

She closed her eyes, seeming to conjure it before her as she remembered, turning the pages over in her mind.

Yes, she said to herself.

She smiled again, a warm, parental smile of seemingly genuine benevolence and affection.

I think you should read it again, she said.

Really? I asked. Why?

I know I've given you a lot of homework, she said. But it won't take you long, and if it doesn't mean anything to you in the end, that's okay. In the meantime, I'll be reading your – what did you call it in our first session? Oh, yes. Your autofiction.

I looked to the clock again. Only forty minutes or so had passed.

Did you want to stop? I asked.

I think so, she said. This happens sometimes. Let's reconvene next week, when I think we'll have more for us to go over. Is that okay with you?

It's fine, I said, a little surprised, though something in me seemed to suggest that ending here felt right to me too.

Do take another look at *The Monster at the End of This Book*, she said. And take care of yourself, Miles.

As we walked to her door, I tried to hand her the money I owed for the week but she refused to accept it, saying it wasn't necessary if we ended early. I took the stairs down and walked to a park where I bought a coffee and thought about the class I was due to teach in an hour, Gothic Fictions in the Scottish City and Country, a cross-disciplinary topic for literature or history students that I didn't feel very much qualified to guide them through but had been compelled to accept on behalf of a permanently-contracted colleague who'd be going on maternity leave in the middle of term. I opened my bag and took out my notepad, sketching for myself the discussion questions I would ask, questions I hoped the answers to might, by the end, carry them towards some kind of understanding for us all.

When the day was through, I ambled home and called for my girlfriend. She wasn't in but had, I saw, left me a message saying she was meeting a friend for dinner and that I could help myself to a curry she'd made which was still on the hob. First, I changed into more comfortable clothes and then cracked open a beer. *Cocktail hour*, I thought. *Chin-chin*.

After I'd done my rounds of Sarah's photos, stopping at the one she'd loved so much, because we looked to be the same height when, beneath the frame, she was standing as tall as she could on her tiptoes, I went into the living room and sat down. It could still make me feel glowy, not just because it was a nice photo of us, but because it was her favourite, and contained a secret meaning only either of us could decipher. I looked over to the boxes again, the one hidden amongst the others jumping out at me as if it was a different colour to them.

After negotiating it from beneath the pile, I found the book at the bottom and in doing so was surprised that I had mentioned it to the therapist at all. Again, it didn't strike me as remarkable, except that the drawings of 'Loveable, Furry Old Grover' had a certain Muppet-y charm. He looked soft, and I could see that his long limbs and oval-shaped body would hold some snuggly appeal.

The premise, as I quickly gathered now, was that Grover does not want you or your child to continue turning the pages, because he knows from the title that there is a monster at the end of the book, which he is afraid of. But the act of reading being what it is, his request is an ontological impossibility: to accept Grover's demand that you stop only withdraws yourself from his predicament, thereby delaying the proceedings rather than providing any real aid to him.

To wit, when you open the book again, you'll find that he remains trapped in the same position. The only way to end his suffering is to usher him onwards with you. However, the more that you progress, the more and more distressed he becomes at your progression, even attempting a series of metafictional illusions to delay the inevitable, appearing to board the pages away, gluing them together. Finally, at the book's conclusion – when his fear is at its most acute, as he is begging that you stop – Grover discovers that monster is himself. Loveable, Furry Old Grover had been the monster waiting at the end of the book the entire time.

I drained what was left of my can and walked over to look out of the window, onto an ordinary scene in front of the bus stop next to the tenement flat where I now stayed: a couple of people milling about; a bit of litter; some wildflowers growing amongst the weeds of an untended patch of grass next to the pavement. I thought of her smile as we'd sat across from each other, the way that she had closed her eyes and said Yes to herself like that, like she had found the perfect gift for me and couldn't wait to give it.

I remained there a while longer as the sun set and then turned away, walked into the kitchen, and put the burner back on. Soon the kitchen filled with the smells of curry.

Each of us is the monster in the end. The key to living is accepting that we are monsters and yet loveable as well. This, I could now see, was the ultimate truth of all literature.

XXV

THIS SECTION IS one that, originally, I deleted not long after writing. It was sometime later that I retrieved it from my computer's rubbish, amongst the old course materials, thesis drafts, the preparation questions I asked myself and completed in advance of my *viva voce* which I managed to attend and pass, despite all the ongoing unpleasantness.

I think it was intended as a record. At the time, I was recording every interaction I had with Sarah's parents in some way. Usually recording them through the voice app on my phone, but not always if that wasn't possible. I'm not sure if there are any legal implications to this but I wasn't concerned because it was they who'd made it a matter of public interest, not I, and if they pushed me into it, I'd just sell my own story. I got rid of most of those once they didn't have much use, once I realised that any story I sold wouldn't be about them at all. But I had already thrown this file away by then, I think because they hadn't factored in it very much to begin with, and because what it was attempting to record was something that wasn't recordable at all, something that neither words nor sound would have ever been able to capture. This isn't a denial or forgetting, no, no. More an acknowledgement of my own limitations, my fundamental inadequacy to the task. Eventually, I realised that, imperfect though it may be, it still had value to me, even if that value was based purely on the recognition that there was no perfect telling, no objectively possible narrative. There was only the embodied experience of the moment, a moment which had already taken place. It therefore makes sense to me that I should reproduce it here, correcting some of the errors I made in the process, to provide that same bathetic catharsis for you, for your own recognition of a pain that is too profound to be expressed in writing.

~~I am jolted awake by my phone vibrating. It's the lawyer calling. My involvement has finished so far as I'm aware, so I assume that this is it. That we have come (finally) to the definitive ruling that none of us had any doubts about but were required to suffer through multiple appeals for. I have always been passionately supportive of the judicial process in all its lethargic scope for those who are aggrieved by systems they perceive as unfair but even I am tried by these abuses of it. I don't know what I feel besides a rush, an overwhelming sense of relief intermingling with Fear.~~

~~Sarah's parents have been barred from witnessing — only I am given permission to overrule this. All my family and friends advise against it. The NHS has concurred in not so many words, suggestively reminding me that it will be an emotional time for everyone and that there could be some aspects to her final moments that could appear like Signs of Life, as though she is fighting against us.~~

~~Bitter though I am — Bitterness has governed every aspect of this process — I cannot be the one to deny them whatever sense of closure they might be able to glean from being in the~~

room with us. I wish that aspect of the ruling had been more ironclad: it's one impossible choice on top of another and I wish that it was out of my hands.

Stuart and I spoke on the phone this evening. I let him know my thoughts on the matter. He sounded tersely grateful, almost like he wanted to be more open with me but wasn't able to. I suspect Lou was with him. I'm reserving the right to kick them out if they are disruptive. Of course, the hospital would do that anyway. Oh fuck, they better not try to actually stop it. Why is this only occurring to me now?

Everyone seems to want this to move as quickly as possible. I had felt the same until the prospect was no longer a theoretical one. It's a matter of resources for most of them, I suppose.

Sarah's parents are still speaking about me to the press. They have completely supplanted Sarah with me in the focus of their myriad institutional criticisms. That's not something I can fix for them but it's Depressing to think they don't know how much it chimes with Sarah's most frequent annoyances over how they treated her.

I'm going by myself. My parents will be waiting in a pub nearby.

Can't eat but not eating makes me feel sick. Did a dumb thing in the shower where I played a playlist of Sarah's favourite songs that I made. Only went and got me sobbing in there, didn't it. Dunno what I was thinking. Useless gesture, and for what purpose other than provoke my own emotional reaction? As if I have to remind myself how much I'm Hurting. Prove to my foggy reflection that I still care and that I'm not doing this because I want to. Might be late now.

Lou has just sent me a text to say they're bringing the pastor who baptised Sarah. I told them that wasn't on, and it's not even my rule. He wouldn't be allowed into that wing of the hospital, anyway. I don't know why I have to think of everything for these people who have spent so much time performatively 'forgiving' me. I tell her there's probably someone in pastoral care from the hospital who could be there, knowing they won't go for it.

Taxi driver asked me if I'm going in for myself or visiting someone. I said visiting.

Shaking all over. Mind is on Fire. I shouldn't have done this. Why couldn't she have just died. Feels like everyone in the hospital today is here specially for this purpose – maybe to stop me from asking them (or myself) too many questions. I keep getting led every which way. They don't seem to want me to go straight into the room for some reason. I don't think they're ready.

Sitting here, can't breathe. Stand up to pace around but room is too small. When I told a nurse I had a headache and wanted some ibuprofen, she said a doctor would have to come in and prescribe it to me first so I told them not to bother. Everything is Oppressive.

It's the brightest day the city has seen in weeks. The sun is pouring into this entire wing. Guess God won't be crying or whatever shite it is people like that tell themselves.

Text from my wee cousin to say she's thinking about me today. Cheers, darling. Which one are you again? I write back and say thanks xx. It means Nothing to me. Almost none of this does.

The doctors are ready. The nurse who has cried in front of me several times won't look at me in the eye today for some reason. Maybe all the stuff about me that's going round has got to her. Oh well. Crosses my mind how twisted it would be to ask her out while we're walking. Obviously, I would never. Feels Weird that I even thought that, even though it's only in my own head, even though I know it's the most private joke possible. Even if there's an afterlife presumably Sarah is still trapped in purgatory. She can't hear me yet.

Just want this over with then feel Guilty because that means I want my wife to die sooner. Theme of the past however many months. I am crying now, mostly out of frustration, which everyone seems to be ignoring. Wish I had a sibling or something. A twin.

Sarah's parents approach from the opposite way in the hall. Now I understand what that holding pen was about: keeping us separated. Doctor in front of them looks annoyed. Wonder if the chief justice or whoever it was thought about what saying it was up to me if they came really meant in practice. Makes me wonder if this is an elaborate Social Experiment.

If Sarah was okay, I wouldn't mind, honest. Even if she was in on it. I don't look at them or say anything. No point.

I'm being Punished. We were in an exclusive relationship and I violated that. Whatever excuses I might make are just that: excuses. I've never taken responsibility for anything in my life. Here's the part where I make a promise that I'm going to turn my life around or something. No bargain seems forthcoming.

We're outside the room. Ask a doctor if she can prescribe me something. She immediately looks away like I've just posed some massive inconvenience on everyone so I say sorry. Almost said, Sorry I'm Drunk, which would have been weird because I'm definitely not.

Heart is bursting. It's kind of Sad that the human body only has so many ways of processing experiences. It feels exactly like I'm about to deliver a conference paper.

Somebody says Everybody ready? and then opens Her door before any of us responds. I have been here so many times now the room is as familiar to me as my own bedroom. Sarah is like a piece of furniture there, a houseplant.

There are some extra chairs for us. This is very macabre. I didn't try to picture this in advance but if I did it wouldn't have looked anything like this. It's like she's going to be executed. Sarah looks the same. Except Brighter? Did someone put makeup on her? I don't know what to feel because — intellectually, sentimentally, bodily — I don't believe it's really Her. She's already dead. She died in the ambulance. And yet.

They are openly weeping at the sight of Her. I was crying before but now I can't seem to. I wonder why I was so ambiguous about asking the doctor to prescribe me something. Was I insinuating or did she correctly assume that I wanted a painkiller?

Different doctor is going through something he has clearly rehearsed about what is about to happen. I can't follow it but I don't think it's for my benefit. Sarah's parents are being remarkably restrained, considering what I think everyone was expecting.

This is happening very quickly. I'm asked if I want to say anything. Not something I planned for. I awkwardly say no and then ask if it is okay if for me to kiss her. I stand up feeling extremely Selfconscious, bend down and kiss her forehead and whisper that I love her in her ear. What else is there to say?

Now Sarah's parents are asked if they want to say anything. Great. Mumbo-jumbo about Christ forgiving us all or something. No-one is listening but we're all Pretending to.

Doctor tells us what he's about to do, which is turn one whirring machine off while some other ones keep going. Reminds us all that no-one can be sure how long this will take but they will be standing there with us. Pointedly reiterates that her brain function has been and remains Zero.

Not sure if I am supposed to feel anything yet. She's still breathing. The phrase Grief in the Postmodern Age passes

~~through me, like I'm spontaneously preparing the bullshit journal article I'll write about this one day.~~

~~Waiting for Death. She's still breathing. Several minutes pass. A restless sort of tedium sets in.~~

~~Then her eyelids start fluttering. I've seen this a few times before and read that it could be caused by seizures that persist even while she's comatose. The idea that some part of her could be continuing to Suffer only strengthened my resolve. Unsurprisingly Sarah's parents don't feel this way. She's fighting it! they yell.~~

~~The scene starts playing out, the one we all rehearsed. A security guard was outside the whole time. He's alerted by their yelling and walks into the room almost as soon as they start kicking off. I remain seated, feeling completely Detached from their pursuit of the dramatic moment.~~

~~Can't you just leave her now? Lou starts to sob. Stuart is being restrained. One of the doctors looks proper angry. I recognise my Mistake but a part of me thinks this is what needed to happen. Sarah's eyes have stopped moving but it's too late. Her parents are escorted out.~~

~~Things are under control again and most of the people in the room leave. It's explained to me that if nothing changes in the next hour or so there are other measures that will be taken.~~

~~It's just me and a nurse now. I ask for a couple of minutes alone. He looks unsure but I think recognises that I don't~~

~~have any Desire to intervene in their process, so walks out but stays where he can still look through a bit of glass.~~

~~For the first time I feel like I am allowed to Grieve. I know that nothing has really changed but I find myself now allowed to feel completely sorry for myself, which I knew was all Sarah believed mourning rituals were for: those still living. I do have something to say now. I'm sorry, I say, through my sobs. I'm sorry for wasting all your time. Your entire adult life spent with me. I didn't deserve it, I say to her. I didn't deserve you.~~

~~Feels like only a minute or two has passed but a few come back in to switch off another machine. Or turn one on. I'm not sure. They check her vital signs. Blood oxygen is lowering, one person says to another, like they're checking on something they're cooking. Like a Vegetable, I guess.~~

~~All the colour is draining from Her. I'm glad Sarah's parents aren't here. This is it. At some point something is going to change. She will, officially, Die. I know that when that happens that I will be fundamentally unchanged and yet it is still significant to me. I'm glad I'm unmedicated for this. I think of my parents grimly drinking a lager in a place that'll be called The Happy Hedgehog or whatever they name those horrible places next to hospitals.~~

~~Colour must be draining from me now. Watching this has become Morbid and Gruesome. I have to look away. I want to leave but feel like I'll regret it if I do. Imagine what it'd be like to be in this room with me. Wonder what they think. Start welling up again at this stupid thought.~~

~~Some beeping happens and there's a bit of chatter. I'm at the window looking at the green grass of the lawn where a family is having a makeshift picnic when someone touches my arm. Sarah is Dead now, I'm told.~~

~~This is the last time that I'll see her. There's a memorial service planned for after she's been cremated but I'm not going to any of it. I'm not sure I was invited, now that I think about it.~~

~~It seems fatuous to say so, but that's life for you. Goodbye, Sarah. I'll miss you forever.~~

~~I am Extinguished.~~

That's where I ended it.

And I did go to the service, in the end. It was a staid affair but her friends who organised it were nice to me and it was the kind of send-off that she would have wanted, understated and optimistic. I read a poem, one of Sarah's favourites: 'The Shampoo' by Elizabeth Bishop. It felt so right in that moment, and looking to the faces of those before me, I thought it seemed to move them as well. Maybe it was wrong to suggest that writing as a medium is incapable of penetrating certain, more extreme or complicated qualities of feeling. Maybe it just requires a different kind of writing altogether.

XXVI

THE WEEKS WERE passing more quickly, days blurring together, the occasional bout of anxiety serving to mainly remind me how long it had been since my last one – a couple of deep breaths and it was gone again; the thin resolution to cut back on the coffee. I had slipped back into being an irrelevance, and I didn't get the impression that any of my students were much fussed over who I was, if they had ever known to begin with. I tried to keep up with their reading and was lucky that the lecturer who'd designed the module was able to talk me through their syllabus so that there wasn't any crucial material I wasn't at least directing them towards. But I was learning a lot in the process: about Scotland, about an entirely new (to me) tradition of fiction, and a sphere of the imagination that was more redolent with scepticism, doubt, and deliberate provocation than any I had previously studied.

As usual, I hopped onto the subway from campus in the direction of her urbanly suburban avenue, bringing with me some extra cash to give to her for our session that had been cut short, which I had suddenly remembered feeling I owed her after the fact. It was still time that she had blocked out for me, and I had ended up getting a lot out of it. Later that same night I had showed my girlfriend what was in the many boxes, making an effort to include her more in what went on inside of my head while I looked through their contents, and I could tell that she appreciated it. I had wanted to do this for myself, too. It helped me feel like I wasn't a basket case, like I was just a guy who'd got caught up in some unusually tragic circumstances but still had the majority of his life ahead of him. There was a lot I still needed to forgive myself for – or maybe simply more acceptance of the past being the past, inalterable and refractive – but this is something I felt would come in time.

I figured that she would agree with this, that we were both anticipating this as our last session together.

On the stairs I started to feel a little apprehensive wondering what she'd say about the journal I'd put together for her, which she had emailed to tell me that she had finished. We hadn't spoken about it much since the beginning, and in the intervening weeks it had remained a mostly abstract endeavour I either was or was not making progress on, rather than something we'd discuss in terms of approach or content. Latterly, she'd mention some aspects of it while she was reading, ask percipient questions regarding how I felt about some of the events now that more time had passed. I just hoped I hadn't done it wrong.

She was ready for me at the door and welcomed me in. Again, she seemed pleased to see me (or perhaps she'd say she was pleased to see how I was starting to see myself?) and I thought that it was good to be meeting on a level in which we both understood that I'd be saying farewell to her, to therapy.

How was your week? I asked when we had sat down.

She laughed. It was fine, she said. And how was yours?

It was okay, I said.

We made some chitchat about for several minutes about how the new term was going before I said, I reread that children's book like you told me to, the one you said that your son liked. I actually read it that same night but I kept forgetting to mention it.

And? she asked, looking expectantly at me.

And I think I took away from it what you wanted me to.

She smiled. You're not a bad person, Miles.

We looked at each other for a moment, each of us perhaps revelling in her revealing phrasing, in the moment of quiet reflection we could share.

But am I a good one? I finally asked.

That you're asking would, to me, suggest that the answer is yes. But what I think isn't particularly meaningful, not compared with what you think.

I paused. I think I'm still working that one out, I said.

That's okay too, she replied. But you'd first have to define what being a good person means to you. Not something we'd be able to do in one hour, I don't think.

Probably not, I agreed.

Would you like to talk about your journal now?

Sure, I said. I guess that's been kind of the project of this whole thing, right?

It's funny you should put it that way, she said. This is something I suggest to everyone I see when we start out. For some it works, for others not so much. But it's a way to train one's eye on the schema of whatever is bothering them, however they might define that. All of which is to say I wasn't expecting you to give the task such – what's the best way to put this – such a literary approach.

I began to blush.

It's a bit much, eh? I said. I mean, you can hardly blame me. I told you I was teaching a course on autofiction.

I have to say, she said, it read like more than that to me.

My blush deepened.

What do you mean? I asked.

I did encourage you to use your name, and to use Sarah's name. I always say this because I think people can get hung up on who's who or what represents what whenever they're writing for themselves − I find it simplifies things to dispense with any need for equivocation while remaining within the experience of what is true for them: what *feels* true. A *nom de plume* would distance you from that. Do you see what I mean?

Yes, I said. But I did do that. Do you mean that you think that I adhered too much to what actually happened? That I didn't stray far enough beyond the truth? Because—

No, she said. I couldn't be the one to judge that, anyway. The gap between whatever has gone on and what you have told me here could be vast; it could be tiny. That's not something I'd have any knowledge of. Although it did intrigue me that you titled what you did. Did you want to speak to that?

Oh, I said. I guess it's a joke.

That Happened? she asked, looking confused.

Yeah, so, like, say somebody writes a story about themselves online. It could be something someone said to them, or something funny or interesting that they said to someone else, or maybe it's just an entertaining scene that they've witnessed. You'll often see other people respond to these anecdotes and they'll say, 'that happened', or some variation on that.

Which they mean ironically, I take it, she said, based on your intonation.

Exactly, I replied. And because these are often fairly mundane circumstances to begin with, there's actually been a kind of a backlash to that recently. Like, why couldn't this have happened? Why do so many people have difficulty believing that witty or unusual or miraculous things occur, occur regularly even?

Why can't we accept that it's the extraordinary that's often ordinary, she said.

Right, I replied. And it doesn't really matter one way or another anyway. My story, it's already so unbelievable. But it happened. It really happened, you know? So, for me, using that title – although I have to admit I didn't give it as much thought as it probably sounds like here; it just occurred to me when I was midway through – is my acknowledgement of that liminal space others would likely see it as inhabiting. When it's really just me; this is just my life.

Yes, she said. We see this in the news every day. Whatever makes the top headline must be on some level abnormal, otherwise it wouldn't be there. Yet this ritual persists day after day. And the people who are involved – British Man Trapped in Cave Abroad – what are their stories? How often do any of us stop to ask?

I think that's what I'm trying to take back, I said. Everybody used everything they could learn about Sarah and me and they distorted it for their own purposes. By the end it wasn't even about her. You can say what I've written is literary; I wrote it in the only way I knew. You say you don't know how big or small the gap is between fact and fiction; I can tell you that, against my best intentions, every word of it is true.

248

She nodded. I understand, she said. But to go back to what I was trying to touch on before, though: what I wanted to ask you about was the perspective you chose.

What about it? I asked.

Well, she said, it's – isn't it Alazon?

I must have appeared confused because she continued.

Your pseudonym? You told me about Alazon in one of our first sessions.

I said, I understand who you're talking about. I think I'm just not sure what you mean. Everything that I wrote was in the first-person.

Yes, she said. That's true. I'm sorry. Maybe I'm not making very much sense. But isn't what you gave to me – I know that what you've written is true; and this doesn't obviate that – the impressions of the events from this self-aggrandising version of you?

She flicked through the notes in front of her. '…deliberately setting himself out for ridicule', she read aloud.

I don't know, I replied. That could be a more charitable reading of it. Than it all just being a reflection of my normal thought processes, I mean. But I don't want to lie to you and say that I did that deliberately. I didn't.

Authors aren't necessarily the best interpreters of their own writing, she said.

They usually aren't, I said. I think I can see why now. The kind of vulnerability and self-knowledge that would require is immense. Perhaps too immense for us any of us, mortals or otherwise.

Don't you think that's what we do here? she asked. Engage in a process of revealing vulnerabilities and deepening self-knowledge?

You could say that, I replied. I see what you mean. Although I think I resisted it for most of our time together.

I think one of the reasons I wanted to clarify what I was interpreting as Alazon's perspective in your story is because I was curious to know how conscious you were of that process, and how you're feeling about it now. You say you might have resisted some of it, but you've shared a lot of yourself with me, and I'm grateful for that. But have you given any thought to the next steps?

Um, I said, stalling. I kind of figured this was it. Maybe I've been too literal about everything, but you said yourself that I seem like I'm in a better place than I was when we started. Much better. I know I'm not cured, or anything. I'm still me.

She laughed at this, and then I began to laugh, although I hadn't actually meant it as a joke.

But, I continued, I don't feel so concerned with my own health any more, which is why I'd wanted help in the first place. I still get some worries, and I'd always prefer to avoid head injuries, internal bleeding, that kind of thing. But that feels more routine to me now, more like it's something to be aware of without obsessing over. I can hold the idea in my mind without being terrified of it. Obviously, a lot more than only that has changed for me in this room, and I'm the one who's grateful, grateful for how you've helped me change the way think about Sarah. I'll always be grateful for that. It's like I can just love her again, without all the other shite coming into it. And I can start to move on from her as well. That sounds like a paradox, but I'm starting to recognise that paradox as a gift. If I hadn't come here, I'd fret over those seemingly oppositional forces for maybe the rest of my life.

I am only a sounding board, she said, putting her hands up. I've made some connections for you, perhaps prodded you into places you might not have gone to alone once or twice. But the work that's been done is your own. Show that gratitude to yourself.

Okay, I said, knowing that I probably wouldn't. That I probably couldn't. That however I looked back on this epilogue to the sorry saga, however many years into the future, it'd always be in the context of someone saving me from myself, saving me by listening to me.

However, you want to proceed is, of course, your decision, she said. I certainly appreciate what you've said here and if you feel equipped to face the world with a new understanding of yourself that will aid you as you go on, then you have my full support. But from my vantage, our work has only begun.

Really? I asked.

This is a process that can last a lifetime, she said. I'm not telling you that you should engage with it in that way if you don't want to, but the point I'm making is that when you think about it, we've just scratched the surface. We all have our own wounds. The one we've discussed here was a gaping one, and perhaps we've sutured it for now. But its enormity shouldn't obscure the many smaller wounds you might have – that we all have, accumulated through our years of struggling to relate to others.

I don't doubt that you're right, I said. But I can't just keep doing this. At some point I have to go out and live my life; stop questioning everything. You'd probably say that those two aren't incompatible. But I think they are for me, at least in the short-term.

Then go, she said, and smiled as she did. If you're no longer mourning for yourself, then perhaps you're correct. I'll still be here if you ever change your mind.

It was slightly awkward when we stood, the formality of the occasion masking the affection we'd gained for each other. We'd never touched, and we weren't going to violate that distance we'd established at this late stage.

Smaller wounds.

My parents. The vanishing number of true friendships I was able to maintain. The wary relationships I now had to what used to be some of my favourite activities: reading, sex, daydreaming. Compulsive habits not yet stamped out, the ways my mind could still torment me. *What if you're epileptic and you don't know it, either?*

I tried to hand her the money, all the notes sticking out of my fist like the so many little slips of plastic that they were. Any therapist must feel like a kind of prostitute on some level, and it was possible, I figured, that I has been exacerbating this feeling for her by refusing a passive exchange conducted by bank transfer. Nothing to do about it now.

She refused them, shaking her head, while I wondered about silly things like propriety, professionalism, and remuneration. I thanked her and turned to go.

Goodbye, I said.

Goodbye, Miles, she said. I hope that we will meet again, in whatever setting you choose.

Yes, I replied.

Students poured into the subway station alongside me; as we waited all of us were all pressed stomach to rucksack. Today, we'd be discussing Victor Frankenstein's sojourn to a 'miserable hut' on Orkney, where the winds on the water are 'but as the play of a lively infant'; his worries there for an impending global disaster, that any rejection by the creation of a female companion towards her intended lover could spell the individual sowing of chaos for them both, or, worse still, their union resulting in a new race of devils. 'I trembled', the doctor writes, 'and my heart failed within me…'

I wasn't sure how to take this in the context as it was to be delivered but I had downloaded an article tying to novel to the British constitution and hoped a diligent skim on the way to the university might yield some answers. I texted the lecturer to ask if she was able to meet before the class, but she told me she wasn't feeling well and had gone back home after only an hour in her office. I responded to say that I was sorry to hear that but that I was confident that they'd have more to say on it than I did in any case.

Once we got on, two first-years standing next to me began chatting about a boy they'd met the night before. How they both thought that he was handsome, smart, and so funny. I could feel a pang of jealousy winding its way through my body. When they alighted, I watched them walk off, up the stairs, to wherever it was they were going. A few seconds later, the doors closed, hurtling us further down the line, taking me away from them yet back towards them as well.

I didn't even take the article out of my bag, and instead sat there, looking at everyone. More wounds than I could count.

XXVII

AFTER CLASS, a few students lingered to ask me questions about their assessment which was due the following week; what would I say the best way to approach it was if they hadn't started it yet and would they be penalised for incorporating multiple texts rather than writing on just one of them as the brief seemed to suggest? I tried to be helpful without conveying the extent of ambivalence I felt towards their plight. *Put on the show*, I thought. *Deliver to them what they're expecting and then you can leave.*

Outside, just as I was stepping away from the New Centre for Research in the Humanities – a construction that the university frequently boasted, for some reason, about how much it had cost – the acting head of the department hailed me to say that a new position was being created to support the American Studies network, and, given the experience I'd accrued in the field, it was hoped that I'd apply, especially given how teaching-focused everyone had to be these days when I was always returning strong feedback numbers.

In my experience, I joked, high scores aren't that difficult to attain if you treat the students like they're people.

The acting head of the department stared blankly at me and then said, Yes. Quite right, too. We've been surprised by how popular the old transatlantic Masters programme has become. Perhaps it's you who's been funnelling them all there. All right, then. Do let me know if you need an internal reference.

Making my way again, I sighed. It would be good to have a permanent contract, and I believed it was only right that I should be offered one. But positioning myself in that way, as a dedicated Americanist, felt as much like an opportunity as it did a jail sentence. I knew that if I took on the role that I'd never leave it, and the mere thought of this attachment made me uneasy. But I'd already seen the ad and knew I had only a few weeks left to deliberate. And I also knew when it came to it that I'd probably apply anyway. Or maybe not.

I decided to walk home, having had enough of life in the underground for one day, and I also thought that I might stop at the chemist on my way.

After their assessments, the students would read *Strange Case of Dr Jekyll and Mr Hyde*, a book I had yet to start myself. Though the story is widely familiar, I wondered what it was about; not what happened in it, but what it was really about. While I could draw some immediate parallels to various dualities or bifurcations that were still very much alive in Scotland (political, cultural, religious) these all seemed somewhat facile, and I figured the students were intended to make more of it than a straightforward representation of good versus evil or mere reflection of something basic like competing nationalisms. I thought of Sarah, and then the image of an ouroboros popped into my head. Something to remember for my next appointment. Or, hang on, I suddenly remembered, I don't have one scheduled actually. Oh well. Probably nothing to that, anyway.

Sarah.

At the chemist I chose a variety of medicines to cover most of the basic eventualities, and then continued my walk. At one of the bridges, I stopped and looked to the water. I must have been stood there for several minutes, or perhaps had allowed my eyes to glaze over to maladaptive effect, because the next thing I knew someone was right next to me asking if I was okay.

Startled, I replied yes, that I was fine. And then I thanked them for checking.

I pressed on. A dark cloud began to spit on me, and I was growing colder in my threadbare, professorial jumper. Neddy. I struggled to remember his second name. Then, Neddy Merrill. *That's right*, I thought, as I crossed through an unlit pedestrian tunnel to the other side of the road, some naughty boys scattering at the sight of me. *I'll keep walking and it'll be like the Cheever story: before I can make it home, I'll be an old man, shuddering and in pain.*

It wasn't to be. In this part of Scotland the sun will shine on you as quickly as the rain can fall, and on the other side I found myself in a bright patch of light filtering through the turning leaves, only the fewest of drops finding their way through the trees onto my head.

I had thrown my portion of Sarah's ashes on a day like today, from the top a hill we'd climbed a few times. Nothing momentous between us had ever happened there but it reminded me of the easy way we'd had with each other, how rarely we failed to have a good time when we were together. Perhaps that's what had worried her when she'd asked me if believed in souls. That I might not have believed that we were soulmates. Not saying yes was just another regret now, appended to end of a list already too long. I'd let my obdurate resistance to any cliché obscure what I really believed, which was that if any such thing could exist then it would certainly have to include us. But I had to concede that many other people would think that she'd got a raw deal ending up with me. Not something to be helped, I supposed.

Once I turned the corner I could see the top-floor flat in the distance. It was a far cry from the house where Sarah and I had stayed but at this point that was by choice. With her life insurance policy paid out, I could live almost anywhere in the city that I'd want to. But it was mostly untouched, used mainly to cover funeral expenditures and estate fees. Something about her parents' insistence it go to them had made me even less likely do anything conspicuous with it. Still, I checked the balance regularly, admired its benign growth in a fixed-rate savings account, and then felt guilty for this admiration though mollified that guilt by reassuring myself that at least it wasn't in stocks and shares. Maybe that's what I thought Sarah would do if our roles were reversed, though this comparison wasn't possible for a number of reasons, more than I'd ever realise.

On the pavement, just a few metres away from the door, I slipped on some muddy detritus and fell backward. As my back made contact with ground, I instinctively jerked my head up. Two people ran over to me from the bus stop.

Are you okay? they asked, helping me up.

I'm fine, I said. And then, twisting my neck this way and that, I started to laugh. It's only whiplash.

You sure? they asked. You don't need us to call anyone?

No, it's just a bit sore, I replied. I only live just here. Cheers, though. I'll make it.

In the close I met Carl, an indigent man who frequently retired here during inclement weather.

Hey Carl, I said. How's it going?

Scattered showers, he replied. Scattered showers.

Ah. I was caught in one of those earlier.

Il pleut, he said and then dazzled the air with his fingers as he moved his hands from above his head to below it.

Non, I replied as I continued up the stairs. *Pas pour le moment.*

I could tell when I opened that door that my girlfriend was still in. The lights were on and her jacket was in its usual spot over the handlebars of her bike which had rested in the hall for several months now.

Hiya, I called.

Hiya, she shouted back.

I took off my shoes and, as I did, she came through, smiling and kissing me.

Class okay? she asked.

It was fine, I said. They spent most of it talking about Frankenstein's particular fears of the female creature and her agency. They were tying this to the burgeoning women's suffrage movement and such. Is that what you wanted?

Those dates don't line up very neatly, she said, looking away as well as quite striking as she became engrossed once again in her material. But it's quite original, I suppose. And why not?

Anyway, why aren't you in bed? I asked. I thought you were ill, but you seem fine.

I am fine, she replied.

Oh, well I needn't have bothered picking all this up, I said, pulling out the various drugs I'd bought for her.

You know I'm trying to not take any of that, she said. Who knows what it might do!

I know, I said. But the way you texted I thought you might give in this time and I wanted to be prepared.

Thank you, anyway, she said, and kissed me again. You'll get through it faster than I could, anyway.

I'm aware, I said. It's why we needed more, in fact. But I'm trying to quit, too.

You're a recovering ibuprofen addict, she said.

Something like that, I replied.

She laughed, although it didn't really seem like she was laughing at this.

Are you sure that you're all right? I asked. You had a phone consultation with the doctor today, right? Everything copacetic?

Aye, we're still fighting fit, apparently.

Good, I said. I'll stop bugging you then.

She followed me into the kitchen where I grabbed a beer from the fridge, handing her a non-alcoholic one. She was still acting a little odd. She wouldn't normally be at my heels like this. But I figured it wasn't for reasons to do with me; we'd patched up all that to do with Sarah's things and I think had grown closer as a result. I didn't envy her for dating someone who'd been widowed, where it would always be relationship between three instead of two, one of them apotheosised beyond comparison.

What should we cheers to? I asked. Oh, I know. They asked me today to apply for that American Studies job. Presumably that means they'd give it to me if I did. Although I'm not sure if they realise that I've not published anything yet. Och, well, you'll help me come up with an answer, won't you? Hey, why are you looking at me like that? You don't think they mean it, do you? You think they're just trying to be nice. Dangling the carrot, as it were. Then they'll go for an outside hire, per usual. Oxbridge or some shite. Still, though, don't ask, don't get, ken. But I might as well apply for it, anyway. At least make them reject me and then I can have a bit of the upper hand next time one of them corners me to take on extra marking. You're looking very unconvinced. Come on, I'm a pretty good candidate at this point. Or at least my CV is able to give that impression when it's massaged just so. Are you practicing being on the interview panel, is that what this is? You're going to watch me make a fool of myself as I try to crank out whatever buzzwords they're waiting for me to say. 'American Studies is, by its nature, an interdisciplinary discipline highly aligned with the university's strategic aims for more inclusive and collaborative projects. This is especially relevant to those of us who specialise in hybrid forms which—'

I don't think you should, she interrupted.

You don't? I had no doubt that you'd encourage me to, not least considering you're the one who sent me the ad in the first place. You really don't think I should even apply? Did someone say something to you? Because that's pretty shit when I was just told today by—

No, she said. It's not that. It's because I got some exciting news this morning.

Fuck me, I said, that consultation better not have been to tell you that we're having twins or something. There can't be any more than two babies in this flat at once. And that includes me.

Better than that, she said. You can't tell anyone yet, but I've just been offered a new job. And, yes, you don't need to say it: I knew that I'd hear from them sometime today, and that's probably 95% of the reason why I felt sick.

No, I said. Not...

Yes! she screamed merrily, doing a wee dance. Georgetown University. Can you believe it?

The truth of the matter was that, no, I couldn't.

THE END

ACKNOWLEDGEMENTS

Gratitude is first owed to the research organisations that made many of the experiences that are described here possible: namely, Fife Kingdom University, the Scottish Research Grant System for Arts and Humanities (in collaboration with the Royal Society for Music), and the Craig Devlin Travel Award. Thank you for your collective belief in me and I'm so sorry that this account should be the only published work which has resulted from your trust.

I am also indebted to the many kind and helpful people at the Library of Congress, and further afield, who made my time spent in the U.S. so fruitful and memorable, and similarly to those at the Morven Writers Colony in Perthshire whose generous support provided the time and space I needed to reflect on many of these events.

Finally, my heartfelt appreciation goes to the McIntyre family, who had understandable concerns about this book, though they never sought to halt its publication. Stuart and Lou, thank you for not trying to stop me from telling my side of your daughter's story. I always loved her, even if I didn't always know what I should do with her.

CREDITS AND PERMISSIONS

'Floor Pile' by Shannon Wright. Copyright © 1999 Tu-Tu 68 Music. Used by permission.

'Maggot Brain' by George Clinton Jr. and Eddie Hazel. Copyright © 1971 Bridgeport Music Publishing and Southfield Music Inc. Permission pending.

'Mingus at the Showplace' by William Matthews. Permission granted by the Estate of William Matthews.

Myself When I Am Real: The Life and Music of Charles Mingus by Geno Santoro. Copyright © 2000 by Geno Santoro. Reproduced with permission of the Licensor through PLSclear.